BLEEDING OUT

A Wim Tierman Novel

CRIME SCENE DO NOT CROSS

Evie Jackson

BLEEDING OUT
ISBN-13: 978-0-9839000-5-4
Copyright © March 6, 2017 by Evie Jackson
Published July 2020

Cover Design & Interior Layout by:
Laura Shinn Designs
http://laurashinn.yolasite.com

BLEEDING OUT

Chapter 1

Had she known what would happen, she never would have gone, but she didn't know, and so she did.

Stacy Tau stood trembling at the entrance of the enormous reception room, her heart pounding within her thin frame with such force that her pulse quivered the skin of her pale neck while blood rushed deafeningly through her ears. Primal instinct ignited the neural pathways of her brain, shrieked in warning, begged her to flee, but the scarlet tapestries and blood red mahogany paneling pressed in around her, holding her in place. Before her, the room hummed, writhing with guests. Women in short, tight skirts hugged and laughed, while men in dark suits nodded and smiled. Had they had drinks in their hands, the gathering would have resembled nothing more than a giant cocktail party. Stacy closed her eyes, and thought of bees.

Bees: a monophyletic lineage within the superfamily Apoidea, classified by the unranked taxon name Anthophila, found on every continent excepting Antarctica. Flying insects closely related to wasps and ants. Approximately 20,000 known species with many as yet undescribed making the actual number of bee species much higher.

Inhaling slowly, Stacy sifted facts and figures from an almost eidetic memory, rapidly composing an impromptu lecture for an audience of her imagination.

All bees have two sets of wings, the hind pair being the smaller, and antennae, composed of thirteen segments in the males and twelve in the females. The probiscus, a long, hollow tongue, is designed for collecting nectar from flowers. Trigona minima is the world's smallest bee, a stingless bee whose workers are approximately 2.1mm long. The largest bee, Megachile pluto, an Indonesian leafcutting bee whose females can attain a length of one and 1/2 inches.

Megachile pluto: Mega meaning "great" plus cheilos or "lip". Pluto derived from Ploutos meaning "wealth", the Latinized name for the Greek god Hades, the god of the underworld, son of Cronus and Rhea, brother to Zeus and Poseidon, with his helmet of invisibility and three-headed dog, who kidnapped the maiden Persephone and carried her off to the land of the dead... carried her off... The Dead... No.

With an effort, Stacy forced her scattering thoughts back to bees.

Bees: Bees can see all colors except the color red. Only the female bee can sting. Honey bees, including the European honey bee, Apis mellifera, live in eusocial communities called colonies; colonies comprised of three types of bees: the worker, the drone, and the queen. Beekeepers, or apiarists, use smoke to calm bees while collecting honey; smoke causing the bees to consume honey in anticipation of abandoning the hive due to fire, and also masking bee alarm pheromones. Bees: active, industrious, important to the ecosystem, so very interesting...

Stacy hadn't thought of bees since grade school. She stood with eyes closed, and smiled.

I must remember to tell Wim, she thought happily, forgetting everything else in the pleasure of anticipation.

Her heart rate slowed and the trembling stopped. She stood quietly, composed, relaxed, and then opening her eyes, turned her attention back to the buzzing humans. A thin line formed above the bridge of Stacy's nose as she frowned, thinking of flies.

Fumbling through her purse, she dropped and retrieved first her keys and then her wallet, before successfully disentangling her iPod and inserting a silver ear bud in each ear. Using her thumb, she selected Classical. While adjusting the volume, Stacy took another deep breath, and then raised her eyes just long enough to identify her father on the opposite side of the room, far across the sea of roiling humanity. Gripping her iPod with white-knuckled determination, Stacy plunged into the crowd.

Stacy's sister, Sierra Martindale, an Amazon in strapless white latex with a cashmere shrug and spiked heels so pointed they could have shaved ice, was working the front of the room, greeting her many admirers.

"Oh my God, how are you... Haven't seen you in ages... So good of you to come..." Hugs and kisses.

Logan, the youngest of the Tau children, with careless dark hair and wearing Armani like it was J. Crew, slouched near the side entrance with some of his friends from school. Both seemed oblivious to Stacy as she struggled not to touch or be touched while making her way through the gyrating horde.

Stacy... Chess Anderson looked up, his ice-blue eyes grey with concern. He hadn't seen her enter the room but was suddenly aware of her presence. Some innate instinct, an uncanny sixth sense, always told him when Stacy was near. She hadn't noticed him of course. He knew that in her circumscribed world she hardly saw what was in front of her face. The noise, the people, not to mention the circumstances that brought them all together must be overwhelming to her. His first impulse was to go to her, but he knew he couldn't. His muscular bicep tensed reflexively as his wife slipped her slim arm through his.

"She's really doing well I think," Page commented, following her husband's gaze. "She seems quite pulled together, considering..."

Page's voice was deep, rich, carefully modulated, without a trace of resentment. Chess nodded thoughtfully, absently squeezing her hand. At least outwardly it appeared Stacy was holding up better than anyone could have hoped or expected.

Stacy shuffled forward, avoiding the other guests as best she could. Awkwardly, advancing an inch at a time, she crept through the crowd until at last she stood before an elderly man in a bespoke navy pin-striped suit. Dr. Marshall Tau's broad shoulders were stiffly erect, though he leaned imperceptibly against a veneered oak sideboard adorned with framed photos of a stern-faced woman at various stages of her life. An impeccably dressed gentleman stood at Dr. Tau's side, but moved away at Stacy's approach.

"I'm sorry," she whispered, leaning in to press her small hand against his blue silk shirt. "Daddy, I'm so sorry."

Stacy knew it was the right thing to say. Wim had told her so.

Her father coughed into monogrammed linen, mumbling something indistinct. He ran thick, arthritic fingers through his curling white hair, and then gestured to the small alcove where the body rested, nestled in its satin-lined box.

"Will you sit with her?" he murmured. "I don't want her to be alone."

It did not occur to Dr. Tau that he might sit with his wife's body; no more did it cross his daughter's mind. His eyes turned back to the photographs as Stacy nodded grimly, her hands fluttering softly at her sides. Though the reception room was teeming with smiling, happy visitors, the viewing area was devoid of the living, her mother shunned by the partygoers who had come to pay their final respects.

Thirty feet. Stacy calculated, focusing her thoughts as she re-inserted her ear buds. Only ten yards from where she stood to the chair at her mother's feet. Moving away from her father, without a backward glance, she began to count softly under her breath. *One, two...* Stacy had reached the midway point when her forward progress was halted by the unexpected appearance of a white shirt and black belt in the exact center of her visual field.

"Hey, Stace."

A quiet voice, barely audible above the strains of *Fer Elise*. Stacy felt an unwelcomed shiver as Rory Vanhurst's fingers touched her bare arm.

"You doing okay?"

Eyes averted, brows contracted, she nodded her head, and tried to pass by, but his hand restrained her. She was blocked from moving forward, but so intent upon reaching the chair in the viewing area that she did not know how to turn back. Stacy's eyes grew wide, shifting rapidly from right to left, as her heart lurched violently, knocking against her ribs, pumping blood and paralyzing fear through her veins. People were all around her, their bodies brushing against her, touching her.

"Eeeeeeeeeeee." A small hiss escaped her lips.

"You okay?"

Rory squeezed her arm tighter and Stacy's hands fluttered faster. The volume of the hiss rose.

"Eeeeeeeeeeeeeeeeeeee."

Heads began to turn, and from across the room her father looked up, frowning first at Sierra and then Logan.

Why won't they do something? he thought, both angry and embarrassed, though making no move to intervene himself. Neither sibling appeared to notice.

Stacy's mind was whirling in panic.

No! Not here! Not now! she thought. *Mother... Oh, please...*

Squeezing her eyes shut, she frantically fumbled with her iPod, turning the volume up. *The Moonlight Sonata*. One of her favorites. She could see the maestro's arrangement before her, anticipate each note before it was played, the bass line so loud that it surpassed mere sound and vibrated in her bones.

"What's wrong with you?"

Rory gave her a shake, and that was it. The music evaporated and Stacy began to wail.

It's common when people are milling about to see the crowd, but lose sight of the individual, in effect not seeing the trees for the forest. As all heads turned toward Stacy, Chess Anderson, using skills retained from his college football days, broke through the line. Slow in thought, but quick in action, he wrapped one great forearm around Stacy's shoulder almost lifting her from the ground as he gripped the knuckles of her opposite hand and began massaging them firmly. Spinning away from Rory, who lost his composure only momentarily before shrugging at the crowd, Chess half led, half carried Stacy from the room.

Page watched intently, and then, turning to her nearest neighbor, quickly began a conversation on irrelevant things. Page's mother hurried to join her, but before Margaret Sheffield could reach her daughter, Sierra Martindale drifted purposefully to her side.

"That's our Stacy," she said, coolly, moving in a bit closer than was comfortable for Page. "une fille très dramatique."

"You know how difficult this must be for her," Page began, taking an involuntary step back, but Sierra interrupted.

"And it's so nice of Chess to take such a *special* interest in her. His devotion is truly remarkable." She smiled cruelly, causing Page to flush in spite of herself.

"He's just trying to help her," Page replied, sounding a bit more defensive than she would have liked. "I didn't see anyone else rushing in," she finished pointedly.

"Stacy's twenty-three," Sierra parried. "She's old enough to take care of herself, though she does like to be the center of attention, especially when Chess is around."

A small crowd was gathering, listening to the verbal sparring between the two women. Though both were tall and athletically built, in a battle of this sort, Sierra was the odds on favorite. Sierra Martindale was smart, beautiful, spoiled, and rich; a golden girl with platinum hair and violet eyes whose caustic sense of humor both amused and permanently scarred those in her social set. Page Sheffield-Anderson, dark and intense, though not lacking in brains or looks was the relatively poor relation, only a cousin to the Tau children, the daughter of the sister of the recently deceased. But then with a flourish that belied her small size, the fiercely protective Margaret Sheffield swept onto the scene, and the odds shifted.

"Sierra, Dear, how well you look," the older woman cooed, standing on tiptoe to kiss her niece's cheek, "...considering *all* you've been through!" She shook her head sympathetically, adding the barb to the complement, and then chattered merrily on. "How are the little ones? And where is that handsome hubby of yours?"

She gazed around the room, wide-eyed and expectant. Sierra smiled, showing perfect white teeth, but her eyes were hard.

"The kids are with Lu, of course. I wouldn't think of bringing them *here*." She raised her palm, and inclined her head discretely toward the open casket. "And Daniel's working. You know how important his research is," she added, with laughing reproach.

"Of course. Of course." Margaret's classic pillbox bob bounced as she nodded agreeably, and she brushed a dramatic bang from her eyes.

"You know, speaking of," she continued smoothly, her voice dripping honey and designed to carry, "I read the most interesting article the other day. In the *New England Journal of Medicine*, I believe it was, or possibly *Urology Today*, or one of those other fancy medical journals."

She paused, pursing her lips as if searching her memory.

"But then again, it may have been *Cosmo*," she

laughed lightly, shrugging thin, elegant shoulders. "I just can't recall."

"Anyway, the article said a Dr. Daniel Martindale had discovered a cure for erectile dysfunction. I think that's what they called it now, "erectile dysfunction". "E.D."? You know, when a man can't..." She straightened, and then slowly curled the manicured index finger of her bejeweled right hand. "Ah, but you know what I mean."

The lines around her eyes tightened and her canines showed, white-veneered and sharp behind the thin red line of her lips. A murmur, "How rude...", "shocking...", followed by suppressed chuckles, rippled through the appreciative crowd.

"Working with some type of study group or focus group, some kind of *group* I'm *sure* it said. You know I'm not up on all that medical lingo." Her tone was self-deprecating. "But, it seemed *several* people were involved." She raised an eyebrow and her voice with the word "several", and saw Sierra flinch.

"That wasn't your Daniel, was it?" she finished sweetly.

Sierra Martindale blushed under her tan. Those standing nearest leaned in expectantly, but even under pressure Marshall Tau's eldest daughter only tossed her fair head.

"Why Aunt Mags," she drawled, with her best Southern twang, "you come up with the most outrageous things!" And laughing stiffly, she turned away.

Chapter 2

Eleanor Tau died on a Tuesday night. The house-keeper found her body, cold and in full rigor, the following morning. She was 58 years old. On one hand her death was not unexpected, she had suffered a major stroke three months earlier and been bed-bound since; nothing suspicious there. On the other hand, prior to her stroke Eleanor Tau had been an extremely healthy, capable woman. The fact is everyone, including the man himself, expected her husband, seven years her senior, to die first. Dr. Marshall Tau, though a brilliant orthopedic surgeon, had the common physician's misconception that, because he cared for the ill, he was somehow bullet proof. He indulged, or more correctly, overindulged, in all the vices we as the health care consuming public are warned against; he drank Glenlivet single malt, smoked Louixs cigars, savored rare red meat, and consorted with women who were *not* his wife on a casual and regular basis.

As a child growing up in Beaumont, Texas, I lacked the sophistication to recognize the extent and inappropriateness of Dr. Tau's behavior. He was a big, boisterous man, with shocking white hair even in his youth, and sparkling blue eyes, always laughing and good with kids, probably because he was one. By contrast, Mrs. Tau seemed rigid and intense, forever disapproving, an autocrat, whose endless rules were strictly enforced under the auspices of law. Mrs. Tau intimidated me, so I never really liked her. Now that I'm older, I can appreciate the pressure she was under, married to an egoist with three children, one of whom had special needs.

Stacy was her "special needs" child and one of my

best friends. I say best because I couldn't in truth call her a close friend. We grew up in the same neighborhood and played together from the time we were old enough to crawl, but it's hard to say how well I actually knew her. Stacy was diagnosed with Asperger's syndrome when she was six years old. She wasn't good with interpersonal communication, and her areas of interest were severely limited, but if a subject was important to her, she could tell you absolutely everything about it. I found that fascinating. Stacy was an encyclopedia, only with some of the letters missing.

Mrs. Tau died in early June. I was an eager, bit-too-brash, 23-year-old medical student, Harvard Medical, first-year, in the middle of my final exams. The fact that Stacy actually called me to tell me her Mom died made me want to drop everything and catch the next flight south. Unfortunately, I couldn't convince even one of my jaded professors, who'd undoubtedly heard every conceivable excuse known to man, that the need to reschedule my tests was pressing or even real. I missed the viewing and the funeral, much to my regret, and only arrived at Stacy's house late Friday night.

My name is Wim McKinley Tierman. Despite what you may think, I was not called "Wim" because my conception and birth were unplanned, or because my parents couldn't spell William, or because one or both of them wished I were a boy. My mother, an elementary schoolteacher and aspiring author, hopeless romantic, and inextinguishable optimist, named me after a Celtic hero she admired in a smartly written but utterly obscure fantasy novel she'd loved as a child. My younger sister, Calliope Myer, had it worse I think. In all other matters, Mom rocked, so I never held the naming thing against her, though at school I went by Mac, short for McKinley, until I was 16. After that I concluded that anyone over the age of 10 who makes fun of you for your name is not worth bothering about anyway.

I tapped on Stacy's door at 9 p.m. on the dot, after

sitting at the curb in the rental car for 35 minutes. Being early or late would have created stress for her. She was staying in the "carriage house", located about 50 yards from the main house: an assertion of her independence but with a safety net.

"Hi Wim."

She smiled shyly as she opened the door, carefully avoiding any eye contact. Stacy never looked anyone in the eye if she could help it. I gripped her hand tightly, but briefly, and moved into the tiny entry hall.

"I'm sorry about your Mom," I said. The cliché, but I meant it. My first impulse was to hug her, but I refrained. A hug would have been as welcomed to Stacy as a slap across the face.

"I know," she sighed softly. "Everyone is. Did you know approximately 150,000 people die each day? That's an average of 107 deaths per minute. That means between the time you knocked on the door and the time you entered the house, at least 214 people died."

A less than cheery thought, but I wasn't surprised to find Stacy'd devoted some time to the study of death in the months leading up to her mother's.

She continued as I followed her up the spiraling stairs and into the kitchen. The carriage house was actually a two-bedroom guesthouse with the living area built above an enclosed garage. Laid out like an efficiency apartment, the bedrooms were defined by heavy hanging fabric instead of drywall. A cook top island and breakfast bar divided the kitchen from the den. The impression was one of Bohemian casual, but with polished stainless steel appliances and a luxury bath. The apartment was relatively neat, which meant the housekeeper had been by shortly before my arrival.

"The mortality rate is highest in South Africa, where 17.23 per 1,000 persons die each year."

"Drink?" she interrupted herself, as she reached into the 'fridge.

I took the cold bottle of Strawberry Crush and sat on one of the high metal stools, pressing the toes of my runners against the silver footrest. I'd loved Strawberry Crush in grade school, something Stacy had apparently remembered, and I wondered how much trouble she'd taken to find it. She retrieved a bottled water for herself and leaned against the counter, walking the fingers of her free hand across the smooth quartz surface like a spider as she talked, then curling her hand back to start again. A wave of pity struck me as she fidgeted, unable to relax.

"But that's based upon the crude death rate. The crude death rate can be misleading because there is no adjustment for age or gender, so developed countries may actually have a higher crude death rate due to people living longer, resulting in a much higher proportion of older people in the population."

She took a gulp of water, carefully replaced the cap, and went on.

"Cardiovascular diseases are one of the most common causes of death, with infectious diseases and respiratory diseases all together making up over 50% of all causes worldwide. Unintentional injuries are more than twice as common as intentional injuries. This seems surprising when you consider that the classification "intentional injuries" includes not only suicide and personal violence, but also war. Falls, drownings, and poisonings are relatively rare causes of death, each less than 1% of total causes."

Stacy was shifting the water bottle from one hand to the other, crinkling the plastic noisily as she gripped it more tightly on each transfer. Her brows drew together and what little color there was in her pale face drained away.

"Strokes, or cerebrovascular events, cause almost 10% of deaths," she pronounced carefully, and her small voice quavered slightly. "Mother had a stroke, but she didn't die immediately. Of course, having one stroke increases your risk of having another. I think it's likely she had another stroke. Don't you?"

She looked up quickly, then down again, seeking assurance or perhaps only confirmation that I was still there.

"Probably so," I agreed, nodding. "Is that what your Dad said?"

"He hasn't said anything to me about it. I brought it up over dinner, that night... He was angry..."

"Let's sit in the den," I suggested, taking the water bottle from her hand and leading the way to the sofa.

She sat on one end and I on the other. Stacy continued on the subject of death, offering various facts and statistics, growing more and more agitated until I took her hand and began massaging her knuckles. People who have Asperger's are as different from each other as people who don't. Stacy exhibited many of the typical features, i.e., inflexibility, poor concentration, impaired social skills, and like many others with Asperger's had a hypersensitivity to light touch, but for some reason she found firm touch and deep pressure calming. So we sat for several hours, Stacy often repeating herself with little variation in topic or tone. Her mother was dead, and I could do nothing except listen, supplying whatever comfort listening provides to those who mourn.

I was tired though, to the bone, having had no real break since Christmas, and a whole week of mind wiping, confidence crushing exams, and her flat, pedantic voice droned on. My body was embracing inertia, sinking into the soft, creamy leather of the couch, while my lizard brain stubbornly snapped my head up each time my chin fell toward my chest, when a sudden unexpected deviation in Stacy's dissertation on Death and Dying and Causes Thereof brought me up with a start.

"No one has proven conclusively what happens when we die," she announced, importantly, "but I have determined, based upon evidence I have personally gathered, that we rise again in a different form."

We rise again...?

The Tau family had attended the local Baptist church, but as far as I knew, Stacy had not. The congregation was too large, the singing too loud, and I could not imagine her being able to sit quietly through a sermon. Before I could ask what she meant, she offered something even more surprising.

"You know of course about Paygo," she said, "and I myself, being baptized by the Holy Spirit, will come back after I die just as he did."

Baptized by the Holy Spirit...? Paygo?

Distracted, I stopped massaging her knuckles, and dropped her hand. Paygo had been Stacy's imaginary childhood friend, but she hadn't mentioned him to me in years. She'd said nothing of his "passing" that I could recall, and certainly nothing of his rising from the grave. I thought she'd simply outgrown him. Now Paygo had apparently died and was resurrected? I felt suddenly afraid, fearful that the stress of her mother's illness and death was proving too much for Stacy with her limited life skills and inadequate support systems. Mrs. Tau had been Stacy's tether, the center and grounding force of her constricted orbit, for her entire life.

Although Stacy abhorred change, she had moved from her room in the main house into the carriage house shortly after her Mom's stroke, offering only the vaguest of explanations, a clear indication that the disruption she felt within familiar surroundings had become more frightening to her than the terrors of the unknown.

"What do you mean?" I interrupted, as Stacy showed no intention of elaborating. "What happened to Paygo?"

My friend never encouraged questions. Stacy preferred to share information as she processed it, organized according to her own selective ranking system, and always at her own pace and so she frowned.

"He's been away at college, like you."

She seemed surprised that I asked, shook her head disapprovingly, as if I should have known. "But of course he came home for Mother's funeral."

Of course he did...

"But you said he...," I hesitated, "rose."

"Well, yes," Stacy answered, impatiently now. "That is why his appearance changed. That is why no one can recognize him except me, and Sierra, and Logan."

I shook my head. "So Paygo... died... when...?" *Why hadn't she told me? Had she told me?*

"Oh, Wim, that was such a long time ago." Stacy covered her mouth as she yawned. "It was a painful transition, no doubt, but he's been quite well since."

She turned suddenly, and pressing her back against the arm of the sofa curled her legs into a lotus position.

"Wim," she said eagerly, leaning forward, "did you know that bees can see all colors except the color red? Even ultraviolet, which of course we can't see? I wonder what ultraviolet looks like to a bee..."

I listened to Stacy talk about bees until 2am. We were just getting ready to go to bed when the doorbell rang. To my surprise, Stacy led Chess Anderson into the room.

"I wanted to be sure you were okay," he was saying as they reached the top of the stairs. "Your lights were on and I thought maybe you couldn't sleep..."

He saw me on the couch and stopped. It occurred to me to wonder what he was doing out at 2 a.m. and if Page knew where he was.

"Hey, Chess!"

Neither of us said what we were thinking. We exchanged the standard greetings, promised to catch up. I could tell he wanted a few minutes with Stacy, and so made the excuse of fatigue from my trip and left them to talk. I heard him saying something like, "you know he didn't mean it" to which Stacy responded, "he said it quite plainly..." and then I hit the mattress and fell straight to sleep.

How long I slept, I'd no idea. I was dreaming about a doorbell, and then I was wide-awake. Harsh light and sound exploded in the darkness, a blast so loud that I felt the reverberation of it even as the ringing in my ears left me momentarily deaf. I fell from the bed, tangled in sheets, and stumbled into the living room. Stacy was on the floor.

The footfalls of someone running down stairs, a crash, the door flying open, were all meaningless background noise as I crouched beside my friend. There was a big, black hole in the center of Stacy's chest, filled with nothing but fragments of gristle and bone. Her eyes were open and tracking and she made a soft clicking sound in the back of her throat. I grabbed her hand, automatically massaging her knuckles, and said, "It's okay, Stacy. You're gonna be alright," terrified that I was lying to her as my mind raced, frantically trying to think of something to do that might help her. Chest compression was out of the question. I could see the dull gray edges of shattered ribs.

Without letting go of her hand, I reached for the cashmere throw from the sofa and pressed it carefully against the wound, hoping in vain to stem the flow of crimson that poured from her body and spread across the hardwood floor. Her pale lips moved soundlessly. She jerked and quivered, tried to raise her head, then squeezed my hand. Blood was oozing into the curls of her white-blond hair, making the bright ends float in a glistening pool of gore.

"It's okay... It's okay..."

Her eyes tracked back, and came up. I thought for once she would actually look me in the face, but her gaze was fixed, corneas clouded. Her hand went limp, and I convulsed into sobs.

Then there were people, all around. Someone had me by the shoulders, trying to pull me away. I screamed and clung to Stacy's hand, fighting, kicking, until arms grabbed me about the waist and carried me from the room.

Then I was sitting on the front steps of the main house wrapped in a blanket, shivering in 80-degree heat. There were legs striding back and forth, mostly male in trousers; dark blue, black, brown. Minutes passed, or maybe hours, and then a gurney rolled by on its way to the ambulance. Leisurely. No siren needed.

Someone handed me a cup of steaming liquid. Coffee. The smell made me want to retch. I warmed my shaking hands on the cup, lifted it to my lips but couldn't drink it. A man sat down beside me.

"You're Kim Tierman, right?" he asked. He gripped my arm to force my attention. I shook my head and turned away.

"Kim?" he said, again.

Running a hand through my tangled hair, I tried to focus.

"No, it's Wim. W. I. M."

I didn't really care. My friend had been shot and bled out before my eyes. He could call me Kim.

"I'm Detective..." He stopped and looked at me. I stared back without seeing.

"My name is Jalen Hawk. I'm with the police." He started over, lowering his voice and leaning in, flashing his badge. "I know this has all been a terrible shock. It's important that you tell me what happened."

"What happened?" Like I would know. Like I could say.

He touched my wrist with two fingers as if he were taking my pulse.

"Someone shot your friend and killed her," he said slowly, emphasizing each word. "I need to know who did that."

I blinked. I'd been thinking of Stacy, dead. It hadn't occurred to me to consider who shot her.

"I don't know. I didn't see," I stammered, as tears burned my eyes. "I was asleep!" I gasped.

The horror, the guilt of being asleep while something so terrible was happening to Stacy was more than I could bear.

He asked more questions, Jalen, the detective. Sometimes I answered, sometimes I nodded, sometimes I shook my head, mostly I stared into space. His voice was deep, and soothing. His eyes were brown, and soft. He was patient, persistent, but nothing he could do or say could reach me. Finally he handed me a card, told me we'd talk more later, asked if he could call someone for me.

My parents were in Europe. I'd planned to meet them there. They'd spent a week in Tuscany, celebrating their anniversary, but the second part of the vacation was all for me. My reward for surviving my first year of medical school was a month-long tour of the EU. When Stacy's mom died, delaying my departure, my folks offered to come home immediately. I'd said "No." that it wasn't necessary, that I would check on Stacy and then join them in a few days. Now I would've given anything to have them with me.

I shook my head. My sister, my friends were all home, in Atlanta. I could think of no one else.

"We'll take care of her."

The voice came from behind me. I turned, and recognized Page, looking young and very pale, dark eyes black against her scrubbed, white face. Margaret Sheffield, equally pale with pink foam rollers in her hair, looking less the Grande dame and more the frightened old woman, laid her small wrinkled hand on my shoulder.

"Honey, come home with us," she said, huskily. "Let's get you away from this awful place."

Chess was helping me to my feet. I clung to him as I rose, staggering. He lifted me in his arms like a child and started down the steps.

"She'll stay here!"

Dr. Tau stood in the doorway, his gaunt frame commanding even in silk pajamas and a dressing gown.

"But she's in shock..." Page began. Dr. Tau inter-rupted.

"Stacy would want her here."

His voice was so cold it made my teeth chatter. I had not seen Dr. Tau since his wife's death, but his expres-sion was one I did not expect. There was no grief in the hollows of his cheeks or the grim lines around his mouth and eyes, only thinly veiled rage.

I shrank against Chess, but nodded my head.

"It's okay," I managed to say. But it wasn't.

Without a word, Chess turned and carried me through the wide double doors and into the massive marbled entry hall, then softly up the densely carpeted stairs, Page and Margaret Sheffield in his wake, the housekeeper trailing behind. I looked back to see Dr. Marshall Tau silhouetted in the open doorway, his face in shadow. Beyond him, the red rim of the sun broke over the horizon, painting the wispy morning clouds the color of Stacy's blood.

Chapter 3

Acute stress reaction or "shock" results from the natural human reaction to fear and the body's automatic shift to survival mode. When confronted with a frightening situation, complex interactions between the sympathetic nervous system and the hypothalamic-pituitary-adrenal axis cause the release of chemical substances that prepare us for fight or flight. We feel the rush of adrenaline, our heart rate increases, blood vessels are selectively constricted and dilated to divert activity from nonessentials, like digestion, to the major muscle groups, and our senses, hearing and vision, focus tightly in on the object of our fear as neural pathways fire, anticipating action.

But when faced with something we can't fight or escape, when physical action is useless and all we can do is stand by watching helplessly in horror, then the flood of physiological reactions overwhelms us. Survival instinct is thwarted, all our fine mechanisms of self-preservation fail, and the mind attempts to deal with a complete system overload by shutting the circuits down. We're left dazed, disoriented, disassociated from a reality we can't understand or control.

I woke the next morning to sunlight streaming through partially opened blinds, and had no idea where I was. It took a while to sort out *who* I was, lying flat on my back in a whitewashed four-poster bed shrouded by pale linen sheers hanging from a bright golden ring suspended from the ceiling. Massive, ornate bookcases lined the walls, brimming with books and journals crammed into disorganized stacks. A slightly scarred viola huddled in the corner next to a brass lyre-shaped music stand, and an antique white dresser stood opposite the foot of the bed. Photographs and pictures cut from magazines were tucked around the hand-carved frame of the dresser's mirror leaving only a tiny reflective oval in the center. Of all the empty bedrooms available in the Taus' 12,000-square-foot mansion, someone had come up with the shiny idea to put me in Stacy's old room.

I could make no sense of what had happened, and so concluded Stacy's death was a dream, a nightmare of the worst possible kind. Obviously I was still dreaming, and my only hope was to wake up, preferably in my own bed, but anywhere outside the Beaumont city limits plus minus State of Texas would have been fine.

For a long while I lay there, eyes open but unfocused, trying to reconcile what had been my relatively normal, ordinary life of school, family, and friends with the jumble of horrifying images and emotions from the night before. I could see Stacy, on the floor, gasping for breath, blood pooling around her, but the scene was too harsh, the colors too bright, artificial, unreal, and impossible. The conviction that there had been a terrible mistake, some horrible hoax, finally became so strong that the need for confirmation drove me from the bed.

As I threw back the covers, a reddish-brown stain on the pillowcase where my head had lain caught my eye. That stopped me cold. The stain on the pillow was from Stacy's blood. The construct of my denial crumbled, rational thought fled, and I broke down, sobbing as my whole body shook. This was no nightmare.

I remembered: the sound of the shot, falling from bed, stumbling to the living room to find Stacy, a gaping hole in her chest, kneeling at her side, dark blood oozing across the heartwood pine floor, blood, warm and sticky against my skin, holding her hand as she gasped and died. Someone had shot Stacy in the chest, and she had died. I had been covered in her blood. The police had come. The ambulance had taken her away. Chess had carried me into the house. Page and her mother had cleaned me up as best they could but stopped short of shoving me half-naked into the shower, and so the blood remained, crusted under my fingernails and matted in my hair. The mind-numbing events of the previous night were proved by a reddish-brown stain on a pale pillowcase. Nauseated, shivering, I climbed from the bed.

To my surprise, I found myself wearing a flowery blue housecoat that probably belonged to the housekeeper judging by the utilitarian design. It looked like a painter's smock, with metal snaps down the front and huge patch pockets. Underneath it was a frilly white beyond floor-length nightgown with pale pink ribbons threaded through the smocked bodice and ruffled hem; a questionable style combination of the practical and the whimsical, possibly put together by the same whiz kid who decided I should stay in Stacy's room.

There was shampoo and soap in the bathroom, so I stripped and stepped into the shower. The tile felt cold and solid beneath my feet, as the warm water washed through my hair, sending riverlets of red down my shoulders and back that dripped onto my bare legs before swirling in tide pools around the drain.

When the water cleared, I moved from beneath the shower head and turned the knob to hot, leaning my forehead against the wall, breathing in the steam, watching small drops of water collecting on the cool marble and then joining other drops, increasing in size as they coalesced, traveling downward, fighting the ache of emptiness in my heart until, without conscious thought, cold fury crept in to take its place. In that moment, I swept past the denial stage of grief and proceeded directly to the anger phase.

Stacy was dead and someone had killed her. Stacy, who had never intentionally hurt another living soul in her entire life, had been shot to death in her own home in the middle of the night. Someone had come to Stacy's house and deliberately blown a hole through her chest. It didn't make sense, could never make sense, but one thing was perfectly clear to me, whoever had shot Stacy was stone-cold evil, and that person had to pay. My mind blazed with thoughts of justice, or maybe revenge.

Calmer, but still shaking, I dried off, ruffling my hair with the towel, and looked around for something to wear. The clothes I had worn the night before were nowhere to be found, and it took me several minutes to realize they were probably in a crime lab somewhere being examined as evidence. Maybe my suitcase was still in the carriage house, but I was pretty sure I didn't want to go back there even if the police would let me in.

Stacy had left some of her winter things in the closet when she moved out of the main house that spring, but she and I were nowhere near the same size; Stacy was tiny, tending to anorexic, wearing a size 2 on her "fat" days. At 5-7, 110 pounds, I was a 6 pushing 8. Nothing she owned would fit. Sadly, there were no other clothing options except the nightgown and housedress.

I had better luck in the footwear department. The closet floor was littered with shoes and boots of all kinds, piled in a disorganized mess. Stacy had big feet for such a small frame, so I picked up one or two and tried them on. I settled on a pair of worn Lucchese's; good, leather cowgirl boots though Stacy didn't ride. They were honey-brown wingtips with a familiar retro feel, reminding me of my barrel racing days. I shoved them on without socks, opened the bedroom door, and strode across the landing, pausing at the top of the staircase to look down past the glittering French crystal chandelier.

"Tress chick!" Sierra called, waving up at me from the entry hall. "You rock that homeless look, Girl!"

Her mispronunciation of très chic was deliberate, obviously a joke. Sierra Tau-Martindale was fluent in three languages in addition to English, besides being a master of the always-popular regional dialect: Southern Belle.

"Sorry," she sighed, shaking her head apologetically as I hurried down the stairs. "It's how I cope."

I hadn't seen Sierra since my family and I left Beaumont. She was five years older than Stacy and always ran in different circles, so even when I'd come back for the rare visit, we never hung out. From a distance she looked just as I remembered her, perfect, Miss Popular, Cheerleading Captain and Homecoming Queen, but as I clomped across the entry hall to join her that impression quickly changed. Of course she wasn't wearing a housedress and her hair was not an untidy towel-dried mess, but she certainly wasn't her usual overly confident, borderline obnoxious self. Lines drew down the corners of her lipsticked mouth, mascara clumped around puffy, red-rimmed eyes, and the matte concealer she'd used to hide the dark circles, evidence of a sleep-disrupted night, had been applied with a less than steady hand.

"The police are here with Daddy," she said. "I'm waiting to see him after they leave."

That was her explanation for camping out on the toile-upholstered bench outside her father's office door. I suspected she was doing more than waiting, more like ease dropping, a suspicion that was immediately confirmed.

"They found the gun in the stairwell," she whispered conspiratorially, patting the seat beside her. I sat, gathering the straggling hem of the nightgown into my lap.

"The killer must have dropped it and just left it there. It was one of Daddy's. But they won't say if there were fingerprints on it or not, only that their forensics guys are working on it." I nodded, and waited expectantly. There was more.

"Of course if it's Daddy's, then anybody's fingerprints could be on it. You know he never locks the gun case, and we all went to the range on Friday after the funeral."

"You went to the firing range? After your Mother's funeral?" I was incredulous, thinking, *Only in Texas...* "Whose idea was that?"

"Don't know," she shrugged without interest. "I think Daddy suggested it first, but it may have been Chess. It was such a gloomy day, not raining, just dreary, sad, you know. We didn't want to sit around the house and stare at each other, so we all went, that is... except for Stacy."

Tears welled in her eyes.

"I don't understand why anyone would want to hurt *Stacy*," she continued, her normally self-possessed expression child-like with disbelief. "I mean, why? She was kind of tiresome, going on like she did, but she never hurt anyone, *ever.*"

"I don't know," I said, patting her shoulder awkwardly in what I hoped was a comforting gesture. "It doesn't make sense to me either."

"But you were *there*." Her voice rose sharply, almost accusingly, as her chin came up and she glared at me with cold violet eyes. "Didn't you see *anything*?"

I shook my head.

"I was asleep." It sounded and felt like an apology.

She stared at me for a moment, and then her face softened. She nodded wordlessly before looking away.

"But they're sure the gun came from the house, from your father's gun case?" I asked.

"Yes, I think they are," Sierra answered, then added firmly, "but that doesn't mean one of *us* did it. People have been in and out of the house all week since Momma died. Anyone could have taken a gun."

Someone might have walked out of the house with a handgun, maybe, I thought, but I was pretty sure the gun used to kill Stacy was something a whole lot larger. I wasn't prepared to argue though and so let it go.

"What else did the police say?"

If she wasn't embarrassed to be caught listening at the keyhole, I wasn't ashamed to ask what she'd heard.

"Only that it was quick, thank God. At least she didn't suffer."

"Quick" is a relative term, and it had taken Stacy several long, lingering minutes to die. I was pretty certain she had suffered immensely, at least for the time it took her brain to stop processing pain and terror, but forced myself to nod in agreement. I wasn't about to add to Sierra's grief by telling her what I thought.

Sierra studied me pensively.

"Not to dis' your daring and eclectic sense of style, Chica," she offered, with a ghost of a grin, "but I can run you by the mall if you like..."

A bright flash-the memory of Sierra, with rimless Dolce readers lending an intellectual look to her carefully composed features, trying hard to convince Stacy that "shopping" was a legitimate college major when she'd actually been studying Art History and Economics at Tulane-almost made me smile, too. Fashion MacGyver Sierra Tau-Martindale would have constructed something sensational from the window curtains in Scarlett O'Hara style before she deigned to wear a housedress. Her head came up suddenly and I could tell she was listening intently. How she could hear anything was a wonder to me, but I was further from the office door.

She stood abruptly, the door opened, and Detective Hawk strode out. He looked different than he'd looked the night before: taller, colder. Seeing me in my granny gown and boots, he did a double take, and then coughed politely into his hand to cover what might have been a laugh. Sierra moved forward.

"Detective, was it Hawk?" she asked, her voice commanding, her gaze direct. "Is there anything at all we can do to help you find this vile person, this monster who hurt my sister? Do you have any idea who could have committed such an unspeakable act?"

"We're pursuing several leads," he answered-a canned response, "and will certainly keep you apprised of our progress."

Turning to me, he added, "I have more questions for you, Ms. Tierman, now that you're awake. Would you mind coming down to my office?"

My sister, my mother, at times even my father has bemoaned the fact that I was born without any sense of personal style. I've never been that concerned with my appearance as long as my teeth are brushed and my hair is clean, but even so, I could not see myself sitting in a police station in nothing but a nightgown and cowboy boots. On the other hand, I wasn't willing to significantly impede progress in the investigation of Stacy's death to satisfy my modesty either.

"I, I don't have my luggage. I'll need to grab some clothes, I guess," I responded, uncertainly. I just wasn't sure where I could grab them fast.

"Take your time," he said, flipping open a spiral notepad. "I have plenty to do here for a while. I can meet you downtown in about an hour and a half."

An hour and a half... the Parkdale Mall was close, but I didn't have my purse, which meant no money, no cell phone, no keys to the rental car...

My mental faculties, normally reasonably sharp, were clouded by the shock of Stacy's death. I stood there, frozen by indecision.

"We can run by my house, see if I have something that will do for now, and then hit the mall later," Sierra offered, as if reading my mind.

She took my arm and took charge, and I felt a surge of gratitude. Sierra seemed to be holding it together rather well, considering. Of course, she hadn't seen what I had seen, and she wasn't the type to show weakness in any case, especially with outsiders in the house.

"Thanks! That would be great," I said, relieved.

"I'm taking the Bimmer," she called to Logan who had wandered unnoticed from his room and was standing at the top of the stairs. He was dressed only in green hunter's plaid pajama bottoms that hung below his narrow hips, and his dark hair fell into his eyes. Nodding wordlessly, he turned away. Sierra selected keys from a china bowl on the marble-topped entry hall table.

Detective Hawk was asking Dr. Tau if he could speak with the household staff.

"I can't talk to Daddy now anyway," Sierra commented, sotto voce, as she led the way through the front doorway. "Let's blow this joint."

Gathering my trailing nightgown, I followed her out.

Chapter 4

The Taus lived in one of the largest privately owned homes in the Oaks Historic District, a much desired section of town that included the former residences of some of the most influential families from Beaumont's glory days. It was a massive old mansion, built in the Beaux-Arts style in the early 1900s shortly after the Lucas gusher at Spindletop marked the beginning of the Texas Oil Boom. Surviving over the years without major damage from any of the various storms and seasons, the exterior had been painstakingly restored to a state of near-newness in accordance with the requirements for a National treasure and the covenants of an Historic District.

Although it was mid day, with the bright Texas sun blazing down from a cloudless azure sky, as we walked out across the circular drive I had the eerie feeling that someone was watching me from the house. I turned back, but saw no one, only the leering faces of the mascarons, the ugly sculpted figureheads that guarded the windows and doors.

Sierra pressed the key fob and the lights of the black convertible blinked in response. We climbed in, she fired the ignition, revved the engine, popped the clutch, and we skidded out of the driveway, the BMW fishtailing as one rear tire caught the curb.

"I love this car!" Sierra enthused, working the clutch and gear shifter while somehow simultaneously managing to press the control to lower the top.

The wind whipped my hair and burned my eyes, but also filled my lungs. It was good to breathe. I felt I hadn't taken a breath since Stacy died.

"The kids should be back by the time we are," Sierra chattered. "I really want you to see them. Lu takes them to the park on Saturdays, so she has the Benz."

"How old are they now?"

I was working under the assumption that Lu was the nanny. Stacy only talked about things that interested her, so I had little information regarding Sierra's marriage, children, or household help.

"Tara is 3 and Faun is 9 months. They are both gorgeous, blond and blue-eyed."

She laughed with pride.

"After my side of the family."

The image of Stacy's blond hair floating in blood flashed into my mind.

"Except for Logan. He's the odd duck," I reminded her quickly, pushing the image away.

"You know, it's funny you should mention that!" Sierra exclaimed. "Someone brought that up just the other day. What did they say? That Logan really was the "black sheep". I think that was it."

"It just doesn't seem real, you know," she said, suddenly somber. "I can't believe it's true..."

I knew she wasn't talking about Logan anymore.

Shaking her head, Sierra sighed. "It just doesn't seem real..."

She seemed to be channeling one of the Andretti's, flying down the two-lane residential streets, barely nodding at the four-way stops. We had turned into the sun, and she reached up to lower the sun visor. A plastic bag dropped into her lap.

"Oh, my God."

Sierra swerved, and then slowed down, holding the bag up so we could both inspect the contents; dried plant material. I was guessing cannabis.

"Oh my God! I can't believe he keeps this where anyone might find it! What if we got caught with it? What are we going to do?"

"Nothing suspicious," I advised, pointedly.

I had as much to lose as she did, if not more. A conviction for possession could end my medical career before it started.

She slipped the bag between the seat and the console.

"You're right," she agreed, taking a breath. "You're right. As long as we act like law-abiding citizens, why should anyone stop us? But I'm going to have a talk with that boy as soon as I get home. He could have warned us."

I knew about Logan's drug problem, not because Stacy ever mentioned it, but because it had taken root when he was only 8 or 9 years old. He started with alcohol, sneaking discarded drinks from the table during his parents' frequent dinner parties, and graduated to smoking pot before he reached Junior High. By the time I left Beaumont, he was snorting coke and had already been in rehab twice at the age of 14.

"I take it he's still not doing so well?" I asked.

Sierra had raised the top on the convertible and was driving like a student taking Driver's Ed. She turned on her blinker 300 feet before reaching the stop sign, braked to a complete halt, and then made the turn at a speed of 2 miles per hour.

"I don't know," she answered, and sighed. "We don't talk much anymore. I don't understand him. He and I were close when we were kids, closer than I was with Stacy, even though he was younger. But then he started getting into trouble all the time... Mom always said, "You can't help those who won't help themselves." I guess I gave up on him after a while."

It was a shame. Logan was messed up, but he'd always been nice to Stacy, and to me.

"Here we are," Sierra announced, turning the car into the driveway of a stately two-story home.

The neighborhood was new construction, green sod and tiny trees. The houses were what my Dad called "McMansions", huge homes built on large lots in a subdivision where no kids played outside.

We went in and Sierra hurried about, opening curtains and raising shades. The house seemed musty, neglected.

"I've been staying at the main house since Momma had her stroke," Sierra explained, "to help out." Her voice took on a resentful tone. "But I've told the housekeeper *a million times* to make it at least *look* like someone *lives here*."

"What about Daniel?" I asked, curiously. "Has he been staying at your parents' house, too?"

Sierra hesitated.

"Daniel keeps an apartment near the University, you know, at Rice. He's so devoted to his research that he often works late. It would be dangerous for him to drive all the way back to Beaumont when he's tired. We always spend time together as a family on the weekends though," she added hastily.

I didn't comment. It wasn't my business.

"Let's see what I have that might fit you."

Sierra had a taste for clothes that showed off her assets, so finding something suitable was not so much a problem. What was snug on her was just about right on me. We found some jeans and rolled the hem, then sorted through tanks and tees. Her style was a bit flashy but still a huge improvement over the housecoat and granny gown. I wasn't about to complain. She made me take more than I hoped I would need, but I kept Stacy's boots.

On the way back, I asked the question that had been weighing on my mind the whole time.

"Who would want to kill Stacy?"

"I can't imagine," Sierra said, shaking her head. "It's not as though anyone could have hated her. I guess people who didn't know about her condition might have found her offensive or annoying. She did go on and on about things. But the world is full of annoying people, many *much* more annoying than *Stacy*. I can't see her being shot for that."

She paused, bringing the car to a complete stop at a stop sign, then looked both ways before proceeding through the intersection.

"Unless, of course, she somehow insulted some gang member. There are some vicious gangs in Beaumont now, lots of drive-bys, some break-ins, shoot-outs, but generally *those people* go after each other."

She considered.

"Now Daddy, or Logan, or even me, I could see someone wanting to do away with any one of us. Why, I can think of at least *a dozen* people who would want Daddy dead, including *most* of his practice partners. And Logan... all those sketchy, druggy friends. Me? The motive would be jealousy, of course." She tossed her head. "But Stacy? Stacy's never had an enemy in her life. She's hardly had any friends except you. She..." Sierra hesitated, frowning, "Well, she just doesn't seem important enough to *murder*. You know what I mean?"

"That's cold," I blurted before I could stop myself, anger flushing my face.

Sierra shrugged unapologetically. "You asked what I thought."

I nodded. She was right. I had.

Chapter 5

Sierra dropped me on College Street in front of the low brick building that housed the investigative branch of the Beaumont Police Department, promising to return as soon as I called. She offered to stay with me, but I wasn't sure how long my interview might last, and so, feeling like a six-year-old on the first day of school, I waved from the curb as she drove sedately away.

During the time I lived in Beaumont, my family and I rarely visited the downtown area, and I, being brought up in a relatively protective environment, had never been to the police station before. To say the building was unimpressive would be an understatement; it's shape and appearance were starkly institutional which made the statues of two police officers, one male and one female, standing at the northeast corner of the entrance all the more evident. The officers guard a five-pointed star that bears the names of those who've fallen in the line of duty.

Feeling a heightened sense of sorrow for the loss of these men and women whose lives had been cut short in the service of their community, I stood for a moment, studying the monument. It was with some sense of surprise that I recognized the first named, Deputy City Marshall William E. Patterson. Patterson had been shot and killed by Pattillo Higgins in 1881. Pattillo Higgins was a key figure in Beaumont history, instrumental in the oil strike that put Beaumont and the State of Texas on the world map, so every school-aged child knew the story well.

It goes like this: Patterson, an eight-year veteran of the Beaumont police force, caught a 17-year-old Higgins and friends in the act of "allegedly" defacing an African American church. In his attempt to capture multiple perpetrators, Patterson fired a warning shot. Higgins turned and shot Patterson, critically injuring the officer. A gun battle of sorts ensued, with Patterson catching another round to the abdomen, and Higgins being wounded in the arm. Patterson died the next day from his injuries, and Higgins, who later lost his arm to gangrene, was arrested for the crime. Higgins pleaded self-defense in the shooting, claiming it was dark and that he did not recognize Patterson as an officer of the law. Higgins was a local. Patterson was not. Higgins was acquitted.

Higgins went on to become an avowed Christian and a self-taught geologist. Convinced there was oil under Sour Hill Mound, he persevered through multiple failed attempts and the loss of his company, enduring the ridicule of the town and formally trained geologists worldwide who claimed that the gulf region could not possibly contain an oilfield. After almost a decade his determination paid off and he was proved right on January 10, 1901, when the Lucas gusher blew crude 150 feet into the air. Production from the oil field at Spindletop surpassed any other oil field in the world at the time, and The United States soon became the world's leading oil producer. Had Higgins been found guilty of murdering Patterson, the history of Beaumont, the U.S. and even the world could have been very different.

History tended to immortalize Pattillo Higgins, a visionary, "The Prophet of Spindletop", a man who stuck to his own views in the face of near financial ruin and public humiliation, and until that day I had never given William E. Patterson a second thought, but as I stood there, in the heat with the sun beating down, staring at his star, I shivered, feeling the presence of a phantom, a shade that stained the reputation of one of Beaumont's favorite sons, the shadow of a dead police officer who was killed in the performance of his job.

As you might expect, this new perspective on an historical event did nothing to lighten my mood, and so I turned and walked quickly across the dark stone steps, through the front door, and into the lobby of the building. The interior was as sparse of decoration as the exterior was stark. There were a few plaques on the walls, black and gold with likenesses of and tributes to the more recently killed officers, and though neat and clean, the lobby was generally as sobering and oppressive as might be intended to deter those visitors that were criminally inclined.

I asked at the desk for Detective Hawk. A phone call and a few minutes later, and I saw him coming out of the elevator. My impression from the night before had been of a soft voice and soft eyes, but in daylight, at the Taus' house and now at the station, he was all hard angles; mid thirties, 6-foot 5 and 200 pounds, whip thin, with long corded arms, a hooked nose, and a jaw like a pit bull. He smiled when he saw me, and the sharp edges softened.

"Thanks for coming in," he said, studying my face intently as he shook my hand.

"I only hope I can help," I replied, trying to reason away my anxiety. My experience with law enforcement had been limited to one personal interaction involving a parking ticket that turned into a warning, plus watching a few old Law & Order reruns.

"Let's walk while we talk."

With hardly a pause, he took my arm, steering me back toward the door.

I was surprised, having pictured something closer to the interrogations I'd viewed on TV and in movies; the poor, witless witness slash suspect slumping over a long, metal table in a stuffy, dark room with a bright light in his/her eyes, being snarled at by some snarky, cigarette-smoking detective while faceless observers leer through a one-way mirror. Instead we headed out into sunlight, walking southwest on College toward Pearl. I had to scramble to match his long-legged strides.

"So you just got into town last night?" he asked, but he already knew the answer.

"Yes, I flew in from Boston to stay with Stacy for a few days," I said, and added, "I was worried about her after her mom's death."

"Bos-ton," he said. A Texan imitating a New Englander. "But you didn't make the funeral?"

"No, I wanted to, but I had my blocks, block exams to finish my first year of medical school. At Mass General, Harvard Medical..."

"Medical school? At Harvard?" He interrupted, snorting his disbelief as he gave me a sidelong appraising look. "So you're pretty smart?"

I got that a lot, the "you've got to be kidding me" gape, sometimes with mouth open, other times with mouth closed. I suppose I've never been that impressive looking. Even some of my closest friends didn't believe me when I first told them I was accepted at Harvard. I've always been "pretty smart", but never tried to flaunt it. Being "smart" was a gift, not something I earned. Still, the detective's manner bothered me. I unconsciously slowed my pace as we turned northwest on Park.

"I guess..." I said, not sure what he was driving at.

"I just meant, if you were going to kill someone, you'd probably come up with a more creative, less conspicuous way to do it than by blowing him or her away with a double-barrel shotgun, especially on your first night in town."

I stopped abruptly. One of the few businessmen walking the street on a Saturday had to sidestep to avoid a collision.

"You think I killed Stacy?" I was stunned.

"Well, no. Not really." He gave a short laugh. "But you were on the scene. That's opportunity. And you could have had a motive..."

He started walking again, leaving the unfinished thought hanging suggestively in his wake. I followed. A spark of anger kindling caused my face to flush and my voice to rise.

"What possible reason could I have to kill Stacy?" I asked angrily of his back, scrambling to catch up. "I came here because she was my friend."

"That's what you say," he answered, shrugging, "but how would I know that?"

I stopped walking again, at a loss for words. He drew up and turned to face me, towering over me.

"I was staying at her house..." I began, licking my lips as my mouth went dry.

"Which means she *thought* you were a friend," he finished, "but maybe you secretly hated her and wanted her dead... or maybe you had a different motive altogether." He paused ominously, the lines around his eyes tight. "We might call it a financial incentive."

He sounded so reasonable as he accused me of killing my friend.

"I don't know what you're talking about. What do you mean? But I didn't..." Already shaky, I was losing it, starting to cry. My distress had no effect on him.

"I never said you did," he said shortly, frowning as he shook his head, "only that you could have."

He turned and started down the street. I stood there, looking after him, unsure of what to do. It seemed to me he was talking in circles and in spite of my being "pretty smart" I was having trouble keeping up, but I had come downtown at his request. What would he do if I tried to leave?

"Are you lost, Honey?"

An elderly woman with snow-white hair, tan orthopedic shoes, and shopping bag in hand, touched my arm. I nodded. I was lost, absolutely.

"Do you want to use my cell to call...?"

"It's okay, Ma'am." Detective Hawk had returned.

The woman looked concerned until he flashed his

badge, then turned distrustful eyes to me. Hawk took my arm and steered me across the street.

"Do you mind?" he said impatiently. "I only have about 20 minutes left for lunch."

~ * ~

He ordered a cup of gumbo and a pecan-crusted goat cheese salad. Suga's was a little expensive for me, besides I didn't have my wallet, so I ordered water no lemon, from the tap.

"How long have you known Stacy?" he asked, as he nodded to the server for more ground pepper.

"Since we were kids."

I didn't like it that he used her first name, casually, as if he knew her, too.

"And you moved to Atlanta...?"

"When I was sixteen."

"But you came back to visit her?"

"A few times."

"Plus you kept in touch by phone?"

"Yes."

He looked up from his salad, chewing, eyebrows raised, expecting more. I looked back, thinking he already seemed to know quite a bit about me. But I was tired, and I was hungry, and he was rude. He had accused me of killing my friend. I wasn't in the mood to chat.

"When can I get my stuff, my cell, my *wallet*, my suitcase, my clothes?" I asked, bluntly. He swallowed deliberately, wiped his mouth with his napkin, took a sip of tea, then pulled a wallet and white iPhone from his pocket and slid them across the table.

"The rest probably by tomorrow," he said.

"Thanks."

I ran through my list of missed calls, Mom, Jordy, Rachel, Jordy again, and then put the phone aside. He turned his attention back to his plate, while I stared out the window. Downtown Beaumont looked gritty in daylight. I wondered what Pattillo Higgins would think of it, if he could see it again over a hundred years after he went from town laughing stock to geologic savant. I wondered where the ghosts of Spindletop might have gone after the Lucas gusher blew the top off their midnight playground. Beaumont was an old mining town despite all the renovations; the starkness only added to my sense of isolation.

Det. Hawk finished his meal, paid the bill and tipped the waitress. It was a generous tip, but failed to garner him any favor with me. On the way out, he opened the door, started to go through, then apparently had an attack of manners and held it while I passed in front of him.

"You already ate."

He made it a statement, but his brows drew together, as if a thought had just occurred to him.

"No," I answered.

"It's 2:30 in the afternoon."

Well yeah. I didn't say anything, just shook my head.

"Why didn't you say so?" he asked, sternly.

"I didn't have my wallet until now, and you didn't ask. What was I supposed to say, "Please Sir, could I have some more?""

"Of course not, but... Why didn't you say something?"

When I'm really tired and someone gets under my skin, I can be a little passive aggressive. It's immature, and totally counterproductive, but what can you do? None of us are perfect. We walked on together in a studied silence that I was determined not to break. Finally he spoke again.

"I thought you would want to help me solve this case," he said, frowning down at me, "if you really cared about your friend."

I spun on my heel so fast he actually took a step back.

"*If I* really cared? *If I cared!*" I was hot. "You want the *facts*? You're some big shot detective working on a *case*.

You don't *know Jack* about Stacy or me!"

"Stacy died last night, right in front of me. She'd never done anything to anyone, not in her life. I loved her like my sister, we grew up together, and I could do nothing, not one stinking thing to help her while she lay there, bleeding to death on the floor. I don't know if she knew what happened to her, or saw who shot her, or if she was scared, or in pain. All I know is there was blood everywhere and she was dying, and I couldn't do anything to stop it."

Suddenly I was shouting, in his face, hysterical.

"You asked me to come to your office to answer questions. I came here to try and help you find who killed her, and you end up accusing me of murdering one of my best friends. Some detective you are! You don't know *anything*! You're the most insensitive, unfeeling..."

I searched for a word, thought of several I couldn't use, burst into tears, and stood there, sobbing in frustration and fury, my hands clenched in fists at my side.

The look on his face was surprise more than sympathy, but he reached out to put his hand on my shoulder. I started to push it away, but he pulled me in, awkwardly, a one-armed hug. It was the most professional, probably the coldest hug I'd ever received in my life, but I surrendered, crying into his stiff cotton shirt. I felt hurt, hollowed out, and I hated him, but it didn't matter. He was there.

Chapter 6

It took a while for me to calm down. Had he been nicer, I'd have been embarrassed by my extreme melt-down, but after the way he pushed me, I thought he was probably expecting it. Then again, maybe he hadn't been pushing at all. Maybe because I was tired and stressed out, I simply took his comments the wrong way. After all, he had never said, "I think you shot Stacy." His actual words were to the effect that he didn't think I did. And realistically, it seemed unlikely a detective would have a true murder suspect tag along at lunch. So whom did he suspect?

I asked him. He dodged me just as he had dodged Sierra.

"It's too early in the investigation."

Back at the station the interview proceeded, follow-ing more along the lines of my original expectations. Det. Hawk sat me at his desk, and left for a few minutes while he retrieved the keys to my rental car and my carry-on bag. Then he sent a young uniformed officer to the vending machine to buy me a Coke and chips while he took out a notepad and began jotting down information.

"Full name? Date of birth? Current address? Occu-pation?" All duly documented.

"Tell me what happened last night."

"In your own words," he added after a pause. "Start with when you left the airport, and then everything that happened after that."

I tried to be brief but accurate, sticking to the things I knew: I arrived at Stacy's house early, probably 8:25, sat in the rental car until 9, went in, Stacy and I talked until 2am, Chess came by...

He looked up with pen poised, a spark of interest in his brown eyes, but then continued his note taking and didn't interrupt me.

...I went to bed, to sleep, heard a doorbell, maybe, I'm not sure, then the gunshot, ran to the living room and found Stacy.

As I paused for breath, I heard a muttered oath from the young officer who had gone for my snacks. The bag-o-chips had caught against the glass on the way down, and his persuasive efforts, i.e., expletives and body slams, were having no effect on the indifferent machine. Det. Hawk grimaced, sighed, "Back in a minute," and went to his comrade's aid.

After assessing the situation, he looked the younger man in the eye while smacking the vending machine once, solidly in what would be the equivalent of the solar plexus, upon which the chips dropped, and he retrieved the bag from the slot. He took the Coke from his speechless colleague's hand, and walked with appropriate swagger back to his desk and me.

Normally this display of male ego would have earned a smirk and an eye roll, but I was grateful for the sugar, caffeine, salt, and grease, and so thanked him quite politely.

"So, what can you tell me about Chess Anderson?" he asked, as I crunched my Ruffles.

"He's a good guy... knew Stacy most of her life. He's from the neighborhood... an only child... We all grew up together. Chess played football in high school and college, but was never your typical jock... just a really nice guy. Parents were well off... think his dad was an investment banker or something like that... Not home much, so I don't remember him clearly, but his Mom was nice... They were in a bad car wreak maybe four or five years ago... drunk driver... head on... his Mom died I think and his Dad was disabled for the rest of his life... Chess and Page took care of him... think the Dad may have died in the last year or so..."

"Actually both his parents are living, though only his father lives here."

He raised his eyebrows. I frowned and shook my head, wondering why I thought they'd both died.

"Chess Anderson and his wife take care of Mr. Anderson in his home, and now Chess Anderson is Dr. Tau's financial advisor and business legal counsel."

"I didn't know that, either."

Stacy only talks about things that interest her...

"Why would he visit..." he hesitated, "Miss Tau at 2am?"

Apparently he had picked up on my disapproval of his casual use of Stacy's first name. Maybe he was more perceptive than I'd thought.

"What was their relationship?"

"I'm sure they weren't lovers, if that's what you mean," I answered, sipped my Coke, and then tried to explain. "Stacy was 23 in calendar-years, but her emotional age was closer to 14 or 15."

"But 14 or 15-year-olds do have sex."

"Yes, some do, but Stacy disliked being touched. I don't think she could have tolerated an intimate encounter, with Chess or with anyone else."

"An intimate encounter?" he repeated, apparently struck by my choice of words. "That sounds so... technical."

I made no comment.

"I guess they teach you to talk like that in medical school."

It wasn't a question, so I felt no need to reply. My personal views against casual extra-marital sex had no bearing on Stacy's death.

"How did his wife feel about their friendship then?" he asked, back on point. "Is Mrs. Anderson the jealous type?"

I considered, remembering that I too had wondered if Page knew about her husband's nocturnal wanderings.

"I really don't know," I answered honestly. "Chess and Page have been together since high school, a couple I mean. Like I said, we all grew up together, though Page and Sierra were older. Chess is a year younger than Page, so four years older than Stacy, and me... She's never seemed insecure about him as far as I can tell, and I've never seen her be anything but kind to Stacy."

Still, if I were married and my husband went to another woman's house at 2am... I thought it, but didn't say it. These people were my friends after all, or had been, and I could no more see Page shooting Stacy than I could imagine Chess cheating on his wife.

"What about Miss Tau's brother or sister?"

"What about them?"

"Maybe one or both of them wanted her dead."

"Neither was particularly close to Stacy, but there was no animosity there."

Not that I knew of anyway.

"Do you know of anyone who might profit from Sta—...your friend's death?"

"No, I really don't," I sighed. "I wish I did."

"No one in the family would benefit if she were out of the picture?"

"I don't think so, plus I can't believe anyone in her family, Sierra, Logan, Page, or Chess, would do this."

"You mean, shoot her?"

"Right."

"What about her father, or her aunt?"

I shook my head.

"It's not possible." I was certain, had no doubts.

"You'd be surprised what people are capable of doing to one another, given the right set of circumstances. Her mother just died?"

"Yes," I confirmed, and then added, "and no, I'm not familiar with the provisions of Mrs. Tau's Will."

He gave me a look of grudging approval for anticipating the question before he asked it. To me it seemed obvious. If he thought someone in the family did it, he'd assume the motive was money. The Taus were in the upper 2%.

"Did Miss Tau have money of her own? Do you know if she had a Will?" he asked casually. He was looking down at his notes, but he'd stopped writing, and he clicked the retractor on his pen.

I thought about it.

"I don't know," I hesitated, "about the money, that is, but I wouldn't be surprised if she did have a Will, of some kind."

I was thinking of Stacy's unexpected revelations about her belief in reincarnation, or the Resurrection, or the Rapture. I wasn't quite sure which.

"But you don't really know?"

"No."

He raised his gaze, leaned across his desk, and his eyes seemed to bore into mine.

"Really?"

"Did she?" I asked.

"Would it surprise you to learn that we found an executed Will Miss Tau had drawn up herself only last week? The housekeeper and the gardener witnessed it, but legality remains to be proved."

"Last week...?" I waited with a mixture of curiosity and dread, thinking, *Stacy made out a Will, and then she died...*

"You, Ms. Tierman, are the sole beneficiary of, and I quote, "all my worldly possessions"."

I couldn't stop my mouth from falling open, but closed it quickly with a snap.

"I didn't know," I blurted, truly shocked, wondering what was in Stacy's mind to make her do such a thing. "I'm not even sure what that means."

"So you did not suggest to your friend that she needed to execute a Will after her mother's death?" he asked.

"No. Of course not."

"Or that she might name you as her beneficiary, since she and her siblings weren't close, as you said?"

"No! I would never do that!"

"And you have no idea how much your friend was worth?" His expression showed skepticism, his tone deliberately doubtful.

"Worth? You mean in dollars and cents?" I asked coldly, suddenly defiant under his cynical gaze. He nodded.

"Stacy, her friendship, was *priceless* to me, when she was *alive.*"

He continued to stare for a moment, his face expressionless as he considered my response, and then he glanced down at his notes.

"Okay, then," he said, shrugging as if the whole thing about the Will didn't matter in the least. "Moving on."

"You said you sat outside the house for some time before going in. Did you see anything unusual, or anyone that looked out of place? Anyone just hanging around? A car circling the block?"

I hadn't considered that; the possibility of someone lying-in-wait.

"No. I didn't notice anything."

I felt hot, and all at once I could no longer meet his eyes as the implications of his question sank in. The truth was, I'd been playing *Ridiculous Fishing* on my iPhone while sitting in the rental car outside Stacy's house and probably wouldn't have noticed Freddy Krueger sharpening his nails on the street lamppost, but I didn't want that in the official police report. I didn't want to say it out loud. It was like being asleep when Stacy was shot.

She'd drawn up a Will and then she died. She had named me her beneficiary. Was it simply that her mother's illness had made her conscious of her own mortality, or had she known something would happen to her? Was she afraid of someone? Would she have told me if I'd been in Beaumont? Could I have prevented her dying if I'd only arrived sooner? Even Friday night, while sitting in the car, if I'd only been paying attention would I have seen the killer lurking nearby? Suddenly I was overwhelmed with the crushing sense that I'd failed Stacy in all possible ways.

Det. Hawk apparently felt a change in the atmosphere and raised his eyes from his notepad, but then nodded and laid his pen aside.

"I guess that covers it for now," he said, closing his notebook and checking his watch. "I can give you a ride home if you can wait about 20 minutes."

"I'd appreciate that," I replied meekly, as he pointed toward a row of scarred wooden chairs that sat against the wall. All my anger had gone, directed inwardly, leaving me weak.

I gathered my meager belongings and moved away. He sorted some files, flipped through some photos, made more notes. I thought about calling Sierra for a ride, but decided not to bother her. Then I considered calling Mom or Jordy to let them know where I was and what had happened, but felt the walls in a police station would certainly have ears. So I sat, hugging my iPhone to my chest, rocking my feet back and forth on the heels of Stacy's boots.

Chapter 7

Det. Hawk dropped me off in the driveway. The front door stood ajar, and so I let myself in, stumbling unintentionally into the middle of the Battle of San Jacinto or the Battle of the Alamo, depending on who's side you took. Sierra was squared off against a tall, dark-haired man in thick, black-rimmed glasses and wearing a white lab coat. Dr. Daniel Martindale, I presumed. From the look of the combatants, this was not the first skirmish in what must have been a long and bloody war.

Reluctant spectators watched from the fringes of the battlefield, unable or unwilling to declare allegiance or look away. At the top of the staircase, Logan stood frozen in his bedroom doorway hand on the doorknob, distress and indecision reflected in his dark eyes.

The door to the kitchen was open, too, but only a crack. The shape behind the louvers was tall but indistinct, most likely the nanny, as underneath the adult bellowing I could almost make out a child's whimper.

In the parlor to the right of the entry hall, the housekeeper seemed inordinately engrossed in adjusting the drape of velvet curtains.

The door to Dr. Tau's office was closed, and I wondered if he was out, suddenly struck deaf, or just immune to the drama of a Texas showdown.

"I'm sorry about your sister," the dark-haired man was shouting, red-faced and flustered. "I liked Stacy, I did, but I can't stay here with you!"

"But I have to stay here and I don't want to be alone. I need you," Sierra pleaded in anguished tones. "Can't you see I need you?"

"This mouse kill has been planned for months! They're exactly 48 weeks old. Professor Ustef is coming over from Switzerland." His voice rose higher. "If we don't harvest the neural tissue now, this week, all our time, all our work will be wasted!"

"But you don't have to be there! Someone else could do it," Sierra retorted, tossing her hair with her hands on her hips. "What about *Te-res-a*?" Her lip curled, as she instantly morphed from despair to rage. "Or one of your other useless techs!"

"No!" the man roared. "I can't have any mistakes! This experiment is crucial. It means everything to me, to my work!"

Sierra's face was crimson as she turned her back on him. For a moment she stood very still, shoulders square. The house was dead quiet except for the low whimper of a child.

"It's good to know what means *everything* to you," she began quietly, then gained volume. "God forbid your *wife* or your *family* should interfere with your precious work." Bitterness caused her voice to tremble, and she placed her hand on the banister for support. "I'm sorry my poor sister could not have been *murdered* at a *more convenient time!*" Sierra screamed, and then broke down and ran sobbing up the stairs.

She rushed right past Logan, who watched her retreat down the hall, then silently turned and closed his door.

Instead of going after his wife, Daniel turned too, almost knocking me down in his haste to escape out the open front door.

A child wailed in earnest now, and the kitchen door clicked shut. The housekeeper disappeared down the hallway.

"What the hell is going on?" Dr. Tau burst out of his office, too late, perhaps by design. Our eyes met.

"So you're back?" he said shortly. "I'd like to see you now."

It was not a request.

~ * ~

"I'm so sorry, Dr. Tau!" The words burst out as we took our seats. "I'm sorry about Mrs. Tau, and I'm sorry about Stacy..."

Emotions welled up, choking me, and I could say no more.

Dr. Tau sat in his enormous ox-blood leather desk chair, leaning forward impassively, elbows propped on a massive mahogany desk cluttered with papers, journals, binders, and pens. An unusual and hopefully one-of-a-kind antique pendant lamp decorated with golden monkeys holding pineapples in their paws dangled overhead. Behind the desk and to the right were wall-length bookcases similar in both style and disorganized content to those in Stacy's room. He cleared his throat.

"I was to die first," he began, musingly, tenting his fingers and gazing up toward the monkeys. "That was the plan. Everything, including the very manner in which we lived our lives, was based upon that assumption. I would die first, and Eleanor would take care of Stacy."

"I see," I said, not sure of the response he was expecting. Another "sorry" didn't seem appropriate.

"But then she had a stroke." His voice sounded strangely distant, as if he doubted the truth of his own words. "She had a stroke."

He sighed heavily.

"And Eleanor, my Eleanor, the beautifully fastidious woman who could not bear a speak of dust on her jacket sleeve, was suddenly drooling down the side of her face. It was *appalling!*" He punctuated his last sentence by slamming his open hand on the desk, causing me to jump and bang my chair sharply against the wall. He didn't appear to notice.

"She looked like the devil! I couldn't stand it! She was repulsive, hideous!" His deep voice rose and the words tripped over each other in the rush for expression. "I couldn't bear to see her. Each time I entered the room, her face would turn toward me, her one bright eye would reach out to me, beseeching me, and her lips would twist into a hideous, clownish grin. It cut me to the bone! It cut me!"

This about his wife of 30-plus years.

"I'm sorry," I repeated, feeling more sorry for Mrs. Tau than her husband, but Dr. Tau wasn't looking for my sympathy. His face grew fierce and his eyes narrowed, almost as if he'd read my thoughts.

"It wasn't fair," he said bitterly. "It wasn't fair at all. What was I supposed to do? It was... unexpected. I was not prepared. I had to hire someone to take care of Eleanor. I couldn't take care of Stacy!"

As a child, I could not appreciate the force of Dr. Tau's personality. He'd seemed perpetually cheerful, always joking, a benign presence but not particularly interesting. Like most other grownups that occasionally intruded upon our egocentric childhood realm, Dr. Tau was only Stacy's father.

Now, as an adult, the intensity and strength of presence of this 65-year-old man surprised me. Despite the white hair, his lined face retained youthful angles, his nose still sharply aquiline, his square jaw set, blue eyes bright, alive, vital even in the face of a double tragedy. I could see how he would be attractive to some women, especially those that had no problem dating a married man. There was a casual arrogance apparent in his manner, but it was not offensive. It set him apart, made his ample frame appear larger, his shoulders broader, his impotent fury more palpable. He rose suddenly and paced the length of the room.

I remembered Sierra telling me she had moved into the mansion to help out. She must have meant to help her mother, but maybe to help Stacy, too. I almost brought that up, but then held my tongue. His anger was boiling over, so I let him vent.

"At first I thought she would rally. After all, Eleanor

was resilient. She'd recovered from far worse. Maybe not physical trauma, but certainly emotional. I thought she'd rally. But there she was, day after day, unable to walk or speak clearly, wearing diapers for God's sake! When I finally accepted she would never get better, she was only a shell. It was *too late*."

"Too late?" I asked, puzzled. "Too late for what?"

He turned toward me, but then his eyes lost focus, and he hesitated before replying.

"Too late... too late to change anything," he answered vaguely, shaking his head and sitting heavily at his desk. He was silent for several long moments, apparently lost in thought. When next he spoke, I could tell he was weighing his words with more care. He pushed back in his chair, placing his hands behind his head, and propped his feet on the desktop giving the appearance of ease.

"Chess came by earlier. He will make all the arrangements for Stacy's funeral once the body is released," he announced to the room.

The body... I nodded, wincing inwardly.

"If there's anything at all I can do..." I began, but he waved my words away.

"Chess handles all my business affairs. He organized the wake and burial of my wife, and he will take care of the business of burying my daughter," he said, his voice brittle, "but the mourning of her..." Dr. Tau paused, and took a deep breath. "The mourning of her, as with Eleanor, will be *personal*." He spat the last word.

"You may stay here as long as you like," he continued with more control, sounding politely detached. "Do not feel that you are in the way, or that you will be an inconvenience to any one of us."

"Thank you, but I..." I hesitated. He'd gone from philosophical to manic to depressed to apathetic in the space of less than 10 minutes. His current calm, impersonal tone was giving me the creeps. Plus I already felt very much in the way. Walking in on Sierra and her husband's screaming match hadn't given me that warm, fuzzy feeling of home. I had my wallet and money for a hotel, so I struggled to think of an excuse to get out of the house and Stacy's room without offending him.

"No." He stopped me before I could start. "Stacy would want you here."

I had no argument for that.

~ * ~

I've often been told that I'm a "good listener". Even when I was a kid, people actively sought me out to over-share often inappropriate personal information. Mom says it's because I have a sympathetic heart and a kind face. I have my own theory. I think it's like the cat that walks into a room full of people and somehow, know-ingly and deliberately, heads straight for that one per-son in the room who least wants a cat to wipe its nose on his or her trousers. People sense that I above all others have zero interest in their affairs. It's not that I don't care about my fellow humans, I do. I care very much. But it's much easier to care about them if I don't know their inner most thoughts, especially their thoughts about their neighbors, their sex life, or how they really felt about their dying spouse. But there it is. People tell me things, and then I have to try to forget.

Thankfully I had some distraction between my en-lightening and unsettling talk with Dr. Tau and the evening meal. Sierra floated down from her room, act-ing as if nothing had happened, and proudly intro-duced me to her two children. They were beautiful. Nine-month-old Faun had a cherubic face, with chubby red checks and a high forehead crowned by rather wispy white hair that looked more like duck fluff than anything else. Three-year-old Tara had violet eyes like her mother's and ringlets of gold down her back, artful-ly arranged I suspected by the slim, and surprisingly young nanny. Luciana Rios, with dark skin and straight black hair that fell almost to her waist, didn't look a day over seventeen. It was her mature manner that after a little conversation convinced me she was closer to my own age or maybe even Sierra's.

Dinner was a singularly gut churning affair, though I think the food would have been delicious. Four relative strangers sat stiffly in the formal dining room at a table for six with two conspicuously empty chairs. Sierra, Logan, and I dined on white fish in apricot sauce with steamed asparagus and rice pilaf, while Dr. Tau enjoyed prime rib au jus with baked potato smothered in sour cream, butter, and chives, shielded from his family behind the Wall Street Journal. We clinked our silver forks and knives on fine china and drank Domaine Ramonet Montrachet Grand Cru from crystal goblets. Everything tasted of sawdust and cardboard to me. Sierra chatted endlessly about her children, their teeth, their steps, their parties and play dates, all the little milestones, as if she didn't have a care in the world.

Logan sat slumped over the table, elbows guarding his plate, and shoveled food into his mouth like a good Catholic after 40 days of Lent.

I tried to engage Logan in conversation once or twice, when Sierra paused for breath or a bite of her fish, but his responses were monosyllabic.

Only once did he look up, when I asked about college. He directed his gaze toward his father's end of the table for the briefest of seconds. "My major?" he repeated, as Dr. Tau shook a wrinkle from his newspaper, and Logan replied, ironically, "Botany, with a minor in Chemistry." Sierra looked at me and rolled her eyes.

We were all so relieved when the meal was over that we bolted from the table and repelled from each other in four different directions; me outside to the porch swing, Sierra to the kitchen where her children waited, Logan back upstairs to his room, and Dr. Tau, still holding the Journal in front of his face, to the sanctuary of his office.

As I sat on the porch, watching the evening fade to night, I thought about Stacy. In spite of what Sierra had said about her being unimportant, someone had deliberately killed her, and had not killed the apparently more appropriate targets of violence in her family, Sierra, Logan, or Dr. Tau. In the last days of her life, she'd made out a Will naming me as the beneficiary of... what? As far as I knew, Stacy was totally dependent upon her parents. She'd never held a job, or had income of her own. And why had she written a Will at all?

I tried to remember what she'd been telling me before she died, wondering if any of it could explain what had happened to her. She'd talked about death and she'd talked about bees, but I'd been so terribly tired I had hardly paid attention to the broad strokes much less focused on the details. There was something else, something I overheard Chess say. "He didn't mean it." And Stacy's response, "but he said it...". Didn't mean what? And *who* was "he"? I planned to ask Chess at the first opportunity. I also planned to get out of the house and Stacy's room as soon as I possibly could, even if I had to scale the back wall under cover of darkness.

In the brief intermission between the Tau-Martindale throw down in the Tau entry hall, Dr. Tau's rabid rant, the Martindale children meet-and-greet, and the drama that was dinner, I'd finally found a few private moments in which to return my missed calls. Both Mom and Dad's phones went directly to voice mail, which I felt was unusual until I realized how late it was in Europe compared with Texas USA. I didn't feel comfortable leaving news of Stacy's death on a recorded message, so just asked for a call back.

I was able to reach Jordy, and he and Rachel, my posse, my peeps, were already on the road. Neither had ever met Stacy, but they'd both insisted on dropping everything and were driving all night from Atlanta to Beaumont to be with me. Despite my relief at having friends on the way, their willingness to come without question also made me wonder: what if I had blown off my exams and been there for Stacy when she needed me most? What if we could have talked more, or I could have listened more? Would she have told me she was afraid of someone? Could I have seen what was coming and saved her somehow?

It's hard not to second-guess your actions when something horrible happens, but it doesn't do any good. Stacy was gone in the instant her heart stopped beating. No matter how hard I wished it, there was no way, in heaven or on earth, to get that instant back.

Chapter 8

At 2:38 a.m. on September 24, 2005, less than four weeks after Katrina surged through New Orleans leaving 1800-plus corpses floating in her wake, Hurricane Rita rode a 20-foot-high wall of water into the coastline between Sabine Pass, Texas and Johnson Bayou, Louisiana while Americans held their collective breath. Fearing an encore of Katrina's pitiless brutality, approximately 3 million coastal residents fled their homes in advance of the storm, the largest evacuation in U.S. history. The mass exodus gridlocked highways as the heat sweltered. More people died in the attempt to escape than in the storm itself.

Mom, Dad, Cal and I were lucky in a way. We hit the road early enough and made it to Dallas, riding out the storm in the relative comfort of a Best Western, only to return two weeks later, when at last allowed back into the city, to find an ancient oak tree, uprooted and lying smack in the middle of the wreckage that had been our home. Virtually every building in the town was damaged by Rita, many destroyed, and we had nowhere to go except back to the hotel. That was the year my family left Beaumont.

After scavenging what we could of our salvageable belongings, which were few, scraping up and hauling off the remnants of our house and selling the lot, we migrated inland, across the country to my father's hometown of Atlanta. Dad said the risk of living on the Gulf was too high, that few things could survive or match the force and destructive power of a hurricane. When Ike hit the region in 2008 his wisdom in initiating the move, though wildly unpopular with some of our family members, me being the most vehemently opposed at the time, was confirmed.

My Dad had weathered his fair share of storms in his life, both literal and figurative storms, but he'd never stood by and watched a friend die. It occurred to me that losing Stacy, in the way she was lost, was shaping up to be a category 5 for me.

A literal and intense electrical storm hit southeastern Texas that evening, and I spent most of the night tucked in a fetal position, shivering beneath the bed covers as thunder rattled the windows and lightning lit the room like mid-day. Around four a.m. the rain stopped and I finally slept, but found myself lost in fitful nightmares of wind, water, and bloated bodies floating in and around the shells of ruined homes. In the midst of the deluge of my dreams, Stacy suddenly appeared to me in stark sunlight, running through fields of wild flowers, toes pointed, her knees too high, arms swinging at awkward angles from her sides, her normal, abnormal gait. She laughed and waved to me, but I couldn't catch her. When I woke up in her room, sweating and chewing my pillow, the world seemed just as inverted as it had on the previous day.

Something was nagging at me, but I couldn't quite put my finger on it. Something that felt obvious, but I just couldn't see it, or more likely chose not to see it. It was early. The rest of the household was quiet, so I passed some time flipping through Stacy's books and sheet music, wondering if these were what she had meant for me under the umbrella of "all my worldly possessions". There were dozens of books on astronomy and almost a library of nature topics, but no Bible or anything about religion or theology. Her sheet music selections included most of the great composers, though there seemed a preponderance of pieces in the key of F-sharp. Stacy always liked the black keys on the piano best.

The pictures around the mirror frame drew my attention. There were tiny portraits, including some of Sierra's and Logan's class photos, and candid shots of the family. Most featured Stacy and her mother, but there were other subjects mixed in. They appeared to be arranged in rough chronological order and I was working my way backward around the circle, when I stopped, staring stunned at the faded photograph of a laughing blond-haired boy in jodhpurs and riding cap, sitting high on the back of a shining black horse. It was Marty. I'd forgotten all about him.

Stacy was not the first child the Taus had lost.

Marty was the Taus' first born, Marshall Tau, Jr., two years older than Sierra and seven years older than Stacy and me. He'd died in a riding accident when he was only 12. I couldn't remember him clearly, being young as I was, but seeing his picture made me feel a great deal more sympathetic toward Dr. Tau than I had the night before. Dr. Tau had lost his son, his wife, and now his daughter. He had plenty of reasons to be embittered, maybe even a bit unhinged.

As I stood gazing at the lined snapshot of a long-dead son, my heart began to ache. At first I thought it was just more sorrow, but then realized it was gratitude, gratitude and relief. As upsetting and horrible as Stacy's death was, my friends, my "cavalry" if you want to call them that, were already on the way. Once I could talk to my Mom or my Dad, then my family would most likely head for Texas, too, or at least to Atlanta to wait for me there. I was grateful to have people I could count on in my life, to be with me, stand by me, and help me through the pain. I could lean on them, any one and all of them, when my own strength wasn't enough.

As far as I could tell, the Taus had no cavalry. No friends or neighbors had stopped by. Dr. Tau's business partners were conspicuously absent. Sierra's own husband refused to stay with her. Logan was locked up alone in his room. According to Dr. Tau, Chess had visited, but in a professional capacity, and I hadn't seen Margaret Sheffield or Page since the wee hours of Saturday morning. It seemed the three remaining Taus only had each other, and they obviously weren't feeling the love.

That's when the idea struck me that my presence in the house might actually be of benefit to Stacy's family, might provide a buffer from all the in-fighting and drama. With an outsider in the house, the Taus would be on their best behavior and perhaps treat each other with some small degree of at least superficial kindness. Plus, I could be kind to them if no one else was. For Stacy's sake, I decided to stay with the Taus at least until after the funeral, and then I would leave Beaumont for the last time.

With a new sense of purpose and a definite plan in mind, I showered, ran a comb through my hair, decided on a plain white shirt and jeans from among Sierra's donated clothing, pulled on Stacy's boots, and wandered downstairs to the kitchen. The kitchen staff, with the help of a bevy of caterers, was preparing Sunday brunch, apparently in anticipation of quite a crowd. Polished but still empty heated silver serving trays were set out on folding tables covered with black linen tablecloths arranged along the windows that overlooked the garden. Peace lilies and pale purple orchids graced with black ribbons and lace mesh were arranged as centerpieces and tucked into corners and cubbies throughout the room.

In stark contrast to the somberness of the house, just beyond the windows the garden was vibrant with spring. Ruby-throated hummingbirds, bumblebees and tiny, gray Hairstreak butterflies fluttered insistently over brilliant red Texas Plume, incandescent Bluebonnets, and vivid yellow Euryops. I stood for a moment, trying to soak in the serenity of the idyllic scene through the glass, when the sound of muted voices drew my attention. Stepping closer to the window, I was surprised to see Page and Chess Anderson, sitting on the back door stoop.

~ * ~

My first friendly impulse was to tap on the window-pane and wave, but I hesitated, stopping the forward motion of my hand in mid-rap. Though not suspicious by nature, Det. Hawk's cynicism had had an effect on me, and that, coupled with the apparent intensity of the conversation going on in front of me led me to step back out of sight behind the edge of the raw silk drapes.

Page was seated on the broad top step with her back to me so that I could not see her face. Chess was two steps down, looking up at her with such grief and des-pair in his eyes as I have rarely seen before or since. His mouth was moving, the words a murmur, but his expression indicated great pain, a question or plea. As I watched, Page reached out and gripped her husband's shoulder. He buried his face in both hands.

Under normal circumstances, had I stumbled upon two friends having such an obviously private and emo-tionally charged discussion, I would have tactfully withdrawn; however, in this instance I found myself feeling frustrated that the scene was playing out with no sound, a silent picture with plenty of angst, but no words. As I looked up, scanning the room for a better vantage point, Sierra suddenly burst through the kitch-en doors with a baby on her hip and a toddler in tow.

"Has anyone seen Lu?" she demanded in exaspera-tion, a question aimed at the busy and bustling food preparers.

She saw me at the window and walked over, head tilted, looking both surprised and then shrewd when she recognized Chess and Page through the glass. Frowning slightly and shaking her head, but without a word, Sierra immediately tapped on the windowpane, bringing the couple quickly to their feet.

Feeling more than a little embarrassed, at least until I recalled Sierra own proclivities for keyhole listening, I made no excuses, but moved to open the door.

"Hi Guys," I said, trying to sound as if I hadn't just been spying on them. "Wouldn't anyone let you in?"

I held the screen door open to allow them to pass through. Page smiled at me as she ducked under my arm. "We didn't ring the bell. We were just enjoying the calm before the storm."

"We're here for the brunch," Chess explained, his voice sounding tight with residual emotion, his smile forced. The way he avoided eye contact reminded me of Stacy.

"Have any of you seen Lu?" Sierra interrupted, impatiently. "It's not like her to wander off. Here, hold this," she instructed, handing the baby to Page as we all responded in the negative.

Faun cooed happily, gazing at Page with china blue eyes as if she'd just found the love of her life, and then extended her hands, stubby fingers outstretched. Page immediately cooed back, began touching each stumpy finger with her own slender ones, singing softly about a spider, completely oblivious to any other audience except the child.

Sierra's face lost all expression as she watching Page intently, and for a moment I inexplicably expected her to snatch the baby away, but then she turned and led Tara from the room, still calling for the nanny.

"We walked over." Chess offered, still distracted as he pointed across the back yard, past the remnants of yellow crime scene tape that fluttered from the corner of the carriage house.

"So you live in your parents' house?" I asked, making polite conversation with two childhood friends I hadn't spoken with in years, "or did you buy one next door?"

"Theirs," he answered. "We moved in after the car accident, to take care of Pop. We're only three doors down from Page's Mom so we can look out for her, too."

He shook his head, though I wasn't sure at what; the accident, his Dad, Page's Mom, I couldn't tell.

"I'm so sorry," Page exclaimed suddenly, turning to me as she bounced the baby in her arms. "Sorry for Stacy, and sorry for you, being there... to... see... how horrible it must have been..."

Her voice trailed off as she struggled to find the right words. Her dark eyes were troubled and she swallowed hard, and then looked away. Apparently sensing a problem with her previously happy playmate, Faun reached out, touching Page's cheek with her dough-girl hand, a funny, serious look on her cherubic face. Page smiled sadly at the baby, ruffled her duck fluff hair and ran a finger down her tiny perfect nose. Faun giggled.

Page was Sierra's age, but lacked the jaded, worldly expression so often seen on her cousin's face. Like Sierra, Page had been on the Cheer Squad, but for some reason always seemed to end up near the bottom of the human pyramid while Sierra soared at the top.

Page's father and my Dad had worked at an engineering firm together in Beaumont where they became fairly close friends. Alex Sheffield was a decent, respectable sort as far as I could remember, but his wife Margaret, five years older than he was and 11 years older than her sister, Eleanor, was considered to have "married down". It occurred to me now that she must have married late. Someone told me once that Page was Mrs. Sheffield's "miracle baby", conceived in her peri-menopausal years when she'd almost given up hope of ever having a child. Neither Page's family nor mine were in anywhere near the same tax bracket as the Taus. Had it not been for the relationship between the sisters, and my Dad's friendship with Mr. Sheffield, we'd probably never have been invited into the Tau's social circle at all, and I'd never have met Stacy though we lived only two doors down.

Like the Taus, Chess came from money. For generations, his family owned a very large house almost directly behind them. As he apparently had control of his father's estate, I suspected Chess was more than well off. I wondered if he worked for Dr. Tau because he really needed the income, or if for personal reasons he wanted to be of use to the family. For as long as I could remember, Chess had played an essential role in Stacy's life, looking out for her welfare in all those areas in which her mother's influence could not reach, particularly in kid-to-kid interactions where Stacy's lack of understanding and literal mind left her vulnerable to the ridicule of her peers. I had always interpreted his interest as brotherly, but maybe things had become more complicated since I'd been gone.

"Thanks," I said to Page. "It was... bad..." *Bad? Words could not convey the depth of "bad"...* "But there's something I wanted to ask Chess... something Stacy said..." I began, turning back to her husband.

At that moment, there was the sound of the porch door swinging open, and Luciana stepped into the room.

We all gazed in her direction. Her face reddened at the scrutiny. She moved to join us, and as she passed me I caught a whiff of reefer.

"I'll take her," she offered, reaching for Faun.

Page held Faun out, and then, wrinkling her nose, immediately drew the baby back into the curve of her shoulder.

"You'd better wash up first," she advised, grimly, a stern and disapproving expression on her face. "And quickly before Sierra finds you," she added pointedly.

Surprise flickered in Luciana's dark eyes, promptly replaced by understanding.

"Oh, but I didn't... I don't..." she stammered.

There was a loud thudding against the porch door-frame as Logan stumbled over the threshold.

Luciana blanched and then, with a horrified look, fled the room.

"People! Friends!" Logan staggered toward us, arms outstretched, apparently intoxicated from more than pot. He recognized me and stopped. "You..." he breathed, black eyes wide, his reaction reflecting both confusion and concern, and turning, he walked unsteadily but quickly away, through the kitchen door without another word.

We all stood for a moment in stunned silence.

"Do you think I should tell Sierra...?" Page began, rocking Faun who grinned up at her, when the screen door opened a third time, this time to admit Margaret Sheffield.

Wow. This is ridiculous, like Grand Central Station! I thought, frustrated. In the back of my mind, I was still waiting to ask Chess my question about the conversation I overheard on the night of Stacy's death.

"Well, I never!" Mrs. Sheffield exclaimed.

"Oh, but I'm sure you have!" Dr. Tau responded laughing, entering the room from the opposite direction through the kitchen doors. "How's everything coming along?" he boomed, sounding like he had when we were children, as if he hadn't just buried his wife and wasn't soon to bury his daughter.

"Everything's well in hand, Sir," Charlotte Nelson, the housekeeper/cook answered immediately. I had not noticed her specifically among the many caterers and house staff bustling about the kitchen, but wondered if she had been a silent witness to the recent conversations, and comings and goings through her domain.

"The preparations for the memorial service may be well in hand," Margaret Sheffield conceded, speaking low as she waved him over to join us, "but you really must do something about your son and that nanny person."

Dr. Tau put his large hand on her slender shoulder and smiled down at her.

"And what must I do, Maggie dear? Are they having a tryst?" He laughed again. "If so, then good for Logan! I was beginning to think he was asexual, staying in his room all day and all night, his only visitor his pharmaceutical rep. And neither he nor she is married, so what's the harm in it?"

"I don't know if they're sleeping together," Mrs. Sheffield answered primly, "and that's certainly not what I meant." She paused to make sure she had everyone's attention. We all drew nearer as she continued in a whisper.

"As I was walking over, I saw them! Out behind the green house, smoking one of those foul cigarettes, you know, the *illegal kind?*"

Dr. Tau shook his head, but his eyes twinkled, and he gave an exaggerated sigh, "Now Mags, you know I've sent Logan to the best rehab facilities money can buy, on more than one occasion, and with no good return for my investment. I'm not about to send the nanny and have the same disappointing results."

"Well." Margaret Sheffield huffed, "If you choose to pretend not to understand me, then you'll have to face the consequences..."

"The guests are arriving," the butler announced, as the doorbell sounded. Dr. Tau clapped his sister-in-law on the shoulder before moving quickly away.

Margaret Sheffield looked perturbed, until Faun's cooing caught her attention. Her face softened as she reached for the child.

"What a cute little baby you are," she laughed, chucking the chubby cheek, causing Faun to squeal with glee.

It's funny that no matter how old you are or how sophisticated you may pretend to be, a baby's laughter can make you act like an idiot.

"Bebe, bebe, beb-be," chattered Mrs. Sheffield, raising Faun above her head and dancing, her steps cha-cha-like.

"Don't grow up to be like your ma-ma," she intoned, in a singsong voice.

Chapter 9

The reception was dubbed a "Celebration of the Life of Stacy Tau", and pictures of Stacy lined the walls and hallways through which the guests passed. Attendance was spotty, the entire uneasy assembly composed of Dr. Tau's six practice partners and their wives and husbands, plus an assortment of nurses and nursing assistants and the office manager, apparently all of whom felt compelled by business allegiances to attend but who were actively seeking the first politely acceptable excuse to leave. Of course I had no idea how many guests had been invited. I suppose Chess or Page had put together a list, but it seemed odd that there were no younger people in the group, no friends of Stacy, Sierra, or Logan, with the exception of our childhood gang.

As Stacy's surrogate, I put on my best game face and circulated through the small crowd, introducing myself, shaking hands, not that Stacy would or could have engaged in that type of social behavior, but because these represented her mourners such as they were. Lu was entertaining Sierra's children in another part of the house, and so Sierra was free to mingle, but seemed unusually subdued and spent most of her time standing in close proximity to Logan, though little conversation passed between them. Logan had somehow pulled himself together after his recent descent into reefer madness, and looked alert, even edgy, much less stoned than I had seen him since my arrival in the house leading me to wonder if his new positive energy was also chemically induced.

Dr. Tau played the part of the ultimate host, making sure everyone had a drink or was fed, managing to cover whatever sense of anger or bitterness he felt beneath a veneer of joviality, as if the afternoon gathering was a private soiree instead of a wake. Chess and Page circled on the periphery, arm-in-arm, speaking only to each other. There was a strange fragility about Chess that I could not account for in a man who had always been such a rock for the rest of us. It would have seemed natural for him to interact with the practice partners, all of whom must have known him reasonable well, but he hung back, while his mother-in-law was the life of the party, telling stories of funny things Stacy did as a child to polite listeners and making sure the caterers kept everything in order. Margaret Sheffield really put herself out to make the reception as successful as possible, and I wondered at that. I didn't believe she was particularly fond of Stacy, or even liked Dr. Tau, and could only conclude she was driven by a desire to act as a stand-in for her late sister, as I was acting as Stacy's ambassador.

The party was winding down, guests were past the point of glancing discretely at watches, some I suspect were on the verge of covertly paging themselves in order to create the charade of a medical or personal emergency as cover for rushing away, and I was as anxious as anyone for the festivities to end. Jordy had texted earlier in the day that he and Rachel, though slowed by the storm, were at last in the area, staying at the Book Nook Inn, a charming and unique little B&B in nearby Lumberton. They had grabbed some sleep after their rather tense drive and were waiting for me there. Things had gone smoothly at Stacy's wake, due in large part to Margaret Sheffield's efforts, and I was just about to sigh with relief and slip out when Sierra abruptly coughed and made her way to the front of the room.

"First of all I... we... my family would like to thank you all for coming," she said, looking around to see that she had everyone's attention. "I can't tell you how much it means to have you here."

She seemed sadder than she had the night before, depressed, shaken, less confident, less poised. The fact of Stacy's death was apparently sinking in; the sense of unreality fading.

"I know Stacy would have appreciated it."

There was a collective nod from the crowd.

"Of course all of you knew who Stacy was, but she was a difficult girl to get to know well." Sierra smiled ruefully. "I thought it would be nice if some of us who were closest to her could share our favorite stories about Stacy."

Her audience looked less than enthusiastic, and I felt panic rising at the thought of having to stand in front of these strangers and talk about my dead friend. The memory of Stacy bleeding on the floor was foremost in my mind and had at present pushed all other memories aside. I couldn't recall one single happy or hopeful story to tell.

"Who would like to go first?" Sierra asked eagerly, as if we'd all be running over each other for the chance.

No one spoke, as all attendees either directed their gazes at each other or the floor. Sierra's expression changed as she scanned the room; a line formed between her eyes and her mouth tightened.

"How about you Chess?" Sierra invited, tossing her hair. "I'm sure you have *lots* of stories to tell."

The way she said it was not quite kind, and caused everyone to turn toward Chess who was standing at the back of the room. His face went white, Page's flushed red, and Margaret Sheffield, well, she seemed to expand to Godzilla-sized from the waves of hatred that suddenly radiated from her petite frame. Page recovered first and squeezed her husband's arm.

"I have a story," she said, her voice even and self-assured, but I saw her swallow hard. Margaret Sheffield took a protective step forward, but then gathered her composure and smiled at her daughter.

"Of course you do, my Dear," she said, managing to

beam encouragement at her daughter while her eyes simultaneously shot daggers at Sierra, as Page made her way through the small crowd to the front of the room, "and I'm sure we'd all love to hear it."

Chess still looked shaken, but Page had successfully diverted the attention of the group from him to her. I casually moved along the wall toward him.

"When Stacy was only..." Page began, and launched into a rather rambling account of Stacy's learning to ride a tricycle, which involved Stacy taking the trike to pieces and then reassembling it to make certain she understood how the mechanics should work before she would consider sitting upon the seat.

"Well... ah... thanks for that Page," Sierra said, sounding slightly dubious, as if she suspected Page of some degree of fabrication. "Who's next? How about you, Wim?"

Her smile and voice were confident, expectant. I'd been making my way across the room, over to Chess, hoping for an opportunity to ask my question in his wife's brief absence from his side, and so looked up with some degree of alarm.

"We don't need any more stories about Stacy," Logan interrupted from the sidelines before I could speak. "No one here wanted to be around her when she was alive. Why pretend? Why talk about her now that she's dead? We all avoided her because she was weird, well, except for Wim. She's the only real friend Stacy ever had, at least until she moved away..."

Logan was angry, his dark eyes flashing as he ran a hand through his thick mop of hair.

"Are you really so self-absorbed?" he chided Sierra. "Can't you see that everyone just wants to leave? They've had their food. They've had their drinks. They've paid their tribute, to Dad, to you. *They want to go!*"

Deftly securing a champagne glass from one of the servers, he moved to the front of the room.

Sierra's initial expression of outrage at the disruption was melting into concern.

"Logan, Honey, please don't, don't make a scene..." she began, reaching for the glass in his hand. He jerked his arm away, spilling a good portion of the golden liquid on the floor.

Faces turned toward Dr. Tau, but he stood silent, watching the proceedings curiously but dispassionately, as if from a great distance.

"Everyone get a glass!" ordered Logan. "Everyone! Now! We're going to drink a toast to Stacy and then you can all go, back to your lives, and forget her as soon as you walk out the door!"

There were murmurs, but no one objected. Even Margaret Sheffield held her tongue. The situation was uncomfortable enough that we all sought the most expedient way out. Servers moved through the room and everyone took a glass, whether of water, soda, or wine.

"To my sister," Logan said, clearly, soberly, and raised his glass. He looked around the room until his eyes met his father's. "Some would say she's better off dead, and maybe she is at that. We all know this place sucks! Some would say she wasn't *my* sister at all." He turned to Sierra and his face darkened. "But she was, in every way that counted. Even though I wasn't a very good brother... still... Here's to her... to my sister Stacy. She deserved so much better than she got from us."

There were no "cheers" but each raised his or her glass and killed it. Then we all fled the room.

~ * ~

Although I had committed to supporting the Taus in their time of stress and grief, I couldn't at that moment manage my own. Without a word to anyone, without looking back, I ran, straight through the front door and to my rental car. Unfortunately in an act of extreme poor judgment I had moved the car to the driveway and so it was impossibly blocked in on all sides. Even though it was probably close to ninety degrees in the shade, I didn't hesitate. I opened the car door and got in, shutting myself into a sauna. My hands were shaking as I gripped the steering wheel and leaned my head against the padded airbag emblem. I wasn't crying, didn't really feel like crying, couldn't begin to put a name to how I felt, but I knew I was coming apart, shattering into pieces, and wanted to see my family or my friends or both, badly.

Knowing that Jordy and Rachel were less than a half hour away only made the waiting harder, but I sat there, sweet gathering in beads and then sliding down my face, chest, and back, until my shirt was soaked, until a sufficient number of guests had departed to clear the way out.

Then I started the car, turned up the A/C, and headed north.

Chapter 10

I'd met my friends, Jordy and Rachel, during my first year in Atlanta. We were science nerds together at Westminster, one of the area's best private schools, and quickly became BFFs.

Jordy, Jorge Castillo, was brilliant, funny, tall, skinny, and had black spiky hair with the suggestion of a widow's peak. His canines were prominent, and he sported the Goth look with great success for several years. The edgy, sexy-scary Edward Cullen smirk was only a façade though. Inside, Jordy was all marshmallows, a fact that some of his earliest girlfriends quickly discovered to their advantage. He'd been hurt to the point that he made casual dating a sport beginning in twelfth grade, his bad boy reputation for loving and leaving only making him more attractive to girls who liked to swim in the deep end. I'd been in love with him since I was sixteen, but never told him of course.

Rachel Sands, shrewd, sincere, sometimes sarcastic, had curly chestnut hair and freckles, so many freckles that her skin looked light brown from a distance until you were close enough to see the fairness between the spots. She wore large round-rimmed glasses that were always sliding down her nose, and sensible, low-heeled shoes that contributed to the untidy intellectual image she chose to portray. Rachel was the most out-spoken in our group, almost always had a cause to argue, and often took up for Jordy or me whether we needed or wished for her to do so or not.

It was extremely fortunate that we had each other at Westminster, as none of us were particularly athletic. Westminster fields 81 athletic teams and has won more than 200 state championships of one sort or another, but also has the 5th highest success rate and 2nd hardest learning program of any non-boarding school in the South. The three of us were academically inclined, definitely not cool individually but we felt a strong sense of belonging together, and helped each other through the acne and angst of Upper School. Upon graduation, we all attended Emory as undergraduates. Jordy and I went premed, but Rachel shocked almost everyone, faculty and family included, when she abandoned her science-techie roots and decided to major in journalism. I could see it. Rachel always had a strong sense of social justice, though she often took exception to the views and questionable ethics of the prevailing liberal press.

Jordy's parents were both professors at Emory; his Dad chaired the Department of Neuroscience while his Mom was a full professor in Microbiology. He was an only child, so the pressure to succeed, and the pressure to stay close to home, had been great. Although he had high marks, in college and on the MCAT, and applied to and was accepted by several prestigious medical schools, Jordy ultimately opted to stay at Emory while I left for Boston. I hadn't seen Jordy or Rachel since Christmas.

The Book Nook Inn was out in the boonies of Lumberton, TX, but easy enough to find. I took 287 to the Cooks Lake Road exit and wove my way down a two-lane country road until I saw the big white sign. I knocked on the main door, asked for Mr. Castillo, and was directed to the "Steam punk room", located at the top of a three-story tower at the rear of the house. A large, black and white cat accompanied me up the first two flights of stairs, but then abandoned me to climb the rest alone. Jordy opened the door. Rachel hugged me, and I was so glad to see them both that I didn't think to consider the two suitcases side-by-side on the floor. There was only one bed.

"We can sit at the table," Rachel said, leading me to an oak pedestal dining table set in an octagon-shaped alcove.

Tree branches right outside the window were visible through the white café curtains. Rachel sat across from me while Jordy leaned against the wall behind her. I noticed that Rachel looked remarkably well, her curly hair tamed and pulled back in a knot at her neck. She wore tight black leggings, and a sheer, flowing blouse cut quite a bit lower than her normal conservative attire. Jordy was Jordy in retrospect, in jeans and faded Lacuna Coil T-shirt.

They offered a drink and I took bottled water, fearing alcohol would exaggerate my already heightened emotional state. Rachel had red wine. Jordy poured wine for himself, but set the glass on the near-by nightstand after one sip. I opened my mouth to speak, and couldn't stop...

I told them everything; beginning from the time Stacy called me to tell me of her Mom's death up until the moment I left the Taus' house that Sunday afternoon. Rachel put in an occasional question, but Jordy stood silently, arms crossed over his chest until I started to cry. Then he came and pulled a chair close beside me, held my hand, brushed wet strands of hair back from my face as I sobbed. Rachel handed me tissues, and more tissues, and then began to cry in sympathy.

"Oh, Rache," I sniffled, "Don't you cry, too! You're such a brat."

We looked at each other's blotchy complexions and red-rimmed eyes and laughed, which made me feel better. I got up and went into the bathroom to wash my face and blow my nose. That's when I noticed the co-mingled toiletries, and a vague sense of panic gripped me.

When I came out, Rachel and Jordy were sitting side-by-side on the edge of the king-sized bed and he had his arm around her, her head against his shoulder. I don't know if my face turned red or white, but my heart gave a pretty good jump when the realization finally struck me that my "besties" had somehow become a couple while I'd been studying my butt off in Boston. I wondered why no one had mentioned this rather significant change in the dynamic of our little trio to me, and voiced the question before I could stop myself.

"So what's up? Are ya'll dating now?" I couldn't quite keep the incredulous tone from my voice.

Luckily Rachel, usually so perceptive, didn't seem to notice. She squeezed Jordy's hand and raised it with hers while smiling broadly, almost triumphantly. A jewel stone sparkled from her left ring finger.

"Yep. Our confirmed free agent's finally seen the light and decided to commit to contract," she said, leaning over to plant a quick kiss on his cheek, and then smoothed away the lingering lipstick smudge with her thumb. "We wanted to surprise you when you came home after vacation, thought it would be a good joke, but now..."

I wanted to throw up. I put my hand on the bathroom doorknob as Rachel's triumph shifted to concern and her smile abruptly faded.

"Wim, I'm sorry about your friend Stacy, we both are, and so we wanted to be here for you. In all the hustle of the trip, the last minute rush, we kind of forgot you didn't already know. We've been together since February, right after Valentine's Day."

"And you're engaged?" *Unbelievable!*

"Engaged to be engaged," Rachel laughed and blushed. "We haven't set a date yet."

I wasn't sure what was significant about "right after Valentine's Day", but felt there must be something. My mind was reeling and I could think of nothing either had said around that time about dating or life changes or really anything at all. I looked from Rachel to Jordy. He didn't say a word, didn't smile, just gazed back at me, his dark eyes searching. He was always so good at reading me, better than anyone else I've ever known.

He knows, I thought in despair.

I picked at the cuticle of my right index finger, flustered, but quickly recovered. They had come because of Stacy. This was about her, not me.

"Oh. I'm happy for you, *surprised*, but *happy...for you*... And thanks for coming," I replied, calmly enough, but sounding a bit too polite. "It's been just horrible. I can't tell you how much I appreciate you being here."

I hugged them both, a gender-neutral hug each. Rachel smiled again, and Jordy nodded, a look of something like relief on his handsome face. I was relieved too, hoping he would believe my distress was all for my friend's death and had nothing to do with a broken heart.

~ * ~

I didn't have a key to the Taus' house, so made that my excuse for an abrupt exit, ably avoiding any dinner plans with the pretense that I didn't want to offend my host or hostess by being absent from Beaumont for too long. I stopped at the first gas station I saw, washed my face again in the bathroom sink, blew my nose, filled the gas tank and headed west, hoping a drive might still the thoughts ricocheting round inside my head, and ease some of the pain in my heart. The sun was still fairly high in the sky, and with sunset after 8p.m. I didn't expect to do much driving in the dark, at least the literal dark. I left the radio off, and Stacy was my co-pilot. Feeling incapable of processing the news about Jordy and Rachel, I soon put my personal concerns aside.

There was something important, probably more than one thing, but something very obvious about Stacy's murder that I knew I was missing. I re-ran everything that had happened, every conversation I could remember, focusing especially on comments made by Det. Hawk. He was convinced it was someone close to Stacy, not some gang banger, not some random home invader, but a family member or friend. I was half way to Houston when I realized he had to be right.

I didn't want to believe it of course, tried every argument I could think of against it, but in the end there was no way around the facts. The front door to the guesthouse was at ground level. Stacy was shot in the living room on the second floor. No one brought a ladder and no one broke in. Stacy either opened the door to her killer, or the killer had a key.

~ * ~

After crossing Old River Lake, I turned around at 565 and headed back. I'd shut my cell off before Stacy's wake, after making sure Jordy and Rachel arrived okay, because I didn't want the ringer going off in front of Dr. Tau's guests and I really didn't feel like talking to anyone anyway. On powering the phone up, I found a short message from Mom. She sounded calm, but reported bad news, more inconvenient than alarming. My parents' bags had been stolen while they were traveling from Florence to Milan via Eurostar Italia on the first leg of their journey to Paris to meet me, with all their papers, passports, cell phones, tickets gone. Cal had wired money from home, but Monday was a bank holiday and so no arrangements could be made for replacement documents until Tuesday at earliest. Until then, they were stuck, if stuck is the right word, in Italy. I sighed and powered the cell down again.

Construction on the Interstate caused traffic delays. It was dusk when I pulled into the driveway in The Oaks. Shadows were falling across the broad porch of the old mansion and only one light was visible from the front of the house when I arrived. It was the one in Stacy's room. I wondered if she was waiting up for me.

Chapter 11

Stacy's funeral was on Monday. I don't remember much about it. I cried. Jordy and Rachel looked on, helpless and grim. Sierra made a point of telling my friends how much help I had been to her and her family, and how glad she was that I was staying with them. I cried more. To this day, I couldn't say who else attended, though I had the impression of a crowd. I don't know if Logan was drunk, high, or inappropriate, or if Chess broke down, or which one of Dr. Tau's dissociative personalities showed up. I do think I remember seeing Det. Hawk, but he said nothing to me. When it was over, Jordy and Rachel came back with me to Stacy's room and sat with me while I struggled to put all the feelings of horror, panic, guilt, and sorrow into words. Then Jordy went to the Book Nook to check out and get the luggage, and Rachel stayed, while I slept soundly for the first time in days.

"Are you coming back with us?" she asked, when I finally woke up.

I considered.

"I want to," I answered, and sighed. "You don't know how much I want to..."

"But you can't." She finished for me.

"No. Not yet any way," I explained, "I need to find out about Stacy's Will. I've no idea what was in her mind when she wrote it, or even what it means, but in any case it'll be easier to deal with now and in person."

Rachel nodded.

"Do you want us to stay?"

Well yes, but... I had to be a grown up.

"No. You and Jordy go on home. Hopefully I'll be

there in a few days."

We were sitting on the bed and I reached over to squeeze her hand.

"Thanks so much for coming."

She nodded again. "Of course, Wim. What are friends for? We should get you something to eat though, before we go. Tex-Mex?"

Practical, Rachel was always so practical about things. She had a way of making the world seem a little less chaotic and a lot less frightening.

~ * ~

On Tuesday morning I at last reached my Mom and told her, as concisely as I could, what had happened. She was shocked, and concerned for me, and sorry that the loss of their luggage and resultant complications had made them unavailable in my time of stress. She promised to sort things out as soon as they possibly could and catch the earliest flight from Milan to Paris and then to The States. I expected to be back in Atlanta by the time they were. It was almost 10 am before I left Stacy's room and headed down the stairs.

I was surprised to find Dr. Tau in his study with Det. Hawk, and the door standing open. Chess was seated on the bench beside the door, possibly to discourage unwanted eavesdroppers or maybe to keep an eye out for someone, namely me.

"Wim," Dr. Tau called, motioning to me with his big hands. "I thought you might have gone."

Gone where? Home to Atlanta? I wish...

"No, of course not," I answered, moving to the study door. "I thought I might need to stay a few more days..."

I didn't want to say, "...for the reading of the Will" so left it at that.

"That's good!" he replied, in his boisterous voice, which sounded somehow lacking in conviction. "Chess and I will talk shortly and then we should all meet with my attorney this afternoon." He hesitated, his brow uncharacteristically furrowed. "There's something I'm told I must discuss with you, but honestly I don't see the point. Stacy made her wishes quite clear."

The light filtering through the blinds fell upon his face and he looked suddenly very old.

"Not that any of it matters in any case..." he trailed off, absently shuffling and stacking papers on his desk.

Up until that point Det. Hawk had remained silent and Dr. Tau appeared almost to have forgotten him. The younger man cleared his throat. Dr. Tau looked up.

"Thank you for your time," Hawk said, rising from the chair. "I'll let you get back to work. If you think of anything else, then please let me know."

Chess got up to go into the study as Det. Hawk came out. I tried to avoid running into both and there was an awkward moment or two as we danced around each other, and then Chess pulled the door closed behind him leaving me alone in the entry hall with a detective. I hesitated. He stood there, towering over me, expectantly, as if he knew what was coming.

"Can I talk to you privately," I asked, and then added, "and confidentially?" I wasn't sure if one could be confidential with a detective. I knew he could use what I said against me, the Miranda warning and all that, but hoped he wouldn't share anything I might say with the Taus or anyone else.

"Sure," Hawk replied, gesturing toward the door. "Would you rather have our conversation outside?"

I nodded and followed him out to the front porch, but even that space felt confining so I led him across the lawn to the rose garden. It was still relatively early for roses, but some varieties were already in bloom, though the majority would bloom nearer Fall. I took a deep breath.

"I think you may be right." I found myself whispering, though clearly no one else was around. The beds were raised, but not so high that a person of normal height or build could hide behind them. "Well, actually I know you're right..."

"About what?" he asked, feigning surprise, "or do you mean I'm right about everything in general?" He smiled, softening the pit bull look. I bit my lip and leaned toward him.

"About who killed Stacy." Still whispering conspiratorially. "About it being someone she knew, someone close..."

"I was sure you'd get there eventually, whether you wanted to or not." His smile faded, and he shook his head. "I'm sorry, but that's the only way to explain the evidence."

"Unless of course you did it," he added, but his tone wasn't accusing, only slightly amused.

I remembered my melt down and flushed red, but then shook off my embarrassment.

"Look," I said, a bit impatiently, "you may or may not consider me a serious suspect. I don't expect you'd tell me if you did, but *I* know it wasn't me, and so my question is "who did it?" Do you know yet?"

He tilted his head and in the sunlight I noticed again how soft his eyes could be, a lighter brown with golden flecks, like they were when he first questioned me on the night Stacy died.

"I have suspicions, but no hard evidence," he frowned, hesitating. "That's as much as I can say right now."

"But what about the gun?" I asked, trying for once to take advantage of my attractiveness to over-sharers and hoping Det. Hawk might be one, or at least have tendencies I could leverage. "Were there any fingerprints?"

He laughed, a genuine laugh, and lost some of his guarded look. "Only everyone's, well, except yours. That's one of the reasons I ruled you out, even with the motive of the Will. There's no evidence the killer wore gloves, but it's as if that gun was passed around to everyone, all family members and friends. Fingerprints over fingerprints, on the gun barrel, the trigger, the shells, all over it. Totally useless."

"Plus the whole lot of them had been at the firing range that afternoon so plenty of ways to explain away gunshot residue on their hands or clothes. The shot was fired from across the room; no blood spatter on the shooter." He shrugged. "No, it was well planned, carefully executed, cold-blooded premeditated murder, and whoever did it just might get away with it."

"You're kidding me?" I was alarmed. "Right? You've got to be kidding me."

He shook his head, looking directly at me and speaking slowly, as if he meant for me to absorb every word.

"We don't have any hard evidence tying anyone in particular to the crime scene. The family's being awfully closed mouthed... don't really think they'd intentionally cover for each other... They don't seem to like each other that much... No one's giving anyone else an alibi or anything like that... If fact, most of them claim to have been alone in their rooms or home in bed... I think there are just so many secrets in this house that everyone's first instinct is to lie, whether he or she has any knowledge of the murder or not."

"Secrets?" I whispered, automatically stepping closer, and that's when we heard the scream.

Chapter 12

The scream belonged to Margaret Sheffield. I recognized her voice immediately, coming from the back of the house. We both took off at a run, but Det. Hawk, having longer legs, easily beat me around the corner. A petite elderly figure was staggering across the lawn, obviously distraught, clutching her chest.

She's having a heart attack, I thought, but when she caught sight of us she stopped staggering and began to run forward.

"She's out there," Margaret Sheffield gasped, stumbling, pointing back over her shoulder, for once inarticulate. "She's out there!"

As she drew nearer, I noticed grass stains on her knees, and runners where she'd torn the fronts of her opaque stockings. Her hands and the cuffs of her blouse were smeared with red.

"Who?" the detective demanded, as Mrs. Sheffield threw herself at me, collapsing in my arms.

"That nanny person," she sputtered. "That poor nanny person. I found her. I *touched* her. She's dead!"

Det. Hawk looked at me, and then, unholstering his gun, stalked purposefully and cautiously across the lawn in the direction from which Mrs. Sheffield had come. I stayed where I was, partly to console Mrs. Sheffield and partly because I'd already seen Stacy dead and didn't need the image of Luciana dead, if she was so, to add to my nightmares.

"Take me inside," Mrs. Sheffield moaned, but I shushed her.

"Let's wait," I said, unable to move from the spot until Hawk returned. I didn't want to leave him out there alone on principle, though I knew I could be of no practical help if the murderer still lurked in the garden. He'd gone beyond the green house, which blocked my view, and so I stood there, holding Page's mother and my breath.

First there were sirens, and then police cars, a van and an ambulance, and then the lush green lawn was covered with officers, examiners, and EMTs. Chess and Dr. Tau came out into the yard and stood with me. Chess tried to take Mrs. Sheffield into the house, but she appeared to have changed her mind about going in. She simply looked at him as if he were speaking a foreign language, confusion and fear clouding her eyes as she clung to my neck. I imagined I'd worn the same look on the night that Stacy died.

After an age or maybe a few minutes, Det. Hawk came back into view. Even before I could make out his features, his posture told me all I needed to know. The tall detective's shoulders were squared in anger but his head hung low and he'd donned his Ray-Bans like a mask. His gun was back in its holster; he was speaking into his cell phone.

"Ok," he said as he snapped the phone shut, and then turned to me still awkwardly supporting my elderly charge.

"Why didn't you take her inside?" he inquired, briskly; very detached, very official. "I'll need to ask her some questions."

"We'll take her now," said Dr. Tau moving forward, his boisterous voice subdued, before I could answer for myself.

Putting his big hand on Margaret Sheffield's shoulder, he stooped to bring his craggy face close to hers.

"Mags?" he said, softly. "Maggie, dear, let's all go into the house."

For a moment she looked into his eyes. Her forehead crinkled, and then without a word she reached up and gripped his hand, her small fingers encircled his, and the three of us walked together toward the back porch, with Chess following. Halfway there, Mrs. Sheffield found her voice, though what she said didn't make a lot of sense.

"I didn't know her name," she murmured. "I couldn't call out because I didn't know her name." She looked away, embarrassed, mumbling incoherently.

At one point she exclaimed, "What *was* she thinking, I mean really?" while gazing directly at me with startled hazel eyes, as if expecting a response.

I patted her reassuringly, and murmured something like, "I can't imagine," and she seemed momentarily mollified, but then shortly turned and asked the same question of Dr. Tau. He simply shrugged and shook his head.

I could hear Chess, vaguely in the background, questioning Det. Hawk for details, but Hawk was as usual noncommittal. Instead he seemed very interested in what time Chess had arrived at the Taus' and if he had walked over. He also asked where Page might be. I didn't need to see Chess to know that one bothered him; I could hear it in his hesitation and then in his voice when he said Page was out running errands and had been all morning.

Just as we mounted the back stairs, the screen door swung open and Sierra stepped out, hands on hips.

"What in the world is going on?" she demanded, as if she'd somehow missed all the sirens. I wondered if she'd deliberately ignored them, telling herself they couldn't possibly be coming back to her house again, and must have been called for someone down the street, but before anyone could reply, she continued angrily. "I had to have *Logan of all people* watch the kids while I got dressed. What's happened now? Where is Lu?"

Detective Hawk brushed past Dr. Tau, Margaret Sheffield and me, and strode across the porch toward Sierra. There was something aggressive, even frightening in his manner. He stopped right in front of her, his pitbull face hard with rage. She stared at him, surprised at first, and then with growing alarm.

"Someone strangled Miss Rios," He threw the words at her, coldly, placing his hands on either side of his neck and illustrating a choking motion. "using a *very thin wire*... sliced right through the flesh and muscle... all the way to bone... Almost cut her head off..."

For once Sierra Tau-Martindale lost her cool. Shock and terror shone in her violet eyes. Her face paled and she fell back, clutching at the doorframe for support. "What...? What...? What did you say?"

I didn't want to hear anymore, wished I could "unhear" what had already been said. Instinctively I took a firmer hold on Mrs. Sheffield as she moaned, "It's true. It's true." and crumpled against me almost insensible. Chess bounded up the stairs to Sierra's side and guided her into the kitchen. Dr. Tau and I half carried, half dragged Mrs. Sheffield up the remaining steps and through the door.

I was concerned for Mrs. Sheffield because of her age and because her sister, while considerable younger, had just died of a stroke. I suggested she lie down, but Det. Hawk insisted she sit at the kitchen table along with everyone else.

Dr. Tau went straight to the liquor cabinet and poured something alcoholic into two shot glasses, giving one to her and one to his daughter, in spite of Hawk's protests. Sierra immediately downed the dark liquid and slammed the empty glass on the table as if demanding another. Poor Mrs. Sheffield's hand was trembling so badly most of her drink was on the floor before it could reach her lips. Chess grabbed a damp paper towel and was trying to wipe the blood from her fingers and sleeves. With a look of disdain, she deliberately pulled her arm away. Chess sat down next to her all the same.

There was nothing else I could do, for Mrs. Sheffield,

for Sierra, certainly not for Luciana, and so I tapped the tabletop next to Det. Hawk to draw his attention and told him I'd wait outside. I doubted he suspected me of killing the nanny, and even if he did, I knew I didn't do it and so didn't need to hear the gory details of how she was murdered or found. I stepped out onto the porch and into the heat, pulling both the paneled door and the screen door shut behind me, and then sat on the top step in about the same position Page had taken when I'd seen her and Chess talking... was it only yesterday... or the day before? The day of the wake, so Sunday, the day before the funeral.

The EMTs came by with the body bag on a gurney, and I quickly stood, at attention so to speak, as they passed. A second murder, but actually a third death if you counted Mrs. Tau's. I hadn't thought there was anything suspicious about the Tau matriarch's demise at the time, but in hindsight I was no longer certain. I slowly sat down again, hugged my knees to my chest, and waited.

The sun moved gradually across the sky, or to be accurate, the earth rotated making it appear as though the sun moved across the sky, while bees and butterflies buzzed and fluttered over the flowers on either side of me. Occasionally one would draw near, in a meandering flight from north to south or south to north. The butterflies I ignored, the bees I waved away. It was hot and bright, and somehow that made Luciana's murder seem even more unreal. How could she have been killed, viciously strangled, almost decapitated as Det. Hawk described, on such a lovely day, in such a beautiful place?

The door opened and closed behind me and I wondered if Luciana had seen her killer coming, if she'd argued with someone who then attacked her, or if she'd been ambushed, without warning, before she had a chance to run.

I looked up into the detective's face as he sat down

beside me.

"I want to go home."

It took me a moment to realize I'd said the words out loud.

Det. Hawk's eyes were soft, liquid gold and brown, the pitbull quiet behind the genuine sympathy in his face. He put a hand on my arm. "It probably would be a lot safer for you if you did go now. I've seen a lot... gang violence... murder, rape, torture... really nasty stuff..." His voice was sad, no longer official but raw with humanity. "The attack on Ms. Rios was brutal, savage, and I don't believe whoever did this is done."

"You think I'll be a target, too?" I was shocked. "Why? Oh..."

The money! He'd always thought the motive was money! Did Stacy really leave me money? But who would benefit most...

Before I could follow my line of reasoning to any logical conclusion, he interrupted.

"Look Wim, Miss Tierman, Wim, I don't want anything to happen to you. I mean of course, I don't want anything to happen to anyone. I feel terrible about Ms. Rios, and that's all on me, but now it seems likely you may be at risk. I mean... I don't want to scare you..."

His words came out awkwardly. He seemed embarrassed, and then he surprised me further by pulling a card from his pocket and writing on the back.

"Look, this is my cell number, my *personal* cell. We're not supposed to give them out, I've never given mine out to anyone involved in an active case before, but you call me if you see anything suspicious, or if something seems off to you, or just, well, if you feel like you need to call me." He blushed. The cynical detective actually blushed. "I can be here in 10 minutes max any time, day or night."

Chapter 13

After Det. Hawk left, I found I had no desire to return to the house or its occupants. Trouble was, I had nowhere else to go. I wandered out across the front lawn toward the rental car, but stopped in the middle of the driveway with the same eerie feeling I'd had earlier, *when? Saturday?* Someone was watching me. Turning quickly, I saw no one, no movement in any of the windows. I walked out to the car and sat on the hood, facing the house, studying it, searching for malevolence in its commanding facade. The twisted faces of the mascarons stared back.

In full daylight, I felt hypervigilent, fearful, anxious. *Someone wants me dead.* Detective Hawk was sure of it. The knowledge, the conviction of the truth in what would have seemed an outrageous supposition only a few days earlier gathered in the humid air around me, pervasive, malignant, suffocating. I wanted to talk to my Mom, but didn't want to freak her out more than she already was, especially since she was thousands of miles away and could do nothing to help. I considered calling Cal, but hadn't even told her about Stacy's death, wasn't sure if Mom or Dad had. Besides, she was just graduating high school and didn't need to hear the outpouring of paranoia that currently consumed my mind in any case. If Jordy wasn't with Rachel, I would have called him, but the comfort in that relationship seemed gone. Thinking of Jordy reminded me: I'd neglected to check to make sure my friends had arrived alive back home in Atlanta and so sent a short text message to Rachel. I was surprised when her number rang back immediately on my cell.

"Hey, Rachel," I said, forcing cheerfulness, "did ya'll make it home ok?"

I was wondering why she hadn't just texted a response.

"Well, no," she answered, and laughed. "We headed in that direction when we left you, but changed our minds and turned around. Now we're back at the Book Nook Inn again. You really should consider leaving your cell on..." she scolded, but I interrupted her.

"What?" I didn't attempt to hide my surprise, couldn't call it relief, more like alarm. "Why would you *do that*? Why come back?"

It sounded rude, the way I said it, ungrateful even, but I was suddenly afraid for my friends. If I was in danger, they might be caught in the cross fire, too.

"Be right back, Babe. Going to get my sunglasses," she said, her voice muffled as she turned her head from the phone speaker. *To Jordy, of course.* And I pictured her, waving gaily as she left him. Then she came back to me.

"We were almost to Baton Rouge when Jordy suddenly decided we had to turn around." Her voice was low and her heals made a soft clumping sound, in the rhythm of climbing stairs. There was another sound, like wind, and then a door closed.

She must have been outside, I thought. *She's gone back into their room.*

I heard the bed or chair creak as she sat.

"He said, he insisted, that you might need us, but he couldn't tell me for what or why," she explained in a less laughing and more sober tone. "Wim, are you okay? I mean seriously, are you okay? Or are you in some kind of trouble? Because you know you can tell me. Do you need us?"

I hesitated. No doubt I needed them; needed them more than I'd ever needed them, desperately, but did my need for my friends, my peeps, to be nearby outweigh my fear for their safety? *No.*

"I'm fine Rache," I lied.

She was quiet for a long moment, and I could imagine my friend's delicate, freckled face, serious, considering... Jordy knew me best, but Rachel knew me, too.

"Well then, come hang out with us," she invited, at last. "We had to move to the pool room, the steam punk room was taken, but it's really pretty here, kind of relaxing with the lake and all. What do you say?"

"Well, I..."

"Come on, Wim. What else do you have to do?"

I've never been good at lying, or making things up on the spot. I blame my Mom. She's always said a person's word is his or her bond. Nowadays Mom's values are old school. Meaningless rhetoric, sly misdirection, or flat out lies are not only condoned, but are encouraged and rewarded, particularly if you're a contestant on reality TV or more so a candidate for the presidency of the United States. The more convincingly a person lies, the more successful the person becomes, but I'm not good at it.

At that moment, I had no where else to go, no one else to turn to, could not conceive of one plausible excuse...

"Sounds great!" I said, mustering enthusiasm, "I'll be there in 30," and wondered how many other lies I'd tell before the night was over.

~ * ~

By the time I arrived at the Book Nook Inn, Jordy and Rachel were in fine form, sitting in lawn chairs by the pool, sipping red wine and laughing in the middle of the afternoon. For just a moment I felt a warm and uncharacteristic resentment toward my dearest friends, almost hated them for being so carefree when all around people were dying. Of course, they knew nothing about Luciana, but they'd been with me at Stacy's funeral only the day before, were intimately familiar with all the details of her murder. Didn't they care?

The laughter died down when they saw me, as I let

myself in through the whitewashed gate and walked across the wooden deck. During the greetings, I found I couldn't quite meet Jordy's eye, and so continued past him to sit in a chair on the other side of Rachel. I accepted a glass of the offered wine, sipped it, and set the glass on one of the little side tables. *Still tasting sawdust.*

"Are you okay, Wim?" Jordy asked, leaning forward to talk around Rachel.

How can he ask me that? No! I'm not okay!

"Sure," I answered, automatically picking up my glass. I looked at it, and then set it back down.

"Of course she's not," Rachel chimed in, sitting up in her chair. Pulling the scrunchie from her hair, she shook her head, spilled curls down her back, and then was momentarily distracted by her swimsuit strap, which had somehow fallen off her shoulder. She straightened the strap, and then continued, smiling, "but she will be. I'm sure she's had a horrible shock, but once we're all back home she'll feel *so* much better."

Though I would have sworn she'd been stone cold sober during our earlier conversation, Rachel now appeared quite lit, slurring her words a bit, which surprised me, not only because it was the middle of the afternoon, but because none of us had ever been heavy into alcohol or drugs. I wondered if this was an "I'm in Beaumont, TX and my best friend's friend was murdered" reaction, or another side I'd never seen of the newly engaged to be engaged Rachel.

Jordy looked uneasily at her, but I couldn't tell if his concern was for her or me.

"I just had a feeling that you might need us to stay, you know," Jordy explained, "I thought... I had a feeling something bad, or something else bad," he corrected, "was going to happen... I..." but Rachel interrupted him, snorting.

"He had *feelings*! Don't you just love him? He's such

a *girl* sometimes," she teased, aiming a pretend sidekick at Jordy, bumping his toes with hers, making both chairs rock. And then she leaned forward, sipped some wine, and licked her lips. Her swimsuit strap again slipped off her shoulder but she didn't appear to notice this time.

I was becoming more and more uncomfortable with the situation, hoping I wasn't going to be forced to watch them grope each other or worse. The melodrama and horror of the Tau mansion was actually beginning to appeal to me in comparison.

"Uh, guys... Uh," I stuttered, as an image of my two friends making out in the swimming pool while half-naked shimmered before my eyes, "I guess I better be getting back. Dr. Tau wanted to talk with me about the Will I think."

Of course I doubted Dr. Tau was really thinking that much about our planned meeting with his attorney now that Luciana had been almost decapitated in his backyard. Wishing I had anywhere or anyone else to go to in Texas, I stood awkwardly and headed for the gate.

"But Wim, you just got here," Jordy called after me, concerned, confused, and obviously less alcohol-soaked than Rachel. "Can't you stay a while? Why do you have to keep running off?"

"Be careful driving," advised Rachel, waving, as she scooted from her chair to sit between Jordy's legs on his. He'd been on the verge of getting up.

"Wim," Jordy called, untangling himself. "Wim, wait."

I stopped with my hand on the gate latch. He approached and put his hand over mine. His fingers were warm. I could see Rachel beyond him, sitting on his chair with her head cocked to one side, blinking as if her mind wasn't quite processing at normal speed.

"I'm sorry, Wim," he began, glancing back at Rachel, "you know we don't mean to intrude."

As if he could... intrude...

"I was just worried, you know. I know this has to be

really hard for you, beyond hard for you. You're family can't be here, you're seriously one of the best friends I'll ever have, and I don't want you to think you have to do this, whatever "this" is, all alone, you know? You don't have to be brave, all by yourself."

I wanted to cry and hug him, really needed to cry and hug him, but instead I looked at Rachel by the pool.

But I do... have to...

I put on my brave face, but couldn't keep my lip from trembling.

"You're not intruding. I do appreciate you being here so much," I said, from my heart, "you just don't know. But you and Rachel should go on home. I have some things to take care of, just paperwork, and then I'll be back in Atlanta before you know it, and we can..."

I stopped, confused, not sure what we could ever all do together again. Like I said, I'm not much good at lying.

Jordy nodded as if he understood, but I hoped he didn't.

"I think we'll stay one more day," he smiled his slightly crooked smile, "just in case you decide you do need us."

"But, Jordy..." I tried to smile, too, but couldn't pull it off. Instead, I sighed.

"So, what's to do and see in Beaumont, Texas?" he asked, brightly.

Chapter 14

No one was left at the crime scene. All the official ve-
hicles were gone, and as I pulled into the Taus' driveway it seemed impossible to believe that someone, a
young and beautiful girl with most of her life ahead of
her, had been brutally murdered there that morning. It
was even harder to believe that two such girls had been
killed on the same premises in less than a week. On
entering the house, I found Dr. Tau seated at his desk
as usual. He looked up and beckoned me over almost
as if nothing had happened, almost.

"Where's Mrs. Sheffield?" I asked, as I approached
the office door. "Is she okay?"

"Margaret has gone home," he responded with casual
indifference, "to the bosom of her family," and all the
energy that had survived the deaths of his son, his wife,
and his daughter, all the forcefulness that represented
the essence of the surgeon's personality had vanished
from his manner, his voice, and his face. His pale blue
eyes were the color of ice, and there seemed to be nothing left except bitterness, frustrating and impotent.

"What did the police say?" I asked insistently, trying
to rouse him. "Do they know who killed Luciana? Or
Stacy? Have they arrested anyone?"

Critical questions to my mind, but not so to his.

"I'm sure I don't know," he answered, vaguely, waving my words away. "Perhaps we'll have news tomorrow, or later in the week."

He sighed, and indicated the chair across from the
huge desk.

"Won't you please take a seat?"

I sat, though I couldn't sit still, and tipped the chair

back onto two legs. He cleared his throat.

"To begin with," he said slowly, in a distant tone, "as I mentioned earlier..." an uncharacteristic hesitation, "...I don't see any need for this conversation."

Then let's skip it, I thought, ungraciously, emotionally exhausted, my patience worn thin, *It can't be that important compared with...* but then I took a breath, and settled the chair with all four legs on the floor. He was Stacy's Dad...

He shook his head slightly and frowned, not looking at me, talking to the room.

"My attorney advised that I speak with you, but Stacy made her wishes clear..."

He raised his gaze intently, almost reverently, to the golden monkeys on the chandelier above him perhaps seeking guidance, but after a moment, apparently receiving none, he continued.

"As you may be aware," he said, reconsidered and then recanted, "actually, you probably are not at all aware..."

He shook his head, and seemed to be conducting an argument with himself.

"We all knew Stacy was very fond of you, but now it seems you were second only to her mother in importance to her. That *must* be why she wanted you to have... *everything...* and who am I to argue with the last wish of my dead child?"

In the silence that followed, the big man clasped his gnarled hands together with the two index fingers pointing upward, and, tilting his head, examined the spire abstractedly from different angles for several minutes. Finally disentangling his grip, he brought both hands to his face, carefully pressed his palms against his eyelids, and then laid his hands flat against the leather desktop with fingers spread. The muscles of his sinewy forearms flexed. When next he spoke, his voice had regained some of its rumble and I thought perhaps the monkeys had been helpful after all.

"Stacy bequeathed you *everything*, all she possessed at the time of her death, in a Will she drafted herself. She had the document signed, witnessed, and notarized almost immediately after Eleanor's death. I had no idea she had done such a thing."

His speech was crisp, concise, business-like.

"What you could not know, what I don't believe Stacy realized, is that everything *she* possessed at the time of her death was essentially all monies *I* possessed, or more precisely all the financial assets Eleanor and I possessed before *she*, I mean Eleanor of course, died."

He took a deep breath, ordering his thoughts, his mind at last firing on all eight.

"It's a bit complicated, but basically a trust was created upon Eleanor's death to the benefit of Stacy, so that funds did not go to Stacy directly but were placed under the control of a trustee for the purpose of Stacy's care and maintenance. At her death any monies held in trust, any remainder, would have been distributed to the beneficiaries of the trust, that is the remaining heirs; however, no one expected Stacy to write her own Will."

He stroked his upper lip.

"Obviously we should have anticipated her doing so. Stacy is, was, a very bright girl, though often single-minded, but as she never worked or had any earnings of her own it seemed so unlikely. In any case, there's quite a bit of money involved, and by the terms of Stacy's Will it all goes to *you*. Of course, Sierra and Logan will most likely contest Stacy's Will, and the wording of the trust agreement must be taken into account, but..."

Dr. Tau stopped speaking abruptly and studied me with a look of cool detachment, as if he had no personal interest in the matter whatsoever.

"I don't want it," I said, shaking my head. "I don't want any of your money."

It was not the response he expected.

"Aren't you going to ask how much it is?" he questioned, taken aback. His pale eyebrows drew together and he glowered at me as if insulted. "Your bequest, the value of Stacy's estate, is no trifling amount! Before you decide you *don't want it*, you should certainly be informed of the monetary value under discussion..."

I put my hand up to stop him. In that moment, the enormity, the possibilities: *Riches, millions of dollars, more money than I could count in a day, spend in a lifetime, the good I could do with it...* all passed through my mind.

"I don't need to know," I declared, firmly. "I don't want a dime."

What good is millions of dollars when every dollar you spend will remind you of someone you loved, shot through the heart, lying in her own blood, dying in her own home, betrayed, killed by someone she probably trusted?

I looked down at the boots on my feet.

"There may be a few personal items that belonged to Stacy, things she meant me to have, to keep to..."

To what? Remember her by? It wasn't as if I'd ever forget her. I hesitated.

"I don't want any money," I repeated. "It wasn't even really Stacy's money. I'm sure she never meant to leave me money, and I don't want it."

The realization that someone who owed him nothing, a person he knew to be less than financially secure from a family he'd always considered inferior, a medical student with the potential for hundreds of thousands of dollars of debt in student loans, was unwilling to take most of his fortune didn't appear to cheer Dr. Tau in the least. If anything he seemed more depressed.

"So you decline the bequest of monies?" he said slowly. "You actually decline the bequest? You may accept a few... personal items... but no monies?"

"Yes, I decline the monies." I nodded quickly in the affirmative.

"And you don't even wish to be informed of the

amount?" He was incredulous.

"No."

"Wim, are you sure? Are you absolutely certain? Believe me when I say, "It is a *great deal of money.*""

Dr. Tau rarely used my name, or anyone's for that matter, but he seemed suddenly solicitous, even troubled.

"Perhaps the shock... the strain... Are you absolutely clear on the consequences of this decision? Do you understand what you are doing? Are you sure you don't want to discuss this with someone? Your parents, your friends? An attorney?"

"I'm sure."

He stared, and then nodded abruptly, resigned.

"All right then. I'll have the papers drawn up as soon as is possible." he said. "Hopefully we can have this settled in short order so that you may return home."

His tone was dismissive, our business concluded in his mind, but I didn't stir from my chair.

"Will Chess be handling this for you, or will your attorney," I asked, wondering if Chess knew about Stacy's Will.

"The attorney," Dr. Tau responded, raising a pale eyebrow. "Chess is my financial advisor, but isn't privy to all my legal dealings." He hesitated, and then smiled weakly. "As you've probably surmised, he's not the sharpest scalpel in the surgical suite."

"How long has he been your financial advisor?" I asked, ignoring the small joke, "and why did you hire him then?"

"I hired Chess straight out of college," Dr. Tau answered, sitting forward slightly. "He asked me for the job and I gave it to him. He's actually done surprisingly well. Chess is slow and methodical, conservative, so he doesn't make many mistakes. Plus I know he'll never steal from me."

I gave him a questioning look, but didn't comment. I wanted his take on Chess, but also sought insight into his own character. This was a man who regularly cheated on his wife without a twinge of guilt, but apparently had significant respect for Stacy's wishes in regards to the disposition of her fortune. A man who seemed more interested in settling any financial matters related to Stacy's Will than with identifying his daughter's killer.

"Not that it's your business," he began, with a curious look on his face that made me feel the surgeon understood me a bit better than I would have liked, "but I've no disinclination to discussing Chess, or his family, with you. I'll tell you the truth."

Ah, the over-sharers... I thought, with some gratitude under the current circumstances.

"When I started my practice, all those years ago, I was not a financially savvy man. Eleanor's family had money, and mine did as well, so I'd never had any reason to consider budgets or the "rationing" of assets, or billing or collection practices; the "business of medicine" if you will. I had a passion for surgery, had an appealing and singularly proficient bedside manner, quickly became one of the most highly recommended, sought after Orthopedists in the area, and so assumed my practice would be profitable. I was shocked to discover that on paper at least, it did not seem so."

"My accountant recommended I hire a practice consultant, possibly a manager, and provided a list of names. One of the names was well known to me, my neighbor, Chet Anderson. Though I knew the name, I did not know the man, but in my naivety expected that, as he had a reputation in his field equal to my reputation in mine, he was a person who could be trusted in all matters financial. His firm was large, had many diverse divisions within the investment banking arena, but he agreed to handle my particular request for assistance personally. I was pleased and flattered not to be assigned to an underling, as I realized my practice could not be considered a sizable client by any measure. Under his direction, the practice grew as my superior surgical skills attracted more patients and I added appropriately vetted partners, and we all prospered."

Inwardly I smiled at his decidedly egotistical "truth" but felt a degree of tolerance toward the old surgeon that approached affection.

"At some point during the course of our association, due to subtle and apparently premeditated advances on his part, I came to consider Chet Anderson a friend. We socialized, our wives and children played together, became entangled with each other, and that more than anything made his betrayal all the more difficult to stomach. Fortunately for me, I found out before the general public and so any losses I might have suffered, at least financial losses, were minimal."

I looked at him. "The betrayal..."

"Ah, he was what they called "skimming", taking money "off the top", you understand, in addition to his agreed upon commission, "helping himself" to the earnings of others without consent, stealing from the very people he was contracted to protect. Oddly enough, the accountant that had recommended Chet was the first to catch on. I'd let him go, in favor of an accountant employed by Chet on Chet's recommendation, but the man apparently felt some loyalty toward me still as he called upon me with the hint of impropriety and the suggestion that I hire someone to independently review my records, a forensic accountant."

"I was appalled to learn that Chet had misappropriated sufficient of my funds to pay for his new Bentley plus most if not all of those extravagant vacations he and his wife were so fond of taking beginning from almost the very moment of his assuming the management of my accounts. When I confronted him with the evidence, he laughed."

"He laughed?"

"He laughed. Said not to worry, he'd put all the money back, and he did. Of course he most likely misappropriated someone else's funds in order to do so. As per our agreement, I did not go to the Feds or anyone else. He and I parted ways, and it was not until several years later that the dominoes began falling, his house of cards collapsed, please excuse the mixed gaming metaphor, and he was arrested. While the authorities were building their case, Chet and Trish were involved in an automobile accident, leaving him mentally incompetent to stand trial. Chess was of age by then, and he and his mother hammered out settlements to satisfy the clients and creditors. After that, Trish disappeared, leaving Chess and Page to care for the ruined old man. I believe Trish moved to Florida, but I could be mistaken. I prefer to think of her in some warm clime..."

"Do you think she knew all along...? So after the settlements, there was no money left, for Chess or his Mom?"

"No, none at all. They would have lost the house, but for me."

"You? And why would you step in to save Chet Anderson from living on the streets?"

Dr. Tau's excesses and indulgences weren't generally known to extend to philanthropy.

"Not to save the father, but to save the son, and I certainly did not do so out of the goodness of my heart. I did it for Eleanor, as she begged me to, for her sister, Margaret, who I suppose begged her to do so for her daughter, Page, who went to her mother for help because she loved the son, Chess." Dr. Tau snorted through his nose. "Family. Love," he said, as if that explained everything.

"And despite what Chet Anderson did to you, you hired his son to be your financial manager. Why?"

"You are referring to the sins of the father, and sons? Chess Anderson is nothing like his father, at least not in his business dealings. Chess has ethics or morals, a conscience developed to the highest degree you may ever see, perhaps because his old man was such a scoundrel. Of all of us, Chess has always drawn a clearer line between good and evil, right and wrong, at least in most cases." He rubbed his chin thoughtfully. "Chess could never steal from me."

He paused.

"Though for the life of me, I'll never understand why Chess couldn't stay away from Stacy, not when he had a wife like *Page*."

He raised his hands and shrugged, indicating he could see nothing in his daughter that might attract a man.

"So Chess *was* having an affair with Stacy?" I asked, taking up the point.

I had denied the possibility of an affair, to myself, to the police, but now wondered if I'd been wrong.

"Why of course he was having an affair," Dr. Tau assured me, "or at least he was interested in having one. Why else would a man follow a woman around like a dog for years?"

Why indeed?

Chapter 15

After leaving Dr. Tau, I headed up the stairs to Stacy's room. It wasn't that I particularly cared to be alone, it's just that given my choices for companionship, "me time" seemed much more desirable than "you and me time" with any of the "yous" that might be in the house. I planned to sit quietly for about an hour, and then maybe call Cal, not to share any of the details of my life at present, but simply to listen to her talk about hers.

Cal had recently gone through her high school graduation-I'd attended via Facetime courtesy of Mom's iPad-and prior to starting college in the fall she was interning at the CDC in Atlanta for the summer instead of beaching it like most of her friends. I wanted to hear about *that*, about what was happening with *her*, at *home*, something real and honest and hopeful, to take the focus from the unreality of the death and dying that seemed to pervade my previous relatively mundane existent. I'd never felt so utterly alone, never felt more isolated than I did just then, from my family and my friends.

As I gained the landing at the top of the stairs, I noticed that for the first time since I'd come to stay with the Taus, Logan's door was open, not wide open, but cracked open enough so that I could see him lying on his back in bed with his laptop resting on his chest. A girl's soft voice was singing in Spanish:

Los pollitos dicen
Pio, pio, pio

*Cuando tienen hambre
Cuando tienen frio...*

I hesitated, wondering why in the world Logan would be watching someone online, on YouTube or something similar, singing about chickens. We hadn't spoken in several years, with the exception of our abbreviated conversations at the dinner table, and our last full exchange before I left Beaumont had not been entirely friendly. I'd commented on some of his lifestyle choices and he'd basically told me to "kiss off". Those weren't his exact words, though.

I knocked on the doorjamb and waited. He let me stand there, while he peered into the computer's glowing screen until the song was done.

"What?" he asked, shortly, turning black eyes toward me.

It wasn't an invitation, but I've been greeted with less enthusiasm.

"What are you doing?" I asked, and added quickly. "How are you holding up?"

I said it as if I cared, and I did. Though we'd never been close, his status as the bereaved and my fondness for Stacy gave Logan a huge and legitimate claim on my compassion.

He frowned, and shrugged.

"Come on in," he said, grudgingly.

His eyes were red-rimmed, maybe from crying, but his nose was red as well. I was pretty sure that was from something else, although he seemed tired and gave no indication that he was high.

"Sit down." He patted the bed beside him. "I'll show you."

Curious, I sat and leaned in so that we could share the laptop screen. As I'd surmised, it was a video clip. Logan pressed *Play* and the video began.

A girl, no a woman, and a child of about 4 were singing and laughing. The child was bouncing barefoot on a threadbare sofa while the woman, her straight, dark hair falling almost to her waist, twirled on a worn rag rug in the middle of the room... scarred side table and a lime green lamp in the background, brightly colored pictures on the walls. Woman and child were both dark-skinned and beautiful with the same smile. Each used her left hand to wave with the words:

Qué	*linda*	*manito*	*que*	*tengo*	*yo,*
(What	pretty	little	hands	have	I)
qué	*linda*	*y*	*blanquita*	*que*	*Dios*	*me*	*dio*
(How pretty and white that God gave me)

My own hand went to my mouth to suppress a groan as tears sprang to my eyes. The woman was Luciana. She was singing a lullaby in Spanish and dancing with a child, her child.

"Is that Luciana's daughter?" I gasped, as my heart sank with the certainty. "How sad!"

Logan looked at me darkly.

"Sad? Because she had a daughter? Whether she had a kid or not, she's still dead. Stacy never had a chance to have any kids. Is that more or less sad?"

He sounded bitter.

"Her husband just posted this," Logan continued. "They're poor. They've got no money to offer for a reward, but they're asking for help to find her killer, trying to show what they've lost..."

His voice trailed off, and he touched the edge of the screen, adjusting the angle for a clearer view.

Qué	*lindos*	*ojitos*	*que*	*tengo*	*yo,*
(What	pretty	eyes	have	I)
qué	*lindos*	*y*	*negritos*	*que*	*Dios*	*me*	*dio*
(How pretty and dark that God gave me)

"Her husband?" I was shocked. "But your father said Luciana was single. He thought you and she were..."

I stopped, confused. Logan shook his head.

"Luciana's husband works as a day laborer," Logan

explained, "and her sister keeps, I mean kept, Lu's daughter while she worked, taking care of Sierra's kids. She has family in Mexico. She was helping them with money, too. Funny, isn't it? Leaving her own kid to take care of someone else's?"

Qué	*linda*	*boquita*	*que*	*tengo*	*yo,*
(What	a	pretty	little	mouth	have	I)

qué	*linda*	*y*	*rojita*	*que*	*Dios*	*me*	*dio*
(How pretty and red that God gave me)

"My father had no reason to know about or to have any interest in Luciana's life, but I'm not even sure Sierra knew about her family. I've no idea why she told me about them."

I sat, not knowing what to say.

Qué	*lindas*	*patitas*	*que*	*tengo*	*yo,*
(What	pretty	little	feet	have	I)

qué	*lindas*	*y*	*gorditas*	*que*	*Dios*	*me*	*dio*
(How pretty and chubby that God gave to me)

On the last note, the little girl leapt from the couch and landed in her mother's arms, giggling as Luciana covered her face with kisses. The video stopped. We both sat there, staring at the still shot at the end.

"I'm sorry," Logan said, finally, heavily, as if to encompass all past sins.

He closed his laptop and put it aside, and then sat up on the edge of his bed beside me. Logan was as tall as his father and his shoulders were as broad, but he weighed at least 80 lbs. less; his wrists, small and bony, protruded from the frayed sleeves of a worn gray hoodie.

"I wish you hadn't been there."

He looked down at me and lightly touched my arm with his fingertips. I felt more than a little uncomfortable, sitting next to him on the bed, but the door was open and I wanted information. I forced myself not to move.

"It was good that I was there." I knew exactly what he meant, and surprised myself by disagreeing.

"I think Stacy knew I was there, at least at first..." I swallowed hard. "I think it was better for *her* that I *was* there."

Logan reached for my hand, and entwined his fingers with mine. It was odd, and personal, but I didn't pull away. I could see nothing, no emotion evident in his dark, flat eyes.

"The police seem to think I killed them both," he said, quietly. "What do you think?"

"The police do seem to suspect someone in the family." I looked down at our hands, twisted together, avoiding the direct question and his gaze.

"No." His voice was deep, insistent. "What do *you* think?"

"Did you?" I raised my face to his, answered his question with my own. "Did you shoot Stacy... and strangle Luciana?"

He was silent, staring back at me without expression, and then his gaze shifted to the ceiling, reminding me of his father and the chandelier.

"You know," he said slowly, "if I did do it, I'd probably confess to you. There's something strange about you... something... quiet... it's hard not to want to tell you things... secrets...."

He twisted my fingers tighter until it almost hurt, and lower his voice to a whisper. "I could have stopped it, you know... saved them both... I think I could have... I don't understand how things got so messed up..."

Cryptic.

"What do you mean?" I asked, frustrated, pulling my hand free. "What does that even mean?"

He shook his head, mutely, looking so fragile; shoulders slumped, tears welling in his deep-set eyes.

Looking at his face, young but tragically lined with care, marked by years of self-abuse, I remembered the ski trip to Snow Mass when I was 15, the year before I moved away from Beaumont. Logan had just turned 14. I was invited to go with the Tau family officially as Stacy's guest, mostly to keep her out of everyone's hair because she was too clumsy even for the bunny slopes. I'd never been snow skiing and was dying to give it a go, but kept my ambitions of becoming the next Janica Kostelic to myself; my role as companion to Stacy having been clearly explained to me at length by the authoritative Mrs. Tau.

Logan at 14, in his early stages of substance abuse and before any permanent damage to his body, brain, or mind had been done, was much like Marty, naturally gifted, an amazing athlete though with different skill sets, Marty's talents being in horseback riding and Logan's anything involving a board beneath his feet. He'd grown up skateboarding, snowboarding, and skiing the blacks, and never in his life had he had a serious fall, but somehow, on the second run of the second day he wiped out, said he hit a snow snake, and got up complaining of a twisted ankle. Refusing medical care, he iced and wrapped the sprain himself, and insisted on staying with Stacy while I hit the slopes. For the rest of the week Stacy and Logan sat in the Lodge by the fire, and read or talked, while I had the time of my life. It was only later that it occurred to me that Logan might not have been injured at all. It was something Sierra said, teasing him that he was limping on the wrong foot.

Could a boy who was that considerate and unselfish, even self-sacrificing at age 14 murder his own sister? I didn't believe it.

"No," I answered, shaking my head. "It wasn't you."

"It wasn't me? You think it wasn't me?"

His face relaxed as he let out a long, slow breath, and turned to lie back on the bed, propping his head on black satin pillows pressed against the padded leather headboard.

"I heard Stacy was talking about dying at dinner

Wednesday night. What exactly did she say?" I tried to make my statement and question sound matter-of-fact, practical not emotional. Logan was obviously on edge, and I didn't want to tip him over.

"I wasn't really paying attention. You know how she runs on about things."

He stopped, considering the verb again, as he had with Luciana.

"Ran on, I meant. Mom had just died and everyone was freaked out and Stacy was making it all worse."

His voice was flat, apathetic, but I sat and waited, watching him.

He looked at me and the lines of his face grew taut.

"It was her usual nonsense. All about how everyone dies and the way people die, natural causes not always being natural, accidents and murder. I can't remember. It was creepy. I don't want to remember."

"Logan?" I touched his shoulder. His hands began to tremble slightly and he clenched his fists, pulling them up into the sleeves of his hoodie, and then crossed both arms tightly across his chest.

"And then at the viewing, she went to pieces, in front of everyone. It was humiliating! Instead of helping her, I was embarrassed of her. I left it to Chess. I went out and got high. Dad was right. She's better off dead then left to us, to her family. We treated her like dirt!"

Logan was shaking all over, crying, looking out the window, away from me. Talking at me, because he couldn't talk to me. I sat there awkwardly, not knowing what to say.

"Your Dad said that, that Stacy would be better off dead?"

Was that what Chess and Stacy had been talking about? Was her father the "he" of their conversation?

"Of course he did! He *meant* it! We all *knew* he meant it. Stacy knew... How could you have been so close, almost a part of this family, and never have realized how horrible we really all are?"

"You need to go now," Logan choked. "It was nice of you to come back. I know you meant well, coming back, but Stacy's dead, Luciana's dead and you're making it all worse... You should go now."

Making it worse? Did Logan think my being there had something to do with Stacy's death?

"How am I making things worse?" I asked, alarmed, and was almost afraid of the answer. "Are you saying Stacy died because I was here?"

"Of course not," Logan answered, taking a breath, shaking his head sadly. "No. You've nothing to do with any of this, anything, you never did, it's just that you don't belong here anymore."

I wanted to say something, do something, to help him, but we were strangers, or as good as. Despite my intention to be a source of comfort to Stacy's family, I was falling short, could come up with nothing to calm her brother's troubled soul.

"What happened wasn't your fault," I offered, weakly. "I don't believe any of this was your fault..."

"It always is, always has been," he said, obscurely. "Everything is... because of me."

"What do you mean?" I asked, again, but got the same response: silence. *The drug connection?*

"Who suggested you all go to the firing range after your Mom's funeral?" I pushed on, convinced the answer to that one question was critical.

He hesitated.

"What's that got to do with anything?" Then considered.

"I think it was the old man," he said, and then added with certainty, "Yeah, it was Dad. Why *did* you come back now, Wim?"

He sat up again, suddenly, and turned to face me, determination reflected in the set of his jaw. He took a deep breath, as I held mine.

"Why did you come back? Why? After all this time... Did you know that when you left, Stacy went catatonic for a solid month? She wouldn't say a word, not to anyone. She refused to leave her room, hardly ate."

My persistence had paid off, but not in the way I'd hoped or expected. Pushed past his limit, Logan decided to unload.

"I was afraid she'd die. I begged Mom to call you, and then I begged Sierra." His eyes grew hard and accusing. "They wouldn't do it."

"What? No! No one ever told me that. Did my Mom and Dad know?"

Was this true, or was Logan lying, confused?

"Logan, I had no..." I began, but he cut me off.

His voice turned bitter as the lines in his face deepened.

"I even went back into rehab. Stupid! I was such a kid! I thought if I did what you wanted, if I quit the drugs like you said, that you would come back!"

He was breathing fast and with some difficulty, his chest rising and falling as if under a great strain, and I could see the veins in his thin neck throbbing, but then he abruptly bowed his head and settle back against his pillows.

"But I couldn't stay clean, and you, you just abandoned me, us, me and Stacy. We, she needed you then. No one needs you now, so why did you come? Why did you come?" His voice fell to a whisper.

"Logan, I'm sorry. I was just a kid, too. My family moved away. I had to go." I was trying to justify myself against an offense I'd never known I committed.

"I came back because Stacy called me, about your Mom."

"It's funny, but Stacy stopped talking when you left. She wouldn't shut up after Mom died; talking about death, talking nonsense, talking about bees for God's sake! I wonder why? She just couldn't shut up."

He looked at me, solemn and sad.

"That's why she's dead you know, 'cause she couldn't shut up, and she's much better off wherever she is. I'm sorry it had to happen the way it did, but glad she doesn't have to suffer anymore. Dad was right, about one thing at least. She never belonged here."

"Don't say that! How can you say that?"

And then I was crying, having had no idea of the pain I'd caused Stacy when I left, and feeling guilty that I'd seldom come back to Beaumont to visit her. I'd no idea Logan had felt such an attachment for me, or that my words regarding his drug addiction had had any effect on him at all.

Logan was silent for a long moment. He was only 23, but the expression in his eyes just then made him look about a hundred.

"Don't you cry now, Wim," he said softly, and something in his voice, the detachment, the false calm, made my skin crawl as he leaned over to wipe my tears and then pressed his cheek against mine. "I'm sorry I said all those things to you. This is going to be another huge regret for me, and I already have so many. Please don't cry anymore."

His breath was in my ear, way too close. Pulling away from him, I stood up, head spinning, and now I was the one with arms crossed. I couldn't look at him, just wanted to be away from him.

"Will you get the light?" he asked quietly, as he lay back against his pillows.

I hit the switch, and saw his knees come up, as he turned and curled his long body into a fetal position, facing the wall, in the dark.

"And please close the door behind you," he instructed, his voice cool, distant.

I did, and wiping my eyes I headed down the hall toward Stacy's room, never expecting that Sierra was waiting for me there.

Chapter 16

My mind was in turmoil, again; thoughts ricocheting like pinballs off the calcified walls of my cranium, but I forced myself not to focus on what may have happened when I left Beaumont, or my crawling skin, and instead concentrated on anything Logan had said that could solve the mystery of Stacy's murder.

So Dr. Tau announces at dinner that his daughter would be better off dead, encourages everyone go to the firing range after his wife's funeral, and then his daughter is shot and killed in her living room, I thought. *Did he kill her? Could Dr. Tau really do such a thing? And why on earth would he?*

Or Logan? He sounded a lot like his Dad; up, down, and sideways. I wondered how much of that might be drug-induced. As far as I'd seen he stayed locked up in his room and without visitors so where did the drugs come from? And his craving for physical intimacy, the inappropriate touching, when had all that started? Maybe Logan had an undiagnosed mental illness, well, maybe his Dad did, too, and actually Sierra with her borderline traits... Mrs. Tau and OCD... but Logan, stoned or sober, believed Stacy was in a better place. He suggested she was killed because she wouldn't stop talking, but talking about what? Could he have killed her to make her stop?

I opened the door to find Sierra standing at the window, staring into darkness.

"So Stacy left you all Daddy's money," she said by way of a greeting. "How *interesting*."

But she could not have sounded less interested. She seemed tired, near exhaustion, and the concealer she

used was doing little good to hide the dark circles surrounding her eyes. Her look of despondency and
mournful tone commanded my immediate sympathy,
but considering her words I couldn't help but wonder if
her Dad told her about the Will, or if she'd been listening at keyholes again.

"I'm not taking it," I commented shortly, laying my
purse on the dresser. "Your Dad and I already talked it
over and I'm declining the bequest. His lawyer will draw
up the papers."

Just then I was feeling the strain, and was pretty
sure my own eyes were as dimly lit as hers were. I'd no
desire for conversation, with Sierra or anyone else for
that matter, and wished she'd just go, but there was an
inner sense of urgency that tightened the muscles in
my gut and along the back of my neck, combined with
a feeling of oppression and dread. The killer was still
out there. Someone else might be at risk. That someone
might even be me...

Sierra had made herself available. I had questions.
Sitting on the end of the bed, I steadied myself as I
considered the best way to approach her about her Dad
and Logan, and the murders. She was a talker, no
doubt, but could I keep her on the track I wished to
take?

"My children are *gone*," Sierra lamented, sliding into
the velvet slipper chair. "Daniel, well rather Daniel *and*
his *mother*, came and picked them up last night. He felt
it was too dangerous for them here, and for the first
time in a very long time I had to agree with him. Really,
what could I say? I'm not sure why I'm still here. I
should go home, too. I just can't seem to leave..."

She gazed gravely around the room.

"If we keep all her things exactly where she left
them," she commented in a slow, small voice, "it seems
as though she really must come back then, doesn't it?
She can't really be gone..."

Oh!

The thought hurt me, struck me through the heart, but I didn't cry. Instead, I gritted my teeth, lifted my chin, and resolutely asked my first question:

"Logan told me dinner on Wednesday night, after your mother died, was traumatic for everyone at the table." A generically true statement, I didn't expect she'd have an argument against. "What happened exactly?"

I didn't use Det. Hawk's qualifier of "in your own words", but knowing Sierra, could not expect her to provide anyone else's.

"When did you talk to Logan? Has he come out of his room at last?"

She countered, surprised, concerned.

"His door was open when I came upstairs, and so we chatted, *briefly*, but he just mentioned the dinner in passing"

I stressed the "briefly" hoping she would fill in the blanks voluntarily. She took the cue.

"And he said dinner was difficult?" she began. "Well, of course it was!"

She obviously needed to spill to someone, and she wasn't about to miss the chance.

"Momma had just been found cold in her bed, and we were all shocked and grieving. Stacy started going on and on about death and strokes. I was devastated, Logan was upset, and Daddy finally lost all patience and first asked her to stop and then told her to stop, but you know Stacy, she never could stop. When I tried to intervene Daddy shouted at me, but actually at the entire room, that Stacy would be better off dead because there was no one to look after her. Chess choked on his wine and I thought he might faint or hit Daddy, and Stacy finally stopped talking and sat there blinking, but she didn't cry because she never really cried, at least not when one might expect that she should. Mrs. Nelson came in and took Stacy back to the carriage house, and the rest of us just sat there staring at each other. It could not have been more mortifying!"

She paused for breath and dramatic effect. I waited, but Sierra suddenly seemed to realize where my mind was going and started backpedaling.

"But Daddy didn't mean it of course, that Stacy would be better off dead. He only said it because he was reeling from Momma's death, but I'm sure Chess repeated it to Aunt Maggie and Page, and they always blow everything out of proportion, and you can't really believe anything *they* say or blame Daddy *at all* for his moment of weakness. I suppose *they're* the ones that told you, and probably everyone else in Beaumont, or the world. Truly you must believe Daddy didn't mean it, at least not in the way it sounded, because of course Stacy was his daughter after all, and he loved her and would never have done anything to hurt her. I'm sure Stacy never thought he meant it."

Liar! I thought, knowing Sierra knew better. Stacy, who took everything literally, who was totally oblivious to subtext, would not have doubted that her father meant exactly what he said. It depressed me to think how my friend must have felt in the last days of her life, her mother dead, her life-long companion and the only truly supportive person she'd ever known gone, and her own father declaring before her entire family that he wished her gone, too. Sierra's attempts to justify Dr. Tau's actions were infuriating, but I clenched my teeth and grimly held my tongue.

She continued, oblivious.

"I tried to cheer everyone up by telling a funny story about Tara and her pink and orange socks. It was quite a funny story as she mismatched them without realizing it until we were in the car, and then what a noise she made... Tara's always been so, well, I guess you could call her "fashion forward" for her age. She's such a little darling! I couldn't believe Luciana didn't notice, but, and not to speak ill of the dead, Luciana never really did have any sense of style. Once she dressed

Faun in..."

"But what happened next?" I interjected, "at dinner I mean."

"Oh, well." Sierra was reluctant to get back to the point. "Well, nothing really. Daddy got up and went to his office, and Logan to his room, and Chess tried to sit with me for a while, to be polite I guess, because I was distraught, but he appeared to be absolutely thunderstruck by what Daddy said and was so very distracted and thoughtful for the rest of the evening."

She stopped and looked at me.

"You know what would have made a lot more sense?" she asked, arching her brows as if startled by unexpected insight, "If Chess had shot Daddy that night..."

But that didn't happen.

"And whose idea was it to go to the firing range after your mother's funeral?" I interrupted again, asking her the same question I'd asked Logan.

She considered.

"It was Chess. That's why I suddenly thought of him... Chess suggested it first." Sierra nodded with certainty. "He said we needed to get some air, to clear our minds of all the sorrow and grief."

"I of course thought it was rather gauche, but Daddy jumped at the idea. I think the rest of us agreed just to be supportive, you know."

Not the answer Logan had given. So why was he as certain it had been his father's idea as Sierra was that the idea came from Chess?

"What exactly was Stacy talking about at dinner on Wednesday night?" I persisted. "You said it was dying and strokes, but I've heard several versions. What did she actually say?"

I'd actually heard exactly one sketchy version of the dinner table conversation, from Logan, but Sierra evidently thought I'd been talking with the Sheffield-Andersons. I didn't feel it necessary to enlighten her.

Sierra sighed. "I can't remember the exact words. I

was too emotional. I'm sure no one else remembers the *exact words* either! You of all people know how she used to run on about any little thing. I think Momma's death addled her already addled little brain even more so, and she became obsessed with dying. She made it sound as if she thought Momma had been murdered!"

Sierra spread her arms in a gesture of incredulity.

This was news. No one, including Stacy, had mentioned that possibility to me before, and I was surprised, but said nothing, watching her.

"You know," she continued in a conspirator's whisper, "I think it would be just as well if they do dig up Momma's body and do an autopsy if only to settle all doubt. We don't want people whispering about us forever!"

"Who's whispering? Who said anything about exhuming your mother's body?" I couldn't help but ask. "When did all this happen?"

Det. Hawk had not mentioned any plans for exhumation to me, or even any suspicions surrounding Mrs. Tau's death, and so Sierra's assertion caught me completely off guard. Before I could thoroughly process this potentially huge bit of game-changing information, I reacted emotionally for my dead friend's sake.

Digging up Stacy's Mom?

"I believe there was a question from the very beginning. Aunt Maggie seemed convinced Momma's death was, well, not natural, but of course Momma was *so much younger* than she was, I mean is. That detective broached the subject of exhumation the first time we talked!" Sierra exclaimed. "I thought it was just an insane idea. I couldn't imagine why he would suggest such a thing, but after all, it is probably the best thing to do."

"You think so?" Beyond surprised, I was shocked.

Most people would not offer up their mother for exhumation and dissection in order to dispel a rumor, but Sierra had always been self-conscious. It was obvious she still cared very much about the neighbors' opinions.

"The police asked to do it, and I'm going to push Daddy to let them. Might as well get it over with. We'll have to do it eventually anyway." There was something like a ghoulish eagerness in her voice.

"You really don't care if they dig up *your mother?*" I couldn't stop myself.

Sierra was immediately offended. Her violet eyes turned to frost.

"Why of course I do!" She was adamant, angry, insulted. "Of course I do! But if the police are going to do it eventually anyway, why resist. Why give them reason to suspect us when everything can be cleared up so easily."

"Exhuming your mother's body won't clear *anything* up *easily*. It won't clear anything up at all." I reminded her, hotly. "There's still Stacy's murder and Luciana's, even if your mother did die of natural causes. Someone shot Stacy! Someone strangled Luciana!"

I was losing it. My intentions of remaining objective while covertly seeking the answers behind Stacy's murder were paving the road to my own personal Hell.

"But it will take the pressure off the *family!*" she snapped, bolting from her chair, striding across the room toward me. She stopped a foot in front of me, closed fists on hips, glaring down at me as my hands clinched over the edges of the coverlet on the bed. The muscles of my legs tensed, and although she had at least 40 pounds over me, I'd no thoughts of flight.

"No one in the *family* killed Momma, just like no one in the *family* shot Stacy! No one in this house *strangled* Luciana! Can't you hear how ridiculous you sound, accusing *us*? It had to be some outsider! The police think it was all for money, but no one in the family needs money! We all have plenty of money."

I felt pretty certain Sierra knew this to be untrue, but her loss of control somehow helped me reclaim mine. My hands relaxed and I gazed up at her mildly. We'd already discussed Logan's drug problem. I wasn't yet clear on her financial situation, but thought she could easily live beyond her means. I took a mental breath, and then another, and decided to try a different tact.

"What does Daniel think?"

Derailed by my pacifistic attitude and the abrupt change in direction, Sierra considered a moment. Her shoulders relaxed, fists left her hips, and after another moment she turned reluctantly and slowly walked back to the chair, sat, crossed her legs, rolled her eyes and gave a dismissive wave of her manicured hand.

"You wouldn't know this," she began, speaking in a tone of distaste and superiority, "after all you're *just* a *medical student*, but Daniel is a PhD, an Assistant Professor, on *the faculty at Rice,* and a brilliant researcher. His name's been on *hundreds* of articles in journals and what not, and when he's not writing he spends the rest of his time peering through microscopes in his lab at the University, trying to discover, well, things... you know... cures for sicknesses... Daniel's absolutely brilliant, but because he's so much smarter than the rest of us, he lives in his own little world, in an ivory tower if you will, and could not possibly care less about the concerns of us mere mortals."

Sierra apparently had no idea of or interest in the type of research in which her husband might be involved. She sounded petulant, resentful, probably of Daniel and certainly of me for asking her what she considered an impertinent question, but she hadn't entirely shut me down. She hadn't walked out, was still sitting in the chair.

"So Daniel wasn't at your mother's funeral? He didn't go to the firing range?"

"Are you absolutely mad?" Sierra exclaimed, exasperated. "Why are you asking all these stupid questions? Yes! Daniel went to the funeral and he went with us to shoot, but he didn't kill Stacy! No sane person could even suggest such a thing!"

She looked at me, but her anger was ebbing, replaced by perplexity.

"How could you even think someone in the family could have done these awful things? You *know* us! No one in the family would hurt Stacy! No one in the family would strangle anyone with their bare hands!" She brought her own pale hands up and clinched them in a circle to emphasize the point.

"And we don't need money! No one in the family..." Sierra circled back to the topic of money, but then stopped. She knew, I knew she was lying.

"Okay," she said, reluctantly. "Okay. Maybe Logan needs money for his..."

She put one finger against the side of her nose and sniffed expressively.

"...but he didn't kill Momma, or Stacy, or Luciana!" she finished. "Logan would not do such a thing."

"But you admit Logan does need money. What about you?" I asked, boldly. "It's obvious you and Daniel are having problems. How are you set for cash?"

The question, including my choice of words, was purposefully crass. Sierra rolled her eyes, again.

~ * ~

"Oh, you're referring to that little dust up in the hall the other day?" She laughed. "Let me explain the facts of marriage to you, *Chica*. When two strong-willed individuals get together, there will be episodes of spontaneous combustion. Daniel and I are very different, but both dramatic, passionate people. We fight; we've always fought. It's what we do. But the making up is just as intense as the breaking up, and, well, I'm sure *you* wouldn't understand, but let's just say Daniel's not about to leave me... and I've no intention of leaving him."

I gave her my *Oh, really?* look of skepticism, no words necessary.

"Even if Daniel and I were having problems in our marriage, and I'm not saying we are, I would not need my Daddy's money," Sierra insisted angrily. "The pre-nup Daniel and I signed was all on my side. He's the one who gets nothing if we split."

"Except what he had at the time of the marriage plus half of his earnings since," I added, though I hadn't a clue if what I was saying was true or not in the state of Texas.

"That's not entirely correct." Sierra was impatient. "You don't know what you're talking about."

"If he cheats, I get it all." She smiled, showing straight white teeth. "So you see, even if Daddy disinherited me, which he has no reason to do, or even if you took all the family money, there's no way Daniel can leave me in the cold."

"He's slept with so many other women, I've lost count," she confided, nonchalantly. Her legs were crossed, and she began bouncing her right foot, her Jimmy Choos hanging from one toe. "I've a PI who's documented them all, well, maybe not all, but more than enough."

"He's just like Daddy, at least in that way, "indiscrete and who cares?", and you can make whatever you want of that, that I married someone like my Daddy... but actually Daniel is much more clever than Daddy, at least in some ways, more careful in his selection of partners, better at covering up... *Anyway*, I have been faithful in my marriage, at least mostly faithful. Since the day of my wedding, I have only slept, well not slept if you know what I mean, but "been with" one other man." She paused for effect. "Daniel's attorney." She laughed, again, but without humor. "No matter what Daniel does now, I'm still set. I won't ever need money.

I looked at her in disbelief. *How could anyone live like that?* I thought, disgusted, but it got worse. Sierra was compelled to make her point.

"So you see," she began nastily, narrowing her eyes,

"it doesn't make any difference to me at all, one way or the other, if Stacy is alive or dead. It has no effect on *me!*"

She heard herself and stopped, dismayed. I could only stare.

For a moment, she sat stunned, still, apparently shocked by her own callousness, but Sierra Tau-Martindale was in the habit of landing on her feet.

"Now I'm sorry for how that sounded. You know I loved Stacy more than anything in the world." Her tone was contrite, but I wasn't sure if she was trying to convince me, or herself. "I've just been under so much pressure lately I don't know what I'm saying anymore. And you, I'd almost think you're deliberately trying to provoke me." Her voice soft, Southern, conciliatory, "But you do see what I mean, don't you?"

I did. I knew exactly what she meant. In that moment, I hated Sierra Martindale as I've hated no other person in my life. That she could say such a thing about Stacy, her own sister... The blond hair, the violet eyes, the perfect skin and teeth, the superficial kindness and supercilious concern were nothing but a thin disguise, hiding the shallow, self-centered shrew that cared for no one but herself. I wanted her to be guilty, of something, anything, to be punished for her heartlessness, but in the end it was her indifference that convinced me of her innocence. She had no motive for wanting Stacy dead, didn't even consider Stacy significant enough to kill. But someone did.

Chapter 17

Sierra left and I could tell I'd never be in her good books again, not that I cared. I didn't have the heart to call Cal to indulge in the luxury of a normal conversation as I'd planned. After everything that had happened, and everything I'd heard from the three Taus, I didn't feel capable of normal conversation with anyone.

I briefly considered calling Det. Hawk, but by then it was late and I thought he'd most likely be off work, maybe throwing back a few after the day he'd had. It wasn't as though I could shed any new light on the investigation, but I would have liked to learn when and why he'd become suspicious of Mrs. Tau's death. I also wanted to share my views on the inhabitants of the Tau mansion. If Logan was right and it had been his father who suggested the trip to the firing range, then Dr. Tau was a strong suspect, but if Sierra was right, could it really have been Chess? And what did Logan mean by his cryptic remarks? I didn't believe he could have shot Stacy or strangled Luciana with his "bare hands", but could he have maybe hired someone to kill his own sister for money?

My mind was whirling with too much and too little information and I knew I was missing something important. I walked about the room, glanced over the photos on the mirror, and then went to Stacy's closet and opened the door. In addition to a taste for shoes and boots, Stacy had an extraordinary fondness for hats. As the floor of the closet was covered with footwear, the shelves were filled with hats and caps; all colors, all styles. I started taking them down, and trying them on one by one. After all, I was already walking in

Stacy's shoes, or more correctly her boots. Now I needed to get into her head.

I settled on a black felt men's Bowler, vintage, probably early1900s. I cocked it to the back of my head, and faced my reflection in the mirror. The black hat crowning dark hair made my eyes look unnaturally blue. Like Texas Blue Bonnets, my Dad had said. Satisfied, I turned on my heel and left the room, striding across the landing to the stairs, past Logan's closed door, and then down, through the entry hall and into the kitchen.

Dr. Tau had instructed me to make myself at home, but I didn't normally drink at home. There were three bottles of wine in the refrigerator that had been brought and left by guests from the wake. I took the bottle of Barefoot Moscato (reasoning that Barefoot Moscato had no business in such an upscale 'fridge anyway) and rummaged through the drawers for a corkscrew. Finding one, I uncorked the bottle and took a swig. As expected, the wine was sweet. I've a theory that you can't really get drunk on sweet red wine. It goes down like syrup, so there's no temptation to slam it.

Not bothering with a glass, I carried the bottle out through the double doors to the patio, propped my cowgirl boots up on the wrought-iron table, pulled the hat brim forward, and sipped slowly, trying to relax. The sun was going down. Insects were humming. The birds had already gone to bed.

For a while, my mind continued to race with thoughts of Stacy, Luciana, Mrs. Tau, and occasionally, unavoidable, Jordy and Rachel, and then began to drift until I found myself thinking, oddly enough, about Pattillo Higgins. Pattillo Higgins, the one-armed, self-educated geologist, the laughing stock of Beaumont and the surrounding counties, who insisted there was oil under the Spindletop salt dome in spite of everything every educated geologist of the time could argue against him. Whose stubbornness or faith was finally rewarded when the Lucas gusher blew, initially producing 100,000 barrels a day and ushering in the Texas oil boom, only after he had been forced to sign away all his rights to the venture. He of course litigated. The other investors settled, so he did receive some pecuniary benefit, but that chapter of his life, the most well known chapter, the one that forever established his place in history, was not what struck me in my near dream state.

What stood out to me was the story around how he lost his arm: caught in the act of defacing an African American church, shot by a police officer, he killed a police officer and was found innocent. Had the same sequence of events surrounding his alleged crime and apprehension occurred in the present time, the outcome for Pattillo would likely have been very different. A possible bigot and unquestionably a cop killer... but innocent... his defense: he didn't know the man he was shooting at was a cop... it was a totally different time... funny how things appear in hindsight... the interpretation and judgment of the past reevaluated under current light... and where had they gone, the ghosts of Spindletop... ghosts from the past... I looked out at the carriage house, wondering.

"Mind if I sit with you?"

I wasn't frightened by the sound of the voice in the dark, having heard footsteps crossing the brick pavers. The approach wasn't made in stealth.

"Nope," I responded, leaning forward just far enough to push the wine bottle toward her.

Page Sheffield-Anderson pulled the chair back, making a loud grating noise with the iron feet, and then sat, propping her elbows on the table and resting her chin in her hands. Not certain the soles of my boots were presentable, I took them off the table and sat up.

"Remember when we use to sit out here at night and tell ghost stories?" Page asked, in her low, pastel-colored voice, as if she'd somehow read my thoughts. "Ghosts were so much scarier than people then." She laughed, but it was the sad laugh of lost youth, or more likely innocence.

She carefully wiped the top of the wine bottle off with her sleeve, and took an experimental sip.

Like that's going to do any good, I thought. I'd already finished my first-year micro and immunology classes, and doubted the small percentage of alcohol in the wine or the wiping of the mouth of the bottle with one's sleeve could prove to be in any way germicidal.

Page took another sip, nodded in approval and passed it back.

"I was just thinking about the night we tried to contact Marty with the Ouija board..." I said, taking another long hit from the bottle.

"And Aunt Eleanor caught us and tried to explain why we were wrong to do it, but broke down crying instead," Page finished, remembering, too. "It wasn't really our fault, though I can see why she was so upset, she had lost a child, but death didn't seem final to us. Children can be really insensitive."

So can adults, I thought, but I said, "You were there though... when he died."

"Yes," she answered, reflectively, "I was there."

"What happened really? Do you remember?"

Page considered.

"Well, you know that Marty was an accomplished rider, even at 12 years old. He rode in dressage and hunter/jumper competitions and always placed highly."

I nodded, trying to retrieve any memories of that time, but I'd only been 5 years old. I could see him, but indistinctly, a tall, well-grown boy, comparatively, in jodhpurs, curling blond hair, big smile, a riding croup in his hand.

"He was so good, that his father had just given over his own horse, Prince Tango, for Marty's use. Prince Tango was amazing, beautiful, athletic, and sound, and could jump like no other horse in the country at that time. Uncle Marshall had received offers for him from almost every other competitive rider in the circuit."

Slipping back into my dream-like state, soothed by the wine and Page's mellow voice, I relaxed as she painted carefully constructed pictures on the canvas of my mind.

"That day Marty was riding well, a practice run, no hurry, just slow, controlled, making his way purposefully around the course. Prince Tango was in high spirits, prancing, but not in the least nervy, just eager and energetic. Marty was happy, you could tell, but not laughing though, he took his riding very seriously. He'd reached the last jump but one, when for some reason, Prince Tango hesitated at the In-and-Out; something spooked him, maybe a rabbit, or a bird, and he shied, and then tried to jump but fell. He'd never been down before. Marty ended up under him; the pommel of the saddle crushed his chest... fractured pelvis, internal bleeding. Marty was DOA." Her tone was subdued but matter-of-fact, appropriate for speaking of a tragedy of long ago.

I started to ask a question, hesitated, then asked a different one. "But you saw the fall?"

"No, I didn't." She shook her head. "I was at the stable, well we all were, except you. Why weren't you there that day? But we were playing you see, me, Sierra, Logan, Chess, and Stacy, too, I think, though Stacy was never very good at games, especially hide-and-seek. She couldn't quite get the point." Page frowned, drawing her penciled eyebrows together in the effort of remembering.

"We heard the fall, and a cry, and all ran from our hiding places... Marty was on the ground... the poles were down... Prince Tango was standing over him..." She stopped and sighed. "It's been so long and I was just a kid... I know it was upsetting at the time, but now seems more like a dream..."

She looked up suddenly.

"You know what?" Page offered, unexpectedly, "You

might ask Mom about it, if you really want to know. She was there, too, of course."

~ * ~

"Page told me you were there the day Marty Tau died," I said, without preamble. "Can you tell me what happened?"

I sat on the sofa beside Mrs. Sheffield without an invitation. Page had taken me to her mother's home and let me into the house before heading off to presumably meet her husband. I say, "presumably" because by that point I was trying not to take anything or anyone for granted.

"It was a tragedy," she sighed. "A real tragedy. So young, so promising, such a life he might have had... not like Stacy."

She was wearing a soft watermelon-pink bathrobe that had a sharply pointed navy silk collar, and that, plus her square face and dramatic bang, for some reason reminded me of Jackie Kennedy Onassis when she was Jackie Kennedy in her pink and navy suit. Though JFK had died long before I was born, shot down in Dallas in front of the world, I'd been impressed by the apparent strength and grace of his particularly iconic first lady captured forever between the pages of our history books.

Buzzing from wine, it occurred to me that I might not be in the best shape to deal with the often unfiltered Mrs. Sheffield, that hearing her views on my friend might provoke me even more than Sierra had. I remembered planning to spend some time alone in Stacy's room, and then calling Cal...

How did I end up here? I wondered suddenly.

She didn't ask why I wanted to know about Marty. I guess the fact that Page had brought me to her was enough of an inducement to talk.

"I hate to say it," Margaret Sheffield went on, "but it's probably for the best."

"What's for the best? You just said it was a tragedy."

"No, not that, I meant Stacy. Well, that the poor child won't be alone," she said, shaking her head, "without her mother."

I should have been shocked, but somehow I wasn't, not anymore. "What are you saying...?"

"That she died. That Stacy died." She shrugged. "I mean, really, Sierra would never have taken her in," she asserted, "and Logan, bless his heart, he can't take care of himself."

There it was again. *Stacy's in a better place... It's for the best... What did that mean: her murderer was a humanitarian? Being shot to death was in Stacy's best interest? How could anyone think that?*

"But she had her Dad..." I said.

"And of course he's dying."

"Dr. Tau is dying? From what?"

"How would *I* know?" she said, sounding slightly irritated. "He doesn't confide in *me*. You're the *doctor*. You tell me."

Was she crazy, or just making stuff up? A mental breath...

"What makes you think that Dr. Tau is ill?" I asked patiently, trying to keep any hint of the anger I felt from creeping into my voice.

"Have you looked at him?" she frowned, answering with a question of her own. "He's obviously lost weight, but it's not just that. There's something about his eyes, a distant, foggy, faraway look. Oh, he still tries to roar, like the old lion he is, but believe you me, he's lost his bite."

"But he just *lost* his wife, and his daughter," I argued, exasperated. "Maybe he's depressed."

"Oh, please!" Margaret Sheffield touched her chin with a manicured fingertip. "Marshall Tau cared very little for his daughter, and never cared at all about his wife. He didn't even like Eleanor. He needed her; she was a necessity, like a paper towel," her voiced dropped, "like toilet paper." She wrinkled her nose, shaking her head. "Marshall Tau doesn't care about anyone except Marshall Tau. He never has."

"Of course my sister was no saint either..." she began, gaining volume, but I didn't want to hear her list of Eleanor Tau's sins. I interrupted.

"But you were there, when Marty died," I said, leading her back to the purpose of our conversation. "What happened?"

"Very well. If you *must* know." she seemed resigned. "Though it's not a thing any of us likes to discuss."

I waited, hoping she shared her daughter's creative storytelling skills, but not entirely optimistic that she did. More likely Page inherited her warmer, more personable traits from her father.

"We were having a picnic and ride at the stables," she began, settling her hands on her knees, "my family, Eleanor's, the Andersons. Everyone seemed happy enough, enjoying the day, it was a lovely day as I recall, all blue skies and sunshine, flowers covering the fields, somehow that made it all the more horrible, when the horse fell. The afternoon was so pleasant... Then suddenly there was the noise of it, and the child screaming, and the horse snorting and blowing and thrashing about. Marshall got to him first, was shouting something, I don't remember what."

She hesitated, forehead crinkling.

"The other children were all terrified of course, began crying, well, except Stacy. She was laughing that funny little laugh she had. It wasn't really a happy sound, if you know what I mean. Then they were all running about, like little chicks in a rain storm, dodging around the barn, trying to get away but not knowing from what, or where to go. Eleanor was kneeling in the dirt beside her son..."

A spasm of pain crossed her face, unexpected, sincere grief, and she paused.

The sounds that came from her throat on that day... were unearthly... I'll never forget it, wish I could forget it, really I would rather forget the whole incident, but that's why I can't be too hard on her, Eleanor I mean. She may have earned misfortune, but no one deserves that... the death of a child... seeing the death of one's own child... if it had been my Page..."

She paused again, taken by a small shiver, but then shook off the memory and continued in a stronger voice.

"*Some people* blamed Marshall... said he should have let the boy ride in the rodeos instead of... but of course he could have died there just as well. And can you imagine, Marshal Tau... bulldogging...?"

She rolled her eyes. I couldn't.

"That chit, Trish Anderson, was acting as though she was the one whose son was dying, wailing and moaning and carrying on. Her husband had to physically restrain her... Chet, such an ass... I of course kept my head, I always do, and did my best to gather the rest of the children up, to get them away and to the house. Alex, dear Alex, my husband, had Page on his shoulders and was leading Chess by the hand. I scooped up Logan and had just herded Sierra out of the tack room, and was trying to pry Stacy out from under the saddle racks, she was petrified, poor soul, but Marshall wouldn't wait."

"Wait for what? The EMTs?"

"No. No. It was the horse."

"What are you talking about? Marty was hurt. He died at the scene, didn't he?"

"Oh, that. Yes, of course he did. The paramedics came, but he was already dead. We all knew he was dead because he stopped crying."

The woman was appalling.

"Why are we talking about the horse, then?"

She looked surprised. "Marshall shot him. Right there in front of the children, if you'll believe it...took a shotgun and shot him, dead! Isn't that what you wanted to know?"

"Dr. Tau shot Marty's horse? Why? Was he mad? Because the horse fell, and killed his son?"

"No! No! Of course not!" she exclaimed, shaking her head emphatically. "He's a callous man, often a cruel unthinking man, but his faults... he's not... no, he wouldn't... not revenge on a dumb brute!"

"Then why?"

"The horse shattered his right fore when he fell. Marshall shot the poor beast out of mercy."

Mercy? In front of all the kids...

~ * ~

"It was not so very long after that that Stacy began acting noticeable strange, though I always thought her odd from the beginning of course, but no one ever listens to me. No one ever has, listened to me that is, well, except my Dear Alex." She sighed. "I'm sure you'll recall just the other day I tried to warn Marshall about that nanny and Logan, and now see what's happened."

She shivered again. She was rambling, getting off track. I steered her back.

"I'm listening to you, Mrs. Sheffield," I assured her politely, remembering my confrontational interview with Sierra. "What do you mean when you say Stacy began acting noticeable strange?"

"Well, she always did seem *odd* to me, but Eleanor refused to consider that there might be something actually *wrong* with the girl," she offered, earnestly, "but after that dear boy died and the horse was shot, and then the incident in the pool, she was so much worse. She started talking to herself, or perhaps to the air. She made up that invisible friend of hers, the one she called Paygo, but we all knew she meant the horse, and how my poor sister suffered every time she heard the name. It just made my heart *ache* to see her. I tried to convince Eleanor to send Stacy away, to a sanitarium or some place like that, at least for a while, so she could be evaluated and taken proper care of, and so that Eleanor could have some peace, but Eleanor wouldn't *hear* of it.

"What incident in the pool? When? Wait, Paygo was Prince Tango? Paygo was a *horse?*" I asked, confused.

Somehow that didn't quite make sense, even in Stacy's universe. *Paygo had done human things, seemed to have human interests. What would a horse be doing in college?*

"Of course he was, Dear," Mrs. Sheffield assured me, as she kindly and quite unexpectedly patted my hand. "Everyone knew, I guess except you. You weren't there that day, were you? When it all happened. Why weren't you there? You and your family were around after, though, at the funeral and that awkward wake. We all knew it was the horse, just never talked about it out of respect for Eleanor."

My calm attention and interest was having a soothing effect upon Mrs. Sheffield. She asked if I'd like some tea.

While she was in the kitchen boiling water and setting up the tray, I took advantage of her hospitality and my alone time to snoop about the room. Mrs. Sheffield was a collector. She had all manner of knickknacks artfully arranged in cabinets and on small tables that suggested souvenirs from a lifetime of traveling the globe. Nothing seemed relevant to my investigation, though it was difficult to visually sort through so many items in the short time available. I walked over to the fireplace mantle and gazed at the assortment of family photos. Mr. Sheffield, my Dad's friend, had died suddenly not very long after we left Beaumont, dropped dead at 54 from cardiac arrest while taking his morning stroll. I remembered my Dad saying that whatever caused his death was hereditary, that he had three brothers who all did the same, dying near and one actually on his 50th birthday. At least I could feel pretty confident Mr. Sheffield wasn't the victim of foul play.

There were pictures of Page, playing softball, fishing with her Dad, at her graduation, in her wedding dress with her Mom beaming at her side. Behind them, arranged in a neat row, were black and white stills of her Mom and Dad from the pre-Page era, laughing while seated in a rusted old rag-top, holding hands on the beach, on their wedding day. You could tell Mrs. Sheffield was older than her husband was, by at least 5 or 6 years, though perhaps she just didn't wear her age as well, but still it must not have mattered. The expression he wore when he looked at his wife was one of pure affection. And her expression, the look on the formidably fierce Margaret Sheffield's face, was as soft and loving as any woman's could be. I touched the edge of the frame of the beach picture, and tried to reconcile who she seemed now as compared to who she might have been then.

There was something very familiar about Mr. Sheffield's face, though I hadn't known him when he was young of course. He reminded me of someone, black eyes, thick dark hair, and then the sudden realization hit me. Young Mr. Sheffield was the spitting image of Logan Tau. *Could it be...? Page's Dad and Stacy's Mom?*

I was considering the possible implications when Mrs. Sheffield returned with the tea things. I held the door open for her, and we moved outside to sit on the porch. With the ceiling fan on and citronella torches burning to discourage mosquitoes, we sat and sipped in companionable silence for some time, both lost in our own private meditations, and then she spoke.

"Some thought I was too hard on the child, on Stacy, I mean," she confessed softly into the darkness. "It wasn't as though I had no sympathy for her. She obviously couldn't help being the way she was."

She sighed.

"If I blame anyone, I blame that oafish son-in-law of mine." Her tone changed, held a note of contempt. "It wasn't *her* fault he was always following her about, making a fool of himself, embarrassing my dear Page... and that Sierra... looking for any excuse to make a nasty remark..."

"Mrs. Sheffield," I said, using my most diplomatic voice, "you don't really think Chess and Stacy were having an affair, do you? Not really?"

She was quiet for a moment as she stirred more sugar into her tea, and then she straightened and pushed back her hair.

"If they were," she answered, and her hazel eyes were cold, "then it's clearly over now."

Chapter 18

I walked back to the Tau mansion, alone in the dark. All around me were the sounds of Beaumont at night. There was some traffic noise, but also the chirping of crickets and flutter of night birds. I chose to call them night birds, though they were more likely bats. Once I stopped abruptly, and listened anxiously, fearing I'd heard the soft swish of fabric on fabric and possible footfalls on the soft, damp lawn, closer than should be without a hail of greeting from anyone, but the night noises continued with no other human sounds, and I convinced myself those I thought I heard were the product of stress, lack of sleep and an overactive imagination.

On checking my phone, I found a text from Jordy. He and Rachel had enjoyed the Spindletop mining camp re-creation, and hoped I would drop by the Inn in the morning. There was no mention of when they might be leaving town.

Trying to sort the important from the irrelevant amongst all I'd learned was proving a daunting task and my head ached with the effort, and from the wine. There were more motives for killing Stacy than I could have imagined for such a gentle and harmless soul.

Her father could have killed her out of pity, worried that no one would take care of her when he was gone, that is supposing he really was dying as Mrs. Sheffield contended. Chess might have killed her out of pity as well, whether knowing of Dr. Tau's alleged illness or not, but foreseeing too many challenges ahead for her after her mother's death and on hearing her own father wish her dead.

Mrs. Sheffield had motive, as did her daughter, if you accepted that Stacy and Chess were having an affair, but I was still unconvinced of that, or Mrs. Sheffield may have had another motive altogether, if Logan was her husband's son and somehow Stacy found out what no one else seemed to know, or at least what no one else openly acknowledged.

Logan seemed to blame himself for both Stacy's death and Luciana's, and may have had Stacy killed for money, or his druggy friends may have killed her because Logan owed them money, though that possibility would not explain the fingerprints on the murder weapon. Sierra, well whether Sierra needed money or not, she might have killed Stacy out of the meanness that filled the empty hole that should have been her heart.

Luciana must have been a witness, or perhaps saw or overheard something that caused the killer to panic and kill her also, but if Luciana did have information about Stacy's murder, then why didn't she just go to the police? She wasn't in the country illegally. Stacy's murder certainly wasn't as straightforward as Det. Hawk initially believed. The real problem was that none of these motives seemed sufficient in my mind for the crime in the way it occurred. The fingerprints were all from family, and I still could not see any of these people taking a shotgun to Stacy's house and shooting her dead in the middle of the night.

~ * ~

I spent another restless night in Stacy's room, though in this instance I could hardly blame the weather. It was actually a perfect night for sleeping, rain falling steadily, but softly, without wind or lightning, until the clouds were drained dry, and dawn broke on a clear, brilliant blue Texas morning. I waited impatiently for the sun to rise, before going in search of Dr. Tau. He was seated at the kitchen counter reading his Wall Street Journal while Mrs. Nelson provided a steady stream of refills for his coffee cup.

Nervy from stress and lack of sleep, I nevertheless felt compelled to continue on the course I'd struck without conscious thought or deliberate decision. Somehow, at some point, I'd taken up the task of finding out who'd killed Stacy and why, and I had more questions for the master of the house.

Chapter 19

"I did it," declared Dr. Tau, looking directly into my eyes, his irises reflecting almost white in the filtered morning light.

When I'd asked if I could speak with him he'd nodded, rose with coffee cup and paper in hand, and led the way to his office without a word. Now we were seated as before, with the great desk between us, and the circle of golden monkeys curiously dangling above our heads.

"I said that to Stacy." He frowned and looked down at his arthritic fingers.

"In front of everyone, at the dinner table," he continued slowly, "I told her, my own daughter, that she'd be better off dead."

I felt sick, could feel anger rising, but remained silent.

"Even now, after all that's happened," he paused, gazing straight ahead, past me and into the entry hall, "I can't say I didn't mean it, or don't believe it to be true. I still believe it to be true..."

Certain that I was going to scream, I gripped the arm of the chair until my knuckles turned white.

"How could you?" The words came out quietly, sounding rational, though I felt far removed from rational thought. "How could you say that to her?"

He turned his pale eyes to mine, an odd, sad smile on his lips.

"Stacy was like me, you see," he explained, "but more so. She was absolutely brilliant about some things, but had no understanding of others, of people especially. I've never understood people either, but I've never cared. I've lived my life as I chose, doing what I would, as my inclinations led me..."

"Stacy did care, and was tortured by what she perceived as her faults, her shortcomings. Eleanor could deal with her, but I had no patience for her insecurities, her constant self-doubt. Always asking others how she should act, what to do, what to say, trying to model her behavior after so called normal people. She never belonged here, should not have been conceived, should never have survived to adulthood, and so I wished she had never been born..."

"But you said..."

"I know exactly what I said." He took a deep breath, and his expression lost its softness.

"She was my daughter," he said, coldly, "and I wanted what was best for her. That certainly does not mean I wanted her to be shot to death, in her own home, in the middle of the night. That's why you're asking isn't it? You think I shot my own daughter? What on Earth could have possibly motivated me to do such a horrendous thing?"

Out of mercy...? I wondered.

"Are you ill, Dr. Tau? I mean seriously ill?"

I avoided the direct question with a question of my own. He seemed surprised, but gazed at me with more curiosity than concern, and hesitated only a moment before replying, "What makes you ask that?"

I didn't answer, didn't care to explain about Margaret Sheffield's suppositions, but instead changed the subject.

"Do you think your attorney will have the papers today? Regarding the bequest?" I asked.

"He expects to have something, a draft for my review, by this afternoon or tomorrow morning at the latest," he answered, and then added, "but if you are anxious to leave, I'm quite sure we can handle everything required via registered mail."

"No," I said, shaking my head in the negative, "I'd rather stay a few more days, if that's alright."

He raised his eyebrows. I responded to the unstated question.

"It's just, when I leave Beaumont this time, I'm never coming back," I hesitated, pretty sure he wouldn't understand. I doubted Dr. Tau was the sentimental type. I sighed. "I'm just not ready to let her go yet."

He looked at me, and then turned and gazed out the window, the lines of his angular face softening again as the early morning sunlight sifted through the blinds.

"I know what you mean," he said finally, so quietly I had to strain my ears. "I know exactly what you mean."

"Do you really think I killed her?" he asked, curiously but dispassionately, turning back to me.

I shook my head.

"I don't see any motive at all," I said.

Chapter 20

Chess and Sierra were sharing the bench seat outside Dr. Tau's office when I left, but weren't engaged in congenial conversation as far as I could tell. If anything, they appeared to be sitting on the very ends of the cushions and leaning outward, as distant from each other as space would allow. Neither looked at me nor spoke to me, so I didn't speak to them. I had no more questions for Sierra, and any I might have for Chess would wait until I could catch him alone. Besides, I had other plans for my morning.

"My Dear," I heard Dr. Tau saying as I strode across the entry hall, indicating his choice of his daughter over Chess for the next interview of the day. A slight movement caused me to look up to see Logan, silently watching from the shadow of his door. On impulse I waved to him, but he turned without acknowledging me and went back into his room.

I headed straight for the kitchen, having already seen and smelled the breakfast on the menu for the morning. Grabbing a plate of chorizo sausage and biscuits smothered in gravy from Mrs. Nelson, I jumped into my rental car and drove out to Lumberton, absolutely determined to send Jordy and Rachel on their way. I hoped not to arrive early enough to find them in bed together, but couldn't really care. As far as I was concerned, they needed to leave Texas and go back to Atlanta, that day, that morning, period.

My hand was shaking as I knocked on the door, thinking perhaps I needed the sight of them as early morning waking up together lovers in order to accept the fact that Jordy was lost to me forever. He answered the door, alone.

Damn! My heart dropped about ten feet or more, towards the Earth's core. He was half dressed, in jeans, but buttoning his shirt, his jet-black hair still damp from the shower.

"Hey," I managed weakly, peering over his shoulder seeking Rachel.

"Hey, yourself," he said, smiling broadly. "It's about time. I've been wondering when you would show up."

He opened the door wide and stood back to let me pass. The bed was immediately within my view, sheets rumpled, clothes strewn about, wine glasses on the bedside tables, a serious reality check, good for the soul...

"I brought breakfast," I offered, with as much enthusiasm as I could muster, moving hurriedly forward, past the bed and toward the dining table.

"Where's Rachel?" I asked, presenting the plate of biscuits. There was no sign of her in the bedroom proper, and no shower noise from the bathroom.

"She's gone out for coffee," he laughed, "promised to bring something back for me, but, hey, let's not wait." He inhaled. "I'm starving!"

"You can save these for later..." I began, but he already had the plate uncovered and was headed for the kitchenette.

"She won't mind," he said. "Rachel's gone all micronutrient-rich and gluten-free. These aren't gluten-free and micronutrient-rich, are they?" he asked, raising the plate ceremoniously, before popping it into the small microwave.

I couldn't help but laugh, too.

"No," I said, with false solemnity. "I can say with absolute certainty that those biscuits and sausages are devoid of any healthful nutritional value whatsoever, or at the very least that any they may have had has been totally obliterated by the gravy."

The microwave binged, Jordy brought out milk from

the tiny refrigerator, we sat across from each other at the table and scarfed down the most deliciously artery-clogging breakfast you could imagine.

It became a contest of sorts, like on the Food Network, both of us grinning while trying to stuff as much food as possible into our mouths before the other could get it. Jordy, the quintessential competitor started it, and ultimately won of course, but only by a crumb, as he grabbed the last bit of biscuit and reached to sop it in my last drop of gravy before popping it in his mouth and chewing with triumph and gusto. It was the first meal I'd enjoyed since Stacy's death.

When it was over, we cleared the table and moved to the couch.

"So you've come to tell us to bugger off."

It was a statement, but Jordy smiled and poked my shoulder when he said it. Another challenge.

"And what if I have?" I answered, trying to keep the tone light, playful, but Jordy's eyes immediately went dark and deep.

"You know we know what you're doing? Right?" he asked, looking at me, seriously, disapprovingly.

I shook my head in the negative, feigning ignorance. "What?"

"You're shutting us out. Rachel and I talked about it on our way to that Gladys Spindletop exhibit. Why did you send us there? We didn't drive all the way to Texas to hang out in a ghost town. We came here for you."

"I know," I sighed.

I turned, pulling my feet up onto the sofa. He did the same, and we sat, crossed-legged facing each other.

"You and Rachel are the best friends I've ever had." I began, looking down at my feet, my hands on my knees, the lotus seeking Zen.

"I'm the best friend you'll ever hope to have." He smiled his crooked, toothy grin. "Rachel has her merits-a close second. But?"

"But, Stacy was *killed*," I said.

"And you can't take chances with Rache or me," he finished for me.

Leaning forward, he placed his hands on my ankles where they crossed. I sat back, folding my arms across my chest, ready for the argument, my mind already made up.

"What makes you think you're a better match for a killer than Rachel or I am?" he asked, still smiling. "You're not smarter, faster, or stronger than either of us, well maybe a little more buff than me, but only a little."

I didn't laugh. I wanted to tell him about Luciana, but knew that revelation would make him even more determined to stay. I was a bit surprised he and Rachel hadn't seen anything about her murder on the news, but concluded perhaps the police were withholding details as the investigation was underway.

Instead, I downplayed the situation.

"Look," I said, trying to believe the lie as I told it so deceit wouldn't show in my eyes, "I'm not trying to catch any killer. The police are doing that. I *want* to go home. I'm just waiting to sign some legal documents so that I don't end up with millions of dollars that don't belong me."

I explained about the Will and the trust. Jordy was quiet for a moment, processing.

"Wow," was his first comment, and then, "wow!"

"But I can see why you can't take it," he said, nodding his head in understanding. "Anyone else might, but not you."

He gripped my shoulder.

"Wim, is that all, everything, really?" he asked, gazing deep into my eyes.

I bit my lip, and looked down. When I looked back up, he was biting his lip, too.

He knows I'm lying... he knows I'm going to lie...

"Jordy," I began earnestly, taking his hand from my shoulder and holding it in both of mine, "please go home…"

His left hand was still on my ankle, his right hand in mine. At that moment, we heard the sound of a key in the lock, the bolt turned, and Rachel entered the room.

~ * ~

She seemed surprised at my presence, and Jordy and I jumped back from each other as if we'd been tazed, but not before she'd had time to note the close physical contact. I couldn't tell if she thought anything about it, at least not at first.

Within the construct of our friendship, Jordy and I had always been "touchy" with each other. I come from a family of "hand-holders" and all his relatives are "huggers". There'd never been any sexual implications attached in the past, but it occurred to me that in our new and dramatically different group hierarchy my touching Jordy, or Jordy touching me, might not be acceptable. He seemed equally uncertain of himself, making the situation appear all the more suspect.

"Hey," he said, bouncing up from the couch and moving to kiss Rachael at the door. She had a brown bag in her hand.

"I brought this for you," Rachel said, and sniffed the air, "but I somehow suspect you've already been fed."

She made it a statement, and didn't smile. Her voice seemed deliberately neutral, not particularly happy, but not offended either.

"I just stopped by to see you both off," I offered by way of explanation. "I thought you'd be heading back to Atlanta today."

Rachel gave Jordy a questioning look.

"Are we going? Really?" she asked him, and couldn't quite keep the hopeful note from her question, or the momentary look of relief from her eyes.

And then it was obvious. The comfort we'd felt when we were all just friends was truly gone. Rachel was not secure in her relationship with Jordy as her lover. She didn't trust him, even with me. That's the trouble in getting the one all the other girls want. No one could ask for a more faithful friend, but Jordy'd been far too casual in his romantic entanglements for far too long.

Jordy was caught. Rachel wanted to go. That was clear. He wanted to stay, because he knew I was lying about something and that I might be in danger, but he had no plausible reason to give Rachel for his concern. He knew I was in trouble because he knew me. Jordy was caught, and had to make a choice. He chose me.

"I was just telling Wim we're staying one more day," he said with forced cheerfulness, as Rachel wilted before our eyes. "I really want to see the historic McFaddin-Ward House. You know, the one in The Oaks, where Wim is staying."

I didn't want them anywhere near the neighborhood, but when you lie you open yourself up for ending in a tight spot. Unable to think of any acceptable excuse for sending them packing, I stood up awkwardly and shifted on my feet.

"Oh. Well," I stammered, not looking directly at either of them, "that sounds great! I guess I'd better get going then, can't leave the Taus alone for too long. Jordy, I expect we'll have all the legal stuff I told you about worked out by tomorrow. Maybe we can all go home together."

Like that was going to happen...

I felt sad and disappointed with myself for becoming such a liar, and for being a sore spot, a source of conflict between my two best friends, but all I could think to do was to get away from them. After a quick hug for each, I fled the room.

Chapter 21

Time for another drive, I thought, but not toward Houston. Rachel and Jordy were staying and might be putting themselves in danger, and I was obviously in over my head. Time to take my information and suspicions to the expert. I wound my way down Cook Lake Road, hopped on 287, and headed for the police station in downtown Beaumont.

The desk sergeant apparently recognized me because when I asked for Det. Hawk, instead of instructing me to wait, he sent me right up. I exited the elevator on two and tried to orient myself. Having only been in the building once before, and having been under considerable stress at the time, I couldn't recall exactly where Hawk's desk was located. Fortunately I ran into the uniformed officer of the vending machine encounter and he pointed me in the right direction.

As I came around the corner, I saw Hawk sitting at his desk with a cute twenty-something blond girl seated in the chair beside him. He was taking notes. She was munching Ruffles and drinking a coke, and appeared to have been crying. Admittedly she was much more stylishly dressed than I'd been on my first visit to the Cop Shop, and her hair was nicely coifed. Still, the feeling of déjà vu was disconcerting.

The thought struck me that I was not unique in Det. Hawk's life. I was just another potential witness to another crime in a long list of crimes he was charged with solving.

He probably gives his cell number to lots of people, I thought, and couldn't help feeling an unanticipated twinge of disappointment.

The detective hadn't seen me, his back was to me, and for a long moment I considered turning around and walking right back out the door, but then, looking down at Stacy's boots, I decided to wait, *as long as it takes, whatever it takes, how I feel is not important,* I told myself grimly.

He looked up as I strode by, and the abrupt change in his expression, from cool professionalism to open concern, made me reconsider my rush to judgment that I was just another witness to him. He raised one finger and then two indicating a short wait. I nodded, continued on without interrupting his interview, walked over to the line of worn chairs, and sat.

~ * ~

I'd felt certain with the breakfast I'd had that I'd never be hungry again, but apparently after almost a week of feeling hollow it was going to take more than one gigantic meal to fill me up.

Det. Hawk and I sat across from each other in Suga's restaurant, apparently a favorite of his. He was paying, so I ordered a couple of appetizers plus an entrée, though we had a side bet as to my ability to finish them all. I'd found I could laugh again with Jordy that morning, and Hawk seemed to appreciate my sometimes quirky sense of humor. By the time I'd cleaned my third plate, and asked for the desert menu, he told me to call him Jalen.

"I was worried when you first showed up, thought something must have happened, but apparently nothing that's adversely affected your appetite. So why have you come to see me, really?" he asked, laughing, "and don't tell me it's payback for the first time I brought you here."

I set down my glass of iced tea. *Time for it...,* I thought, as I wiped my mouth.

I told him everything, with my own commentary provided; everything I'd been told by members of the family, everything I'd seen in my comings and goings, everything I'd heard, felt, smelled, touched, wondered about, believed and disbelieved.

I told him that Mrs. Sheffield thought Stacy and Chess were having an affair and so might Page, though I continued to consider it unlikely; however, if either of them thought it true, one of them might have wanted Stacy dead. I told him that Dr. Tau had shot a horse out of mercy and might have shot his own daughter out of pity, but I seriously doubted it. I told him Logan was using and felt guilty for Stacy and Luciana's deaths, but I could not see him committing either crime. I told him Sierra was a heinous unfeeling monster, but she didn't consider Stacy important enough to kill, actually didn't consider Stacy of any consequence at all. In a house full of suspects, I seemed to have eliminated them all.

I had not of course talked to Chess, and perhaps in the time since I'd left Beaumont he had somehow transformed from a gentle caring giant into a crazed psychotic sociopath, but in my mind that possibility was as farfetched as the others, if not more so. I gave Jalen every detail, every sliver of information, every tiny factoid that I could remember, whether it seemed important or insignificant to me, in the vain hope that he could put it all together and come up with the murderer.

When I stopped for breath he simply stared, his pitbull face puzzled.

"Why were you doing this?" he asked finally. "Why were you interviewing all these people?"

You're missing the point. I shook my head.

"Because you said you might not catch the killer," I answered, matter-of-factly. "What was I supposed to do?"

"Walk away?" He said it like it was a question and an answer all in one. "That's what any sane person would do."

"But you said..." I began, flustered. *Sane...?* I'd been counting on him to put all my clues and puzzles pieces together. I never expected he would simply shut me down.

"Look, I never meant for you to run your own personal investigation into your friend's murder!" He was angry. "I told you to go home!"

"I'm not about to let Stacy's killer get away," I replied, feeling something of a burn myself but fighting to keep my tone civil, "and I can't go home anyway, not until the Will is sorted out!"

I hadn't told him the part about inheriting millions of dollars, yet.

"Stacy left me some money, accidentally," I began, trying to explain. "She didn't really understand..."

"Great! So you're getting money. Take it and go home! I'm not going to let her killer get away!" he snapped, cutting me off. "It's *my job* to solve this case!"

That again! The "case".

"This is not a "case" to me and I don't care about *your* job," I said, carefully enunciating each word. "One of my best friends was shot to death practically in front of me..."

At that moment we were interrupted by AT&T's standard ringtone: his cell. He checked the number and put his hand up to halt further conversation while he took the call.

The caller was speaking rapidly, but all I could hear were Hawk's responses: "Uhuh, uhuh, uhuh..." and then he hung up, stood up, bent down, and looked me straight in the face.

"There's been a major break in one of my cases," he announced. "I have to go, *now.*"

I nodded, unsmiling.

"Don't do anything *I'm* going to regret; don't talk to anyone about your friend's murder until I get back to you." It was an order, not a request. "I'll call you as soon as I can. Okay?"

He took several bills from his wallet and laid them on the table.

I nodded, again.

"Okay?" he asked, again, determined to get a verbal response: my word I guess.

"Okay," I said, and meant it. I'd pretty much hit the wall anyway.

Chapter 22

I sat in the restaurant sipping my sweet tea until Det. Hawk was well out of sight, preferring to walk back to the station parking lot alone, and strongly suspecting I was satisfying both of us on that point. In my heart I knew he was only trying to protect me, but I was mad all the same.

How dare he? Treating me like a child!

The thought made me want to stamp my foot. The impulse to stamp made me realize that maybe I was being childish, which made me sigh and almost laugh at myself, and so I forgave him in about three minutes. Hawk, despite his brusqueness, wasn't the enemy. He was on my side and Stacy's side and Luciana's side. The enemy was a vicious killer who'd brutally snuffed out the lives of two young women.

Brutally. But none of the suspects seem brutal, or not brutal enough... I thought.

As I left Suga's, pondering the viciousness, the true brutality of the attacks, the whole thing seemed impossible. Could any of the Taus or Andersons or Sheffields really have committed the murders? I tried to imagine Margaret Sheffield, wearing her Jackie O dressing gown, with shotgun against her shoulder throwing down on Stacy for tempting her son-in-law to stray, or Logan, with his weakness for addiction and tragic black eyes mercilessly strangling Luciana with a wire because she did what, threatened to blackmail him? *Impossible!*

My iPhone buzzed. Mom was trying to Facetime with me, and my thumb hovered over *Decline*.

"Hey, Mom," I greeted her, and then quickly added, "I'm outside in downtown Beaumont." I flashed her a quick look around through the phone's camera lens. "Let me call you back..." not caring to have everyone within 10 feet overhearing our conversation. I could walk and talk as long as I didn't have to look at her while I did so. Besides, if I needed to skirt the truth, as was fast becoming my habit with family and friends, at least I wouldn't be lying to her face.

Standing on the curb, I scrolled through my contacts and dialed Mom, and then, waiting for her to answer, glanced both ways before stepping into the street. Before I'd time to cross the narrow two-lane road, a black BMW convertible was bearing down on me literally from out of nowhere. It was easy enough to avoid being hit, the car didn't swerve to pursue me as I scrambled for the safety of the sidewalk, and so my initial thought was not one of suspicion only irritation, but as I followed it's path, heading west, speeding rapidly away from me, I found myself squinting, trying to make out the numbers on the license plate.

The car was similar, if not the same model, as Logan's black Bimmer. The windows were tinted like his, but tinting windows is common in Texas, more to do with the sun and heat and not so much due to a criminal inclination, and so I'd not seen the driver's face.

Mom was talking in my ear, concerned, requesting information, "are you okay?".

"Yeah, sorry, I'm fine," I responded, a bit breathlessly. "Some stupid Texan almost ran me down is all. Crazy drivers!" I laughed for her benefit and, filing thoughts of the car away for future contemplation, turned my attention to her.

She and Dad had made it home safely without any further drama, and were settling in, doing laundry and such. They'd had a wonderful time in Europe, despite the aggravation of the stolen passports, and Cal was enjoying her internship a great deal. She sounded bubbly and so happy, and excited, and normal, that tears sprang to my eyes and my throat tightened up.

I want to go home! Please! I thought, though not sure to whom my plea was addressed. No one was keeping me in Beaumont. The police, Dr. Tau, Logan, Jordy, Rachel, all said I could go home. Some even encouraged me to go. *So why am I still here?*

"Wim, are you listening?" my Mom asked. "You're awfully quiet."

"Yeah," I said, quickly. "Just tired. Would rather be sleeping in my own bed, you know. I'm almost back to the parking lot, so I'd better let you go. Think I'll be home in just another day or so."

"Can't wait to see you!" she said, and I could feel her smile radiating off the cell towers.

"Can't wait to see *you!*" I replied, and meant it from my heart.

~ * ~

It was late in the afternoon after what seemed a very long day when I at last pulled into the Taus' circular drive. Logan's BMW was parked in the usual spot, behind Sierra's Benz, not that he couldn't have pulled out around her and then come back after almost running me down outside of Suga's. The hood was warm to touch, but as the Texas sun was beating down, I couldn't prove the car hadn't been sitting in the same spot all day.

If I'd only been quick enough in trying to read the plates, I thought, but I hadn't.

Det. Hawk wanted me "off the case" and asked, if not ordered, me not to talk with anyone else about Stacy's death, and so in the spirit of compliance, and because I wasn't feeling particularly social anyway, I decided to avoid my hosts and hostess and sit out at the patio table that was rapidly becoming my favorite haunt. The weather was hot, of course, but there was shade, and an unseasonably cool breeze, the usual southern wind, but with just a hint of the east, making the idea of sitting outside appealing. All I needed was a short bio break, a quick freshening up, and something to drink, no wine this time.

My stealth paid off, as I made it through the front entry, up the stairs to Stacy's room, back down to the kitchen, raided the 'fridge, and was just about to sneak out the door without having had any human contact whatsoever, when I found to my dismay that my re-served table was already occupied by none other than the heir-apparent and possible vehicularly homicidal Logan Tau.

A heated debate among my better angels followed: *You promised Det. Hawk... but I won't talk about Stacy or the murders... how can you not... I'll just ask what he's been up to, find out if he went downtown today... ran over any pedestrians...*

Either my least best angel was most compelling, or I grew tired of their collective indecisiveness. Turning the doorknob with one hand and pushing with my shoul-der, I exited the kitchen with my Coke and a plate of cheese and crackers, and made my way across the porch and down the steps to the patio.

Logan heard me coming, but didn't turn his head. He didn't so much drop the joint he was holding as let it fall from between his fingers, and then ground it into the pavers beneath his heel. It mattered little. The entire area reeked of the distinctive smell of cannabis.

"Mind if I sit?" I asked, stifling a cough.

On considering the direction of the wind, I chose a seat to his left and hoped the air would clear before the minute particles of ash could attach themselves to my hair and force me to shower again before I went to bed.

"Of course not," he said, though he was slow to re-spond and I was already seated. Logan spread his arms expansively, smiling broadly. His speech was slightly slurred and I wondered if he'd been drinking as well. His black eyes looked glassy and doll-like, and he squinted, blinked, and then opened them again.

"What's up, Wim?" he said, grabbing my shoulder and shaking it. "Tell me, wha's up?"

This is probably not going to go well, I thought uncomfortably, and wished my better better angel had made a more convincing argument before letting me trot out the door.

"Gonna have a snack," I answered, non-threateningly. "I've been running around all day, and finally have a chance to relax. Want some?" I offered the plate.

He looked puzzled for just a moment as he was apparently having difficulty processing: *cheese? crackers?*, but then looked up at me and smiled again.

"Thank you!" he exclaimed loudly, eyes growing wide. "I'm starving!" And grabbing the plate, he set it on the table in front of him, and began to scarf down cheese and crackers so rapidly and ravenously that I didn't risk putting my hand in for fear of losing a finger. I wasn't really hungry anyway, having eaten more in that one day than I'd eaten in all the others days combined since Stacy's death.

"So what have you been doing today?" I asked casually. "Been out and about?"

The question apparently caused him some confusion, as he stopped chewing and gazed toward the greenhouse. He frowned.

"Out?" he repeated, as if the word was new to his vocabulary. He ran a hand through his thick, black hair.

"No..." he answered, slowly, "I've not been out... or about."

On adding the "or about" he laughed smartly, like a clever child.

"Wim!" he exclaimed, eyes wide again as he grasped my hand with his, still sticky with cheese. Wim! Have you been about?"

Groaning inward, I realized Logan was too far gone for any sensible conversation. In all likelihood, he'd no idea, no memory of what he'd been doing earlier, and would not likely remember later what he was doing now.

"No, Logan," I answered as patiently as I could. "I've not been about, only out."

I gave him a gentle laugh and sad smile, hating to see him like that, so wasted, so lost. Somehow, my sadness seemed to touch him, broke through the clouds of inebriation in his mind, for he suddenly let go of my hand and leaning forward said clearly, "I didn't want any of this to happen. You know that, right?"

I nodded.

"I'd never intentionally hurt Stacy, or anyone else," he said insistently. "You know that!"

Logan banged the table with his open hand, reminding me of his father, in his office talking about his wife.

"Yes, I know." I agreed.

"But..." He stared down at the tabletop, but I didn't think he was seeing it. "But things happen..."

His jaw went slack and his mouth hung open, and the clouds, from drugs, alcohol, either or both, returned as quickly as they had cleared.

"I don't *understand!*" he cried. "I... I... don't understand..."

He gazed again at the greenhouse, and then at the carriage house.

"Wim, I just don't understand..."

And without another word, he rose unsteadily and stumbled away.

~ * ~

Though off-balance, Logan didn't appear at risk for a fall. I couldn't bring myself to watch him go, staggering as he was toward the porch, and so I sipped my Coke and contemplated the flowers surrounding me, and the insects swarming them. Several of the red wasps appeared particularly hungry, or at least interested in the almost empty plate on the table, and so I threw them the last crumbs, wondering if wasps were in any way fond of cheese. The wasps hovered suspiciously for a moment, and then slowly and cautiously flew away leaving the crumbs to the tiny black ants that seemed to appear from spontaneous generation at my feet.

When I heard the door pulled shut behind me, I pushed my chair back from the table and propped my feet up on the top, stretching out and pulling my most recent selection from Stacy's chapeau collection forward to shade my face. It was warmer than anticipated, the promise of the breeze unfulfilled, and sweat gathered in the hair at the nape of my neck. Still I stayed, delaying re-entry into the house until the last possible moment, until my presence at dinner was required.

I must have dozed off, as I didn't hear a thing, until I felt warm breath on my neck and woke to a whisper in my ear...

Chapter 23

"Sleeping?"

I jumped four feet straight up and two feet sideways, slamming my knee into the wrought-iron table, grabbing my hat with one hand while somehow managing to catch my chair with the other to keep it from tipping, and turned, red-faced to meet... Mr. Anderson?

There was certainly *some* resemblance to Chess in the man standing before me: stocky, with the same cleft chin, but with a massive belly, wisps for hair, and skin so pale and thin that contorted blue veins luminesced around his cadaverous temples.

"What the...?" My heart, throbbing in my throat temporarily blocked coherent speech, as the old man cackled with laughter.

He rubbed knobby hands together and moved forward. Letting go of the chair, I backed up.

He stopped, and his expression went from one of glee to one of confusion, and then disappointment and indignation.

"You're not *her*!" he said, accusingly. "*Who* are *you*?"

"Who are you?" I replied, with some irritation, more with myself than with him, thinking about what Hawk would say if he knew I'd let someone, even this old guy, sneak up on me after he'd warned me to be careful.

"I am Mr. Chet," he replied, importantly, "and sometimes I am Dr. Chet and Captain Chet. This is my garden. Who are you and what are you doing here?"

He moved his head back and forth as he spoke, undulating like a snake, as if he could not see what was directly in front of him, but was looking at me from the sides of his eyes.

Mr. Chet? I thought, and wondered. *Peripheral vision? Macular degeneration?* His pupils seemed unnaturally dilated in the bright afternoon light.

"I'm Wim," I said, "Stacy's friend, Wim."

"Wim?" he laughed. "Oh, Wim! Yes, I remember Wim, but that was a long time ago... in the long ago... there was a Wim... I had a whim..." He laughed again, but then frowned, looking down at the ground.

"Stacy is dead," he mused quietly, under his breath as he stroked his chin, "so why would her friend be in my garden?"

His eyes narrowed. "Is she a ghost, too?" He moved toward me. I stood my ground. He reached out and pinched my arm hard.

"Ow!" I exclaimed, and slapped his hand away.

He giggled.

"You are still alive," he pronounced with a bow, as if it was an official proclamation, "and that is good. There are too many bodies and ghosts in my garden already. It cannot accommodate many more. Overcrowding you know... can't stack the corpses on top of one another... the neighbors will complain."

He's cracked, I thought, and sighed, but then Mr. Chet looked up and in that moment I could have sworn I saw something very canny in his eyes, but almost instantly the shrewd look vanished, replaced by vacancy signs.

"No one else knows, but I do," he whispered, reaching to take my arm, and leaning in a bit closer than I liked. "I've seen them, at night, when everyone else is asleep. I've seen where they go and what they do."

"Who have you seen?" I asked, fighting my desire to pull away while vaguely wondering who might haunt a man of his age with such a colorful, possibly criminal past. Some of the investors he defrauded?

"Girls, them young girls." His fingernails dug into my skin.

I wasn't sure what he meant, but the recent murders

were foremost in my mind.

"You saw Stacy and Luciana, together?" I asked, in disbelief. "Before they were killed?"

"Oh, no!" He seemed surprised by my misinterpretation, and momentarily loosened his grip, but then leered at me and added, "but I would have liked to have seen them together, yes, I would have liked that *very much!*"

"Then what *did* you see?" I asked shortly, disgusted by the leering and suggestiveness behind his remark, but determined to find out if he knew anything at all that might actually be helpful.

"All the pretty little girls!" He let go of my arm and began rubbing his hands together again. "They come in, they never go out again, or sometimes they go out, but they cry... sometimes they stay in the garden..."

"What are you talking about? What girls? Coming in where?" I asked, feeling instinctively repulsed by his words, but genuinely puzzled.

"Pop!"

Chess Anderson closed the space across the lawn with surprising speed, though he never broke stride from a brisk walk.

"We've been looking everywhere for you."

Chet Anderson appeared to shrink at first sight of his son, but then stood taller. His face took on a fierce look.

"Chester!" he snarled, "Chester, the molester!"

What are *you* doing here?" he shouted, belligerently, springing forward. "*You* have chores! *You* have homework! *You* should be home, not out here playing in the garden!"

"And that girl, that harlot, that whore," he continued, his voice rising to an even louder pitch. "Where is she? You think I don't know, but I know... what you do, late at night, when you think I'm sleeping, locked in my room. I hear every grunt, every moan! You're pigs! You swine!"

As they rushed together, the older man aimed a clenched fist at his son's chin, but Chess, adroitly grasping his father's wrist before the blow could land, and pivoted him so that the confrontation ended quickly with Mr. Chet's arm pinioned behind his own back. He struggled for a moment, spewing curses, but then relaxed and glared angrily at the ground.

"Ready to go home now?" Chess asked, quietly, when the older man was still.

Wordlessly, Chet nodded, kicking the ground with his toe.

"Sorry, Wim," Chess said, not meeting my eyes. "I'm really sorry about this."

"Sorry, Wim," his father parroted him in a nasty, mocking tone. "I'm *really sorry.*"

The son's cheeks were flaming as he hurriedly led his father away. I watched them cross the lawn until they passed behind the greenhouse and were lost from sight.

~ * ~

"I rang the doorbell, but the housekeeper said you were out here."

Jordy's voice surprised me, though this time I'd heard the footsteps on the pavers. I was sitting back at the table, but with no inclination to nap. Instead, I was considering whether my nerves might not benefit from a shot of whatever Dr. Tau had given his daughter and Margaret Sheffield on the day Luciana's body was found.

Jordy smiled, pulled up a chair, and sat uninvited. "Nice hat."

Stacy's dark tan Stetson, classic, maybe 1940s though I'm obviously no expert, chosen to match the boots.

"Thanks." I tried to smile back, but only managed a rather rueful look. All in all, it had been one heck of a day.

Jordy seemed relaxed, stretched his long legs out and rested his Converse high tops on the empty chair beside me. I guessed he and Rachel must have sorted things out.

"Can I ask you something?" I blurted, on impulse.

"Sure, anything, always." His crooked grin widened, and he bumped my knee with his toe. "Go."

I hesitated, not sure what to say, and then held my breath and took the plunge.

"What happened around Valentine's Day? That's when Rachel said you and she got together." I asked, then added, "not that I'm being nosy..." *But I was...*

My smile wasn't quite as heart-felt as his, but I thought I carried it off. *Casual question from an interested friend...*

Jordy frowned slightly, and considered.

"Wow... I'm not sure how to answer that..."

He reached across the table for my Coke and took a sip, grimaced because by then it was both warm and flat.

"I guess I finally faced facts. I realized that you and I could only be friends, and that I should move on and give Rachel a chance. She'd let me know she was interested, you know, in, well, a relationship, a long time ago."

I stared at him, hard.

"What?"

Obviously not the response he expected. Something that was apparently very clear to him was totally obscure to me.

"Wim, you didn't respond, you didn't even call." He looked troubled, as if he was remembering something painful, but at a distance. "But in the end I understood, you know, because you do love me, just not that way, and you just couldn't bring yourself to hurt me, or maybe couldn't stand to see me hurt, so you answered me... with silence."

Now gaping, I shook my head slowly.

"Didn't respond to *what*?" I asked, with a rising sense of alarm.

"The flowers, Wim, the roses and the card I sent you on Valentine's Day." His smile was returning. "I was pretty sure you weren't feeling it for me, but thought you'd at least say something. Don't tell me you didn't get it, what I meant. I thought I made everything pretty clear."

I was thinking fast, trying to separate and recall one day out of the month of February when all days and months had been running together since I returned to med school right after Christmas break. I was fairly certain I had not received flowers on Valentine's Day. I would have remembered that... but my suitemate, Remy, "Everybody Wants You" Remy, had received flowers, dozens of flowers, some were roses... Not that she would have taken them deliberately from me, but the card must somehow have been misplaced... unlabeled flowers, she would have assumed were for her...

"It's not that I didn't "get it" get it. I didn't receive a card, or any roses!" I answered, dismayed. "If they were delivered my suitemate must have thought they were for her!"

Now it was his turn to stare, and then his eyes lit up and relief spread over his handsome face and he reached across the table to take my hand.

"That's so great! I wondered why you never said anything!" he exclaimed. "I tried to make it all make sense in my own mind, but I couldn't understand how you could say nothing!" He was excited, half-rising from the table, so I brought him back.

"What did the card say, Jordy? What did you send me?" I asked earnestly, squeezing his fingers to draw his attention. He sat down slowly.

His face changed, from wonderment to confusion, and then concern. He looked down at the table top, then back up at me.

"Wim, I wrote in the card that I had a ticket to fly to Boston, that I had something to ask you about, but before I got on the plane I needed to know if you wanted to be asked or not. I was afraid you see, that I'd spoil everything... It's kind of, you know, awkward to talk about now..."

He chewed his lip. I waited, and then the words came in a rush.

"Wim, I said I loved you, that I, you know, was in love with you, wanted to be with you. I've been in love with you since we were sixteen, but I always knew you didn't really feel that way about me. I hoped maybe you'd change you know, that when we got older you'd change. And then you went away to Boston, and I missed you so much. I couldn't wait anymore. I had to know if I had any chance at all."

"Jordy, I..."

"But you didn't get the card... It's okay," he assured me, entwining his fingers in mine, "really. You love me as a friend, and that's great. I'm glad to know though that you didn't just ignore me, cause that kind of hurt, when I thought you did..."

My mind should have been used to spinning by then, after all I'd been through, but I still felt the vertigo, and the nausea.

Jordy's engaged to Rachel! I thought, *It's June now, but he was coming to Boston in February to tell me he loved me!*

What could I say? Obviously not what I wanted to say. *Jordy, I love you. Please don't marry Rachel...*

"Jordy, I'm so sorry." And I was, but not for the reason he thought. "I honestly never knew you felt that way about me. All this time, I thought you were the one that only wanted to be friends."

He laughed and shook his head.

"How can you say that? I've always been crazy about you." He grinned at me shyly. "Do you remember our first kiss, or should I say kisses?"

Well yeah. I nodded, as my face flushed red.

"We were playing spin the bottle at Danny Dessler's house. You were sitting across from me, next to Chris

D. I paid Chris five for every time he put out his toe to stop the bottle on you, every time. I kissed you six times that night... cost me a week's allowance. Did you really think that was chance?"

I was blushing like I was still sixteen. At the time I'd been totally naïve, only thinking how very lucky I was, to be able to kiss Jordy...

"You were my first kiss," Jordy said, his black eyes went deep and his voice soft, "and I... I hoped would be my last, but things changed..."

He sighed, his embarrassment gone, all his cards on the table. Mine were still close to the chest and I'd every intention of keeping them there.

The faraway look faded, as he squeezed my hand one last time and then let go.

"I'm glad we had a chance to talk," he said. "I'm glad I know now that you never even read the card and, well, that we're good."

"We're good." I repeated, stunned, but it felt more like a question than a fact to me.

"Guess I'd better get back to Rachel," he said as he stood to go. "We're going out to eat. I'd invite you but, not to hurt your feelings, you look beat. You should get some rest."

I nodded, wanting to stop him, to make him stay.

He put his hand up in farewell, turned, took two steps, and then turned back.

"But Rache and I are not going home until you do... not until you're done here. Got it?" He gave me his stern look.

My heart melted and sank. I felt defeated on so many levels, could think of nothing to say except, "Okay, Jordy."

As he walked away, I buried my face in my hands, and cried.

Chapter 24

There were unexpected guests at dinner that night, at least unexpected by me, which in a way made up for Logan's conspicuous absence.

Page sat in Eleanor Tau's empty seat at the foot of the table, while Chess occupied what must have been Stacy's former place to Dr. Tau's left and across from Sierra. I was opposite Logan's empty chair and so between Chess and Page.

Sierra gave me one icy glance on entering the room, and then directed all her attention to the rest of the group, appearing especially gregarious and gracious; the perfect hostess at her father's table. I wondered that she had not claimed her mother's chair at the end during our earlier meals together, but as her father's dinner etiquette seemed one of his few enforceable laws I suspected any encroachments Sierra might have attempted to usurp her mother's previous position would have been firmly and not too politely rebuffed.

The infusion of new blood brought actual conversation to accompany the fine food and drink. I was only able to ask Page briefly how her mother was doing, to which she responded, "As well as can be expected," before Dr Tau set his reading materials aside and engaged in a lively discussion with Chess, primarily on business matters, while Page, looking elegant and serene in the dancing light from the candles, added a word here and there, generally supporting her husband and showing that she had more than a passing interest and understanding of the finer points of his chosen profession.

Sierra was essentially put on mute; she had nothing

to contribute and the few comments she made only served to illustrate her ignorance of any medical practice-related concerns as all would stop talking and look at her curiously for a moment without response before continuing on. She made a weak attempt to gain Page's attention with references to her absent children, but the physical distance between them, due to seating, and Page's distinct lack of interest or sympathy put an early end to any exchange on that point.

I was accustomed to being the odd-man-out at the Taus' table, and being a doctor-in-training was interested to learn as much as possible about the challenges of navigating the choppy and often murky waters of the U.S. health care system, so was not self-conscious about sitting quietly while the others talked. It was good to see Dr. Tau appear more his cheerful, boisterous self, and I began to hope that Mrs. Sheffield was mistaken in her assessment of his allegedly dire state of health.

By the time dessert came around, a ridiculously rich and decadently creamy dark chocolate mousse, Dr. Tau was beaming, Chess was laughing, and Page was glowing with satisfaction. Seeing the others so relaxed and happy in spite of the challenges I knew must be present in their own individual lives, I found I could smile with them, and only Sierra's tightly pinched face showed any signs that the evening meal had not been a complete success. Chess and Dr. Tau took their dessert plates and drinks and removed to Dr. Tau's office for further discussion as they determined the need for a review of certain spreadsheets. It was only then that the party took a sideways turn.

Chess walked past me to kiss his wife prior to leaving the room and to indicate that he would meet her at home. I touched his sleeve quickly as he went by to ask if I could speak with him later, temporarily and conveniently forgetting my promise to Hawk not to discuss Stacy's murder with anyone else. Chess seemed surprised at my request, but then agreed to text me regarding scheduling, and carefully entered my phone number into his contacts list. He and Dr. Tau exited through the door, and the entire room fell silent.

Sierra and Page looked across the table at each other, and some unspoken communication occurred, though I was not sure exactly what was "said". Sierra looked angry; Page just a bit triumphant, and then Page placed her hands upon the table and rose.

"I'll be going," she announced deliberately, in her low, carefully modulated voice, "Wim, it was really good to see you."

"You, too," I responded, automatically.

"So that's the way it's going to be then?" Sierra rose, too, violet eyes flashing, and placed her hands on her hips: Scarlett O'Hara on the verge of civil war.

"I'm sure I don't know what you mean," Page replied coolly, "but there is no real need to explain yourself," she added. "I've absolutely no interest in anything you have to say."

Page was walking as she talked and so gained the head of the table by the time she made her last comment. Sierra lunged forward and grabbed her by the forearm. I had been in no hurry to get up, but stood quickly and moved to Page's aid. As it turned out, Page didn't need any help from me.

"So you and Chess think you can just waltz in here and take my place and my Momma's place, and expect my Daddy just to forget about me and ignore me because you and Chess are oh so smart, and oh so helpful, and oh so reliable."

She yanked Page's arm, pulling her against the table, but Page kept her balance and slipped adroitly around Dr. Tau's chair. Then she was facing her cousin, and her dark eyes glowed as her cheeks flushed red.

With a quick move that spoke of many hours of self-defense training, Page twisted her arm from Sierra's grip, and using both hands shoved her cousin roughly

back against the wall with such force that the chandelier shimmered from the intensity of the impact that
radiated up and across the ceiling of the room. I was
shocked by the violence, both in the reaction itself and
in the sudden change in Page's beautiful face as anger
narrowed her dark eyes to slits and strung tight the
cords of her neck. Sierra lost her footing and slid to the
floor.

"We aren't waltzing, Sierra," Page said coldly, her
voice no longer mellow, but hard and brittle. "We've
never been waltzing, but we are done with tiptoeing,
around you or anyone else. You can no longer "keep us
in our place". You have no power over us. Your father
will do as he pleases. *You...* are irrelevant."

For a moment, stunned, Sierra's pale eyes glazed
with real fear, but then scrambling to her feet she posi-
tioned herself behind her former seat and gripped the
laddered back of the chair either for support, as a defensive barrier, or possibly as a potential weapon.

"You're wrong!" the Taus' eldest daughter roared,
red-faced, while stamping a foot, but she couldn't help
ducking her head just slightly as she spoke, as if expecting further assault. "I'm not done yet! I've not even
started!"

"No," Page answered, quietly, arms crossed loosely
over her chest and feet slightly apart, her face serene
once more. "You are wrong, and you are done. Your
mother's not here to take your side. Once the Will is
settled, everything else will be up to your Dad."

"Ah, but... You just wait..." Sierra was fuming and
blustering, knuckles starkly white against carved mahogany, but she seemed to be all bark with no teeth for
once and I was at sea about the entire conversation.
Page turned to go.

"Good night, Sierra." she said, without a backward
glance, apparently unconcerned that her cousin might
be preparing to smash her over the head with an antique dining room chair.

"Walk with me?" she asked, an invitation, for me. I was feeling a bit afraid of her at that moment, but on consideration of Sierra's face I decided Page was my safer bet and so I nodded and followed her out.

~ * ~

"I'm sorry you had to see that," Page said solemnly, as we exited to the rear porch, "but as you did, I feel an explanation is required."

"Oh, no. You don't owe me any..." I began, but Page interrupted.

"I do. I very seldom lose my temper, even in the face of extreme provocation, and believe me I have had my share of extreme provocation," she laughed lightly, "but Sierra... well, we grew up together. She's known me long enough to know just the right, or perhaps wrong, buttons to push."

I nodded, mutely. *No argument there...*

"In any case, we all know that Stacy left you a great deal of money in her Will, most of the Tau fortune as a matter for fact, whether intentionally or not. We also know that you intend to decline the bequest," she stated simply. "The motivations for and wisdom of your decision are obviously not for me to judge. It is a great deal of money, and I honestly can't say I would do the same were I in your position, but that is neither here nor there..."

She paused, considering, as we wandered slowly across the yard toward the greenhouse. The night was warm, the air thick, oppressively humid. Another storm was brewing.

"Not many weeks prior to aunt Eleanor's stroke, uncle Marshall became determined to, we can call it, reorder his Will. He wanted to keep the provision for Stacy's trust intact of course, but expressed a desire to include at least some individual provisions for my mother and for Chess and for me. I'm not entirely certain of the reasoning behind or impetus for his sudden interest in my family's welfare, but he seemed absolutely sincere and was in the process of working with his attorney and making changes when my aunt fell ill."

"Oh," I said, as Page was quiet, apparently expecting some response. I could think of nothing else to say. Then I recalled her mother's opinion regarding Dr. Tau's health.

"Your mother mentioned Dr. Tau may be ill. Do you know if he is?" I asked, wondering if the old surgeon might share details of his life with Chess as his practice manager that he did not feel comfortable discussing with his own children. "Perhaps that would account for his interest in your family and the changes he was considering for his Will."

"I've no information concerning Uncle Marshall's state of health," Page replied, carefully, "but to tell you the truth I felt there was something..." She hesitated, and then apparently succumbing to my appeal to over-sharers, she sighed.

"To be honest, Wim, I personally felt that something happened, possibly within the Tau family or to one or more of its members, something drastic, maybe shock-ing, that affected the way both my aunt and uncle either viewed themselves, each other, or all of us to-gether. It was not like Uncle Marshall to ever think of us, at least not of his own volition, although he had helped us out financially and quite significantly so once, but that was at Aunt Eleanor's request. This was different. The changing of the Will seemed something he had thought of himself and decided upon on his own, something that he felt compelled to do. Aunt Eleanor was not entirely on board with his decision, and then she had a stroke. I wish I knew more..."

We'd unconsciously slowed our pace and finally came to a halt. We stood quietly for a moment as Page apparently gathered her thoughts, the soles of our shoes sinking into the soft grass, and then Page moved forward and continued.

"After Aunt Eleanor's stroke, all discussion of the

Will and any potential changes was suspended pending her expected, or at least hoped for, recovery, but she didn't recover. It was almost as if she didn't wish to recover, as if she'd given up..." she said, "but that was only my personal impression," she added quickly.

"In any case, Sierra felt threatened when she learned of Uncle Marshall's intention to change his Will in my family's favor, and still feels threatened, though I believe her concerns are more a matter of pride than based upon a true financial need for any of the Tau assets. Her insecurities, and my failure in patience," her tone held a rueful note, "led to our rather heated altercation, which you witnessed, and so now I've provided the explanation."

I nodded. Page had finished in a hurry, and I wondered what she'd decided to leave out while we'd been standing still on the lawn.

"You didn't need to explain to me," I said, "but thank you."

Page had given me a lot more to think about than her explanation of her violent smack down with Sierra. I was trying to process all she'd said about the Taus and Dr. Tau's abrupt change in attitude toward Mrs. Sheffield and the Sheffield-Andersons, and the timing of Mrs. Tau's stroke. It was too much to take in all at once, and so I decided to sort it out later at my leisure when I was alone in Stacy's room for the night.

"I met your father-in-law today," I said, breaking the silence abruptly, changing the subject, interested in how Page felt about being one of the caregivers for her husband's apparently demented and at least occasionally violent parent.

"Chess told me," she answered, shortly. "I'm sorry if he disturbed you."

"I heard his parents were in an automobile accident a while ago, but didn't know his dad was living with you."

I paused. Page made no response, and so I continued.

"Mr. Anderson doesn't seem altogether well, though he was quite spry when motivated." I remembered how agile he had seemed when he sprang at Chess with his fist raised.

Still no comment from my companion.

"He said some odd things though, and also appeared to have at least some visual impairment. I thought the vision problems might be due to his age?" I added, hoping for at least a confirmation of a neutral question of fact.

"Yes," she said, vaguely, "due to his age."

Page wasn't giving me anything to work with, and normally I hated to pry, but feeling there might be something important to learn about Chet or Chess, or even Page herself, I pushed on. My attractiveness as a good listener apparently was not strong enough in this instant to illicit full disclosure.

"Did he have a closed head injury? Is that what made him kind of..." I shrugged, in the dark, trying to think of a politically correct term for "mean", "spiteful", "hateful", "abusive", "violent"...

"Oh, no," Page sighed deeply, as if she'd completed the sentence as I'd intended without my saying the words.

"Well, I mean, yes, he did have a closed head injury which does affect his balance. That plus poor vision due to macular degeneration causes him to fall, frequently, which is the reason he needs our help. That's why we live with him, the fall risk and vision difficulties I mean. Chet can't see to prepare food, and he needs help to shower and dress, but otherwise, his mind, his personality, his behavior... The head injury had no effect on any of that. He's the same..." She took a deep breath, and shook her head sadly. "Chet Anderson is the same man he has always been. He hasn't changed one bit, not one bit..."

Her answer puzzled me exceedingly. *How could Chet*

Anderson possibly be the same? Dr. Tau had described him as mentally incompetent to stand trial. Was he faking it? Could he have faked mental incompetence to avoid prosecution? There had been that shrewd look in his eyes: that glimmer of canny intelligence right before he'd gone back to acting crazed. Acting...?

But there was no time for further probing. We'd reached the fence and gate between the Tau's yard and the walkthrough to the street. Page stopped and turned toward me. The light from the streetlamps reflecting on damp grass provided no illumination, but instead only served to blind me so that I could not see my companion's face.

"It's always good to see you, Wim," Page said, in her carefully modulated tone. "I'm sorry we could not have met again under happier circumstances."

Happier circumstances...? Less tragic circumstances...? Stacy's murder was a "circumstance"? I forgot my promise to Detective Hawk and remembered my questions.

"Page," I said, somewhat cautiously in light of her recent explosive behavior toward Sierra, "do you know who suggested the trip to the firing range after your aunt's funeral?"

If it had been Chess, would she lie?

"I don't," she replied, immediately. "My mother and I were not present when the decision was made."

Moving on then... Page had her hand on the gate.

"And at dinner, that night, before Stacy was shot in the chest and bled out on the floor," I added the harsh words intentionally, hoping to shock her into an impulsive, unedited response, "what was Stacy saying about death and dying?"

In the darkness, I could feel Page shudder. It was if a sudden chill radiated from her body.

"Chess was at dinner," she pronounced, succinctly. "My mother and I declined to attend."

Her voice sounded formal and stiff, almost resentful,

but then she sighed heavily, and I could see the outline of her head shaking in apology.

"Wim, I am aware, I think we are all aware, that you have taken it upon yourself to look into Stacy's murder," she said, softly, "even though the police are conducting an investigation of their own," she reminded me pointedly. "It's because you loved her, like she was your sister, and I can understand and respect that."

"What no one else seems to understand is how hard Aunt Eleanor's death was on my mother," she explained. "Everyone acts as though it should be nothing to her. But she and Aunt Eleanor were so close growing up, though there was a significant difference in their ages. And even after they both married and had families of their own, it didn't matter. My mother loved her younger sister at least as much as you loved Stacy."

"I'm sorry," I said, and I was, "and you're right," I said, and she was, "I was thinking of the Taus' loss and didn't really consider your Mom's."

"It was too much to ask her to sit through one of their dysfunctional family dinner parties right after the funeral, especially after dragging us all out to the firing range. *That* was dreadful! We'd had enough of the bickering and sniping, of Uncle Marshall's blustering, Sierra's backbiting, Daniel's pouting, and Logan's, well, I guess Logan's misery. My mother's nerves were shot. She just wanted to go home, and so I took her home."

We'd had enough... I didn't think Page's Mom was the only one fed up with the Taus' behavior.

Chapter 25

Page and I had separated, she exiting through the gate and heading *presumably* home, and I turning back and aiming myself at the Taus' manse when I received a text message from Chess. He and Dr. Tau were finished with business for the evening and he asked if I still wanted to meet.

After deliberating a moment, I decided a discussion of Stacy's murder inside the Taus' house, with Taus possibly wandering about, would not be entirely appropriate and might even be considered rude by my hosts. I suggested we meet outside on the Taus' patio in 10.

With the lights from the road behind me, I found I could see a bit better in the dark: a good thing as I was feeling just a little, well, more than a little creeped out, walking alone, past the spot where Luciana had died. My mind added the unwanted descriptors: *thin wire* and a*lmost decapitated,* before I could halt the thought.

As I approached the greenhouse, I found myself shivering and goose bumps popped up on my arms, the pilomotor reflex that occurs sometimes in response to fear or stress causing the affected hair follicles to stand the hairs on end perhaps designed to make us appear larger than actual size. The pilomotor reflex can be used to great advantage by some animals, such as cats, and porcupines, but the hair on my arms being rather thin and in no way barbed could not be expected to provide much by way of presenting an intimidating front. I rubbed my arms to chase the sudden chill, and quickened my steps, averting my eyes from the spot where Luciana must have lain.

Once past the greenhouse, the light from the road

behind me was blocked, the night was dark as pitch so that I couldn't see my own hand in front of my face much less the ground at my feet. Something small whizzed past my left ear, *night bird? vampire bat? unknown miniature flying Creature from the Black Lagoon?,* and the urge to run for the illusionary safety of the main house became almost overwhelming. Problem was, I knew once I started running, for one thing, giving in to the urge would only increase my fright, and another, I would not be able to hear anyone *or anything* else approaching in the soft grass over my own footfalls and pounding pulse. I forced myself to keep a steady walking pace, eyes forward, but purposefully listening in 360 degrees.

Up ahead, small lights flickered from windows of neighboring houses and the occasional passing car, and after what seemed an eternity, but was actually more likely 5 minutes, the outlines of the Taus' mansion and outbuildings appeared as vague but distinct shapes. It was then that I became aware of the presence of someone else walking with me, following closely, matching my steps, but not trying to overtake me. I could not say how long my shadow had been present, and hoping my mind was playing tricks, I stopped short. The person following was not quick enough, and continued one step too many, and I knew: there really was someone, a voiceless, potentially malevolent someone, with me, alone, in the dark... Heart pounding, mouth suddenly dry, I swallowed hard, trying quickly to decide on fight or flight. Unlike Page, I'd never trained in self-defense. My angels were more decisive this time.

This might be the person that shot Stacy and strangled Luciana. Did he or she have a gun, knife, more wire? Don't know? Easy choice. Flight it is, then. Only remaining decision to make: in which direction to run?

In that moment I caught sight of the form of a large man reflected in the porch light against the carriage house wall.

Chess, I thought, and breathing a sigh of relief, I sprinted forward to meet him.

Unfortunately, the man waiting for me wasn't exactly the Chess I remembered from childhood.

~ * ~

"What's the matter? What's the rush?" Chess asked, frowning, striding forward to meet me as I dodged through the raised beds on the edge of the rose garden and catapulted across the pavers.

Glancing quickly over my shoulder for any sign of pursuit, I slipped and lost my footing, the leather soles of Stacy's boots providing little traction on the smooth stones. Chess leapt forward and caught me by both wrists, pulling me up to prevent a face plant in the dirt.

"There was someone..." I panted, holding my side, trying to catch my breath. "There was someone out there." I waved toward the greenhouse, and then straightening, turned to look back.

Darkness. No movement on the lawn, nothing. But it hadn't been my imagination.

"Are you sure?" he quizzed, skeptical, as if he didn't quite believe me. "Are you sure it was *someone*? After all, even though we're technically in the city, there are lots of raccoons that come out into the neighborhood at night. Maybe it was a *something* instead?" he laughed, a short barking sound.

I found this attitude interesting if not alarming. Two women had been murdered, and not by raccoons. My immediate impulse was to shake my head, assure him I'd not been mistaken, but then I realized there was nothing to gain in pressing my point, and so held my tongue. I'd no proof. The *someone*, whoever he or she might have been, had not followed me into the light.

We were standing near the entryway to the carriage house apartment, Stacy's apartment, and motion sensor-activated floodlamps over the garage doors cast eerie, rippling shadows across the white railing and columns of the small porch as they flicked on and off with our movement, or rather with my movement as I was agitated, having been badly frightened, and could not stand still. Chess, in contrast, seemed chiseled from granite, solidly rooted to one spot.

"It's good to see you, Wim," he said, echoing his wife's earlier expressed sentiments. "I just wish you could have come home under better circumstances."

I nodded: *better, yes*, but wondered at his use of the word "home". Of course it had been his home for his entire life and so maybe he considered Beaumont home for everyone who grew up there. He seemed very different from the Chess I remembered though, detached, his voice without inflection, not like the often sensitive, always emotionally available Chess I had known.

Anti-depressants? I wondered, *or illegal drugs like Logan?*

"Chess, are you okay?"

The question came out before I could stop myself.

This honest expression of concern apparently startled him. His jaw twitched, as his fair, almost invisible eyebrows rose and he frowned again.

"Yes. Of course, yes," he answered, in rapid succession, but his speech came in staccato bursts. "Of course, I'm okay, well, not really *okay*, none of us are *really okay*, how could we ever be, okay again, I mean, after what happened, after all that's happened...? But I'm as well as can be expected... under the circumstances. Why would you ask that? What makes you ask? Are you... okay?"

"No, not really," I replied, shaking my head sadly, "kind of like you: just as well as can be expected." I sighed, and placed my hand lightly on his jacket sleeve.

The physical contact seemed to both calm him, and provide a sudden focus. He stared at my hand, and then at me. His eyes grew wide, and then the big man glanced around, furtively.

"Wim," he whispered, leaning toward me as if he were afraid someone might overhear, "Wim, I think I know who shot Stacy, and why. I think I'm the only one who does know, well, except the killer."

~ * ~

Chess paused ominously, and I held my breath, as winged insects spun crazily in the fluorescent light. Chess moved closer, draped one great arm around my shoulder and pulled me in: co-conspirators, our shadows one on the carriage house wall.

"Do you remember when Stacy almost drown?" he continued in his deep, Southern voice. As close as his face was to mine, I still had to strain to hear.

I shook my head, and whispered, "No."

Margaret Sheffield had mentioned a near drowning but I'd no memory of it at all.

"It was a few days after Marty died, after the funeral, at the wake. Everyone was outside, in the backyard at the Taus': a Celebration of the Life of Marty Tau, just like the family had for Stacy, only somehow Stacy ended up almost drowning in the pool. She was dragged out... by Page's Dad... Rescued, but almost too late..."

I concentrated, trying to recall: Marty, a funeral, an event, but I'd only been 5 years old when Marty died. I finally managed to conjure a vague image of people, upset, shouting, and crowding around a small, pale, wet figure lying on the pavers near the Taus' pool, being pushed back and out of the way, busied activity on the ground, peering around adult bodies to see what in hindsight may have been someone performing CPR, but I wasn't convinced I'd actually seen any of those things. The recollection, if that's what it was, was all too hazy. Maybe I was just imagining scenes from a story I'd heard as a child, or the whole thing could have been something I'd watched on TV. I shook my head.

"We were all just kids," I explained, apologetically. "I can't really say I remember anything with certainty from that time."

"That's okay," Chess nodded reassuringly, squeezing my shoulder, reminding me momentarily of the old

Chess. "I guess I remember because I was older. Plus what happened was partly my fault..."

"Your fault? How could any of that have been your fault?" I interrupted, surprised, before he could finish. "Did you push Stacy in?"

"Oh, no!" he answered, shocked, stepping back from me and no longer whispering. "Of course not! I would never..."

Now it was his turn to pace, as he wrung his hands, muscular arms bulging the sleeves of his expensive, tailored suit coat.

"I would never intentionally have hurt Stacy! Not ever, not for anything in this world, or the next!" He shouted and his voice trembled with anguish. He didn't appear to be shouting at me though, but looked up as if speaking to the night sky, or perhaps to God in the Heavens. "Not for anything... No... not Stacy..." he was beginning to sob.

"Chess," I called, as he stalked back and forth, the floodlight continuously activated as the motion sensor clicked on each pass, "Chess, I know. Chess..."

He stopped, turned, and looked at me, face white, and lined with pain. I held his gaze and believed him.

"Chess, I *know* you would never hurt Stacy," I assured him, "not for *anything...*"

He came back to me, shaking his head, and took my hand.

"It's just been so hard," he said, softly again, sounding and looking more and more like the Chess from childhood, my friend, Chess, Stacy's loyal defender. "I can't believe she's gone. I still think I'm going to wake up and everything will be fine and Stacy will be here, home where she belongs."

Home, again.

"But Chess, you said you know who killed her. Who did it? Why haven't you told the police?"

"I know," he whispered, "but I can't prove it. I just know."

"Then tell me," I pleaded, urgently. "Tell me, and I'll help you prove it. Whatever it takes..."

~ * ~

"Well," Chess began, as I hoped without hope he would not be as rambling as his mother-in-law. "As I was saying..."

He paused.

"...but I guess I have to back track a little..." Chess sighed softly. I bit my lip and kept my sigh to myself.

"I don't know if you know anything about my Dad... the things he did... what he did to Dr. Tau... and to everyone else he worked with... he stole money you see, embezzled funds..."

I nodded, almost patiently. "Yes, I heard about that."

Chess hung his head. "I didn't understand it all then. My Dad was a hard man, not the best Dad in the world, but I thought he was a good businessman. I'd no idea anything was wrong, at least not at first."

"My Dad had stopped working for Dr. Tau, but our families still socialized so I didn't realize he'd been fired or why he'd been fired, or think that his not working for Dr. Tau was a big deal. Then the Feds came to our house. They talked to my Dad and then my Mom, and then even to me. My Dad was angry. My Mom cried, and I was scared. That was the week before Marty died. The Feds came around on Wednesday and on Saturday Marty was dead."

"You think your father...?" I began, but Chess shook his head.

"Wait," he said, and then continued.

"Everyone was there when Marty died, my Mom and Dad, Page's family, all the Taus, everyone that is except you. Where were you that day? Anyway, I remember my Dad and Dr. Tau arguing loudly outside the barn door before my Dad stalked off, while my Mom tried to put on a brave face, circling around the picnic tables, loading and unloading trays, fussing over the food, staying away from my Dad. We, I mean us, the kids, were all playing, all afternoon, different games, archery, crochet, whiffle ball, and then finally hide-and-seek, but in a distracted way as we could all kind of feel the tension coming from the adults. Page's Mom was having an intense conversation with Mrs. Tau and they'd walked out and were leaning on the paddock fence. I could see them from my hiding place behind the tack room door. I could also see Stacy, in clear view, leaning out the window of the hayloft. I guess she meant to hide up there but then forgot or lost interest in the game. Stacy never was any good at concealment..."

He stopped and looked at me, serious, troubled.

"That's when Marty fell," he said, in a hushed, solemn tone. "He fell, and he died."

Sadness. In that moment I felt an overwhelming sense of sadness, for Marty of course, but also for Mrs. Tau, Dr. Tau, Chess, Stacy, Sierra, Logan, Page, everyone who had been there to witness the tragic death of a very young boy. Chess and I stood together silently, and I suspected his heart was aching as mine was.

Shaking his head slowly, Chess gathered his thoughts and then began again.

"After the funeral, there was a gathering, a wake I guess, at the Taus' house. It was called a celebration of the Life of Marty Tau, kind of like Stacy's, but different. A huge crowd had gathered in the Taus' backyard." His brow furrowed as he fell silent for a moment, considering, and then continued.

"I guess Marty had a lot more friends than Stacy, and well, a lot of people just knew him, because of the riding, and he was in some school clubs, Math, I think and Science. I think he won some sort of award in the Science Fair. Some of his teachers were there. And maybe Dr. and Mrs. Tau had more friends then, when their kids were younger, maybe other parents from school. It seems like there were always people around their house in those days, dropping by, staying for dinner. I know my family was invited over a lot back then, at least before the Feds came. My mom spent hours getting ready to go to the Taus' house. My dad always griped about her primping, as he called it, but he always griped about everything she did..."

Inwardly by then I was groaning with impatience, and it took all my self-control and "good listener" skills to keep my mouth shut. I wanted to grab Chess, shake him and scream, "Who did it? Who did it? Who did it?" but instead I clinched my teeth until I thought the enamel might crack and stood quietly.

"There were lots of adults, but also lots of kids. Of course the kids weren't taking it all very seriously. We didn't really understand death then, and especially the guests, you know, the kids that weren't part of the family..."

He stopped again, and looked at me.

"I don't mean you, Wim. I've always considered you family, just as much a part of the family as everyone else who was, you know, a member of our gang. I still do consider you family, though we've not been in touch, and I guess we don't really know what's going on in each other's lives anymore, but even distant family is family. Don't you agree?"

He needed my reassurance, needed me to confirm a tangible bond, a solid connection, before he could feel comfortable going further with his story.

"We'll always be family, Chess," I replied sincerely, and felt it was true. Chess had been my big brother growing up, in all ways except for blood.

He took a deep breath, seemed to be steeling himself.

"Only Page knows the whole story," he said. "I've never told another living soul..."

His voice dropped, and I leaned in, eager to catch every word.

Then the soft night sounds exploded into chaos: an ominous revving engine, impossibly close by, followed with the immediate and violent screeching of tires, and suddenly we were blinded, deer in the jolting headlights of a motorized vehicle that jumped the curb and headed straight for us. I froze, stunned like the proverbial deer, as the car accelerated and bore down upon me, crashing through manicured shrubs and over the low stone border along the driveway, wheels spinning and sliding across the lawn while dirt and showers of turf filled the air, but Chess, always slow in thought, always quick to act, grabbed me by the shoulders and shoved me hard, sending me flying backward and over the low white railing surrounding Stacy's front porch.

"Chess!" I screamed, as the big man charged after me, but not fast enough.

There was a sickening sound as the car struck him and dragged him several feet before slamming into the wall. The light above the garage was knocked loose, swung crazily from it's wiring, creating a strobe effect. Amid flashes of light I saw Sierra's silver Mercedes, hood crushed into accordion folds against the wall of the garage, front tires half-buried in the soft earth. Scrambling to my feet, I ran to find Chess, but he was buried underneath the car. Throwing myself flat, belly down in the turf and dirt, I could barely make out a human shape but could not see his face.

"Chess? Chess?" I cried, urgently, stretching my arm as far as I could under the car to try to reach him.

He didn't answer, or move at all.

The passenger door of the Benz groaned open, and in the space between the undercarriage of the car and earth, I saw a foot emerge. Rising awkwardly from the ground, I approached, cautiously. Someone was moaning softly. It was Sierra. Her air bag had inflated on impact, and hit her in the face. She was bleeding from her nose and upper lip.

"He didn't mean it," she whimpered, touching her lip tentatively. "He didn't mean to do it."

Looking across her, I saw whom she meant. Logan had not been wearing a seatbelt and his air bag, though deployed, had somehow collapsed. He was crushed between the driver's seat and the steering wheel, bleeding heavily from his face and head.

"You're ok?" I asked Sierra, but knew by looking at her that she was not in immediate crisis. Without waiting for a response, I lifted myself onto what was left of the hood and crawled over to Logan's side, trying not to see the blood on the crumpled fender or on the shattered glass of the windshield.

Logan's pulse was strong and regular, pupils reactive, but he was unconscious, didn't respond to a sternal rub. His skin looked not only pale, but greenish gray under the flashing light. Scalp wounds always bleed like crazy so it was hard to tell how serious his head injuries were, but obviously the unconsciousness was concerning. His breathing seemed shallow, but examination of his chest, abdomen and lower extremities was prevented by the loss of space in the driver's compartment. Pealing off my shirt, I folded it into a rough square and pressed the fabric against the largest head lac, right above Logan's left ear, while operating my iPhone with my other hand.

The first number I called was 9-1-1, the second my favorite detective's personal cell. His promise of fifteen minutes or less was no exaggeration. He was there in eight. Within ten, the place was once again crawling with police, EMTs, even the fire department this time. By then Dr. Tau and Mrs. Nelson had come out into the yard. Mrs. Nelson brought towels and Dr. Tau assisted with Logan's assessment and care, freeing me up to re-dress in my now bloody shirt.

It was a nasty feeling, the cold, crinkly cotton still sticky with blood against my shoulders and back, but I couldn't bring myself to leave the scene even to find a clean shirt, not while Chess was trapped under the car. Getting him out was not going to be an easy task as the Mercedes weighed almost two tons, was half buried in dirt, and had partially punched though a panel of one of the garage doors.

My interaction with Det. Hawk was short and sweet: I assured him that I was entirely ok, that none of the blood on my shirt was actually mine, gave him the story, briefly. He listened with an air of professional detachment, said he'd circle back to me with any further questions, started to walk away, then turned and awkwardly grasped both my hands tightly in his, no words, but his eyes reflected relief. He raised his gaze to the night sky for the briefest of seconds, and then he let go and was moving through the crowd, conducting his investigation. Page arrived and stood with me, though we'd little to say to each other and could only wait anxiously on the sidelines. Her husband had saved my life, possibly at the cost of his own. What was there to say?

In the early hours of morning it began to drizzle rain. Sierra, crying, frantic about Logan, calling for her father, was taken from the scene first as she was easiest to extract, and then Logan was prized free of the driver's seat. Though he wasn't moving, I was relieved to note his face was covered with an oxygen mask and not a sheet. Logan was still alive.

Seconds, minutes ticked by, and it took what seemed an eternity before Chess was finally pulled from underneath the vehicle. There was a great deal of conversation, activity, and noise associated with the big man's excavation, but once he was freed, the night suddenly went silent; the absence of sound jarring in it's abruptness. All voices fell to a whisper, and the crowd of people who had been practically crawling all over themselves and each other in order to unearth Chess rapidly dissipated, leaving only two or three paramedics to quietly load the big man into the bus. From a distance and in the falling rain, we couldn't see clearly, but Chess looked a real mess as the EMTs quickly strapped him to the body board and lifted him to the gurney. Page cried out her husband's name and tried to run to him, but was restrained. The EMTs wouldn't even let her ride with him in the ambulance, and so Page and I shared a ride to the hospital, along with Mrs. Sheffield, who seemed more than a little dazed and disoriented. I didn't really wonder at that, after the day she'd already had, and it turned into an even longer night...

Chapter 26

Chess Anderson clung tenaciously to life through the multiple surgeries required to stabilize internal bleeding and fix his various fixable fractures. In all, roughly a fourth of his 206 bones were broken, cracked or at least chipped. He remained in Recovery for hours, teetering on the brink of death, but seemed to improve with the sunrise and was finally transferred to the hospital intensive care unit around 10 am the following day.

His room in the ICU was directly across from Logan's in the Neuro ICU. Logan also managed to survive the night, after a mere three hours of surgeries during which the Neurosurgeon drilled holes through his skull to relieve pressure from bleeding in his head to prevent his brain from herniating into his spinal column and killing him, and Ortho reduced and stabilized open comminuted fractures of both tibias and crush injuries to his ankles. So Chess and Logan, practically side-by-side in the ICU, were each intubated, on respirators, and in medically induced comas.

Sierra was treated and placed in 23-hour OBS for possible concussion with multiple contusions, but had no injuries thought to be life threatening. I was checked out in the ER and released, pretty sure my backward collision with and summersault over the porch rail would catch up with me eventually, but too wired from adrenaline, and numb with shock to feel any type of physical pain. Emotionally I was a complete wreck.

Logan Tau, sad, drug-addicted, self-destructive Logan Tau, had tried to kill me, to run me down with a car. The kind-hearted, sweet, thoughtful, messed up boy from my childhood had coldly and deliberately tried to end my life in a horribly brutal and painful way, but why? Was it about money, as Detective Hawk had long suspected, or something else? Logan had failed, injuring Chess instead of me, and now he and Chess might both die. There were too many unanswered questions, and I was running out of people to ask.

The night dragged on. Page and Dr. Tau sat together in the waiting room while Logan and Chess were in surgery, and I made frequent coffee runs for both until Dr. Tau was allowed into Logan's room. Steely Margaret Sheffield had finally given in to exhaustion and on urging from her daughter had agreed to let one of the officers take her home. Then it was just Page and me.

"Chess was just about to tell me who he thought killed Stacy," I announced to the room. "Did he think it was Logan?"

In my own mind the attempt on my life was not necessarily directly related to Stacy and Luciana's deaths. My interactions with Logan and his odd and somewhat obsessive behavior toward me led me to consider alternative motives for his attack.

I was absolutely certain if Chess suspected his wife of Stacy's murder, he would never have agreed to meet with me, not even to try to throw me off the scent *if* he thought her guilty. He knew, and I knew, that he was not that good of a liar. Therefore, the person Chess suspected was not Page. The killer could still be Page though, and I wanted to find out what she knew or thought she knew.

"He didn't tell me," she said softly, sitting up in her chair, hugging a sofa pillow to her chest, gazing at me with dark, tragic eyes.

I didn't respond, just waited.

"He was afraid to tell me," she explained, her voice cracking as she succumbed to the pressure of filling the uncomfortable silence. "He thought telling me might put me in danger." She sighed. "And now see what's happened..."

The same thing her Mom had said about Luciana's murder.

"He said you were the only other person who knew,"

"No," she said slowly, shaking her head. "No, you must have misunderstood."

I considered what Chess had told me, the words he used, the topic of our conversation just before the car hit him... before Logan ran him down...

I shook my head, too.

"We were talking about... Wait... Maybe he meant he told you about something else, something about Stacy, something he thought was significant, about how she almost drowned at Marty's wake."

Page looked surprised.

"Why were you talking about that?" she asked, and then nodded. "Oh, you were talking about Stacy's murder, and of course he would think of that, when she almost died, when we were kids. It was really a traumatic experience for Chess. He never got over it."

"Traumatic for Chess?" I was puzzled. "What do you mean? I can see that nearly drowning would have been traumatic for Stacy, but how could that have been traumatic for Chess? Was Chess in love with Stacy, even back then?"

It was a stretch; implying an assumed love connection when I was almost certain there'd been none, especially not at that age.

Page simply shook her head. "No."

She fell silent, and this time I spoke first.

"Detective Hawk, and some other people... *who shall remain nameless, Dr. Tau, your Mom...* think Chess and Stacy were having an affair."

"No." She hugged the pillow closer, and squeezed her eyes shut. A single tear crept slowly down her cheek.

I wanted to apply pressure, make her answer, make her talk, but instead I broke.

"I would never believe you killed Stacy," I assured her, impulsively, but found I meant it. "Never. Just like

I'd never believe Chess would cheat on you. He just wouldn't do that. He loves you, has always loved you, only you."

A sob burst from her throat, and her beautiful face contorted as the serenely composed Page fell apart. She cried as if she'd never stop. I grabbed one of the handy tissue boxes, fortunately it was a well-stocked ICU waiting room, and handed her a new one as each used one was drenched with tears and discarded.

"I was never jealous of Stacy," Page choked brokenly. "I felt sorry for her. I even liked her in a way. And, Chess was never in love with her. There was never an affair. All that was Sierra, trying to stir up trouble."

She mopped her eyes, crumpled and dropped the spent tissue in the garbage can, accepted another solicitously offered by me.

"The thing at Marty's wake, the pool... He never told anyone but me... he was so ashamed... and he made me promise not to ever tell, but it seems he was going to tell you himself..." She hesitated, torn between her promise to her husband and the urgent need to spill, to find some release for the emotional strain that was threatening to break her heart.

She dabbed at her face, blew her nose, took a deep breath, and made up her mind. Accepting another tissue, she composed herself as she carefully folded the thin sheet in half and then quarters, pressed creases into four corners, and then held the square between her palms, on top of the pillow now in her lap. Her eyes were red-rimmed, bloodshot, but dry, as she kept her gaze fixed on the linoleum squares of the floor at her feet.

"Chess felt responsible for Stacy, for the way she was, because he was there when she almost drown in the pool, at the wake, right after Marty died. She was under water a long time, may have been oxygen deprived. He didn't try to save her, you see."

But I didn't. Page explained.

"It was summer, the weather was nice, and so the wake was held outside. There were people everywhere, wandering around the grounds. Caterers were bringing food, in and out. For us, the kids, it was almost like a garden party. We weren't really thinking about Marty, or at least not considering that Marty was dead. We had all been playing at Tag."

"Chess had run around some of the pool chairs, trying to dodge whoever was "it", when something, some pink "thing" caught his eye in the dappled water of the pool. As he moved to the edge of the water, he saw what he initially thought was a scarf, submerged and swirling near the grate, the shape distorted further by the shadow of the diving board and sunlight filtered through the leaves of the trees. It took him a good minute or two to realize the "scarf" was actually not a something, but was instead a someone. It was Stacy, floating a few inches above the bottom."

Page took a slow breath, laid the tissue on the pillow, unfolded it and smooth out the creases, and then tucked an unruly strand of dark hair behind her left ear. She licked her dry lips.

"Chess was a child. We were all children. He didn't understand what he was seeing. He thought Stacy was swimming, like a turtle. She wasn't struggling, didn't appear to be distressed, and so he didn't realize she was in any trouble or danger, that she was drowning, or that by then she was almost drowned. He just stood there, watching her floating quietly at the bottom of the pool, that is, until Aunt Eleanor came up beside him, I suppose to see what had engrossed him so. "

"When Aunt Eleanor saw Stacy, she, of course, immediately screamed, sending everyone into a panic. My dad jumped in, pulled Stacy out, and performed CPR, and Stacy was alright, I guess, or everyone seemed to think she was... alright. But soon afterward, she developed... well, problems. Chess felt horrible, blaming himself; he always thought Stacy's Asperger's was his fault because he didn't recognize that she was drowning. He didn't see that she was in trouble. She stayed under water too long because he didn't save her."

I nodded with new understanding.

"And, that's why he kept trying to save her, for the rest of her life," I said, thoughtfully. I hesitated, and then asked my question, "But when her Mom died, and Stacy's Dad wished her dead in front of the entire family, when she was alone and had no one to take care of her, would Chess have killed Stacy to keep her safe? Did Chess think Stacy would be better off dead?"

Page looked at me then, surprised.

"Of course not," Page replied firmly. "That's the most ridiculous thing I've ever heard. Chess isn't crazy and only a crazy person would think killing someone was a kindness."

At last, someone who didn't think Stacy murderer was a humanitarian. Which had been my conviction all along.

~ * ~

Patients in the ICU are allowed only one visitor at a time and only during specified visiting hours. The rooms are usually small; people in critical condition aren't generally up for company and all the equipment necessary to keep someone alive on life support takes up most of the space. Page was kind enough to allow me to see Chess for a few moments on his arrival to the floor. She was going to stay, with him when allowed and in the waiting room when not, but knew I needed to assure myself that he was all right, or at least not dead yet on my account.

The big man looked very small under the stiff white sheets and blanket of the ICU bed, and his face was almost unrecognizable, swollen, discolored, and pumpkin-shaped. I felt a twinge of guilt for having critical thoughts about the shape of his face.

"Chess?" I called his name softly as I took his hand and squeezed it. There was no response.

The respirator made a constant low humming sound, with clicks and shudders as oxygen hissed in and out through blue plastic tubing. His chest rose and fell in rhythm with the machine. Tears came to my eyes.

"Chess, I'm so sorry," I said, crying softly. "It should have been me. If not for you, it would have been me."

His fingers felt cold and so I carefully folded his hands on his chest and tucked the sheet around his arms and shoulders. Then I straightened the blanket, pulling it up toward his chin.

"Page is waiting." I forced a semblance of cheerfulness into my voice. "I'd better go. Feel better soon." No response. I turned and walked away.

Chapter 27

I'd just left Chess and Page when Jordy and Rachel showed up. At first I thought I was seeing things, but there they both were. How they learned about the attempt on my life, and the form it had taken, and the consequences for Chess, I didn't know, but thought perhaps Det. Hawk had told them I was at the hospital and they had somehow tracked me to the ICU.

Each of them hugged me and told me they were glad I was okay. Jordy kept his hand on my arm, and I found myself leaning against him in spite of myself. I felt numb, chilled to the bone.

"You're white as a sheet," Rachel said, as she rubbed my shoulder and the back of my neck. "You need some coffee." She offered a steaming cup from Starbucks. "Something to brace you."

The smell of coffee took me back to the night of Stacy's death, sitting on the Taus' porch, and my stomach turned over, twice. Clasping my hands together to keep them from shaking, I shook my head.

"Maybe just some water," I stammered, "or some tea... maybe hot tea..."

Something warm... but something not coffee...

Rachel nodded. "Be right back." She headed off to locate the nearest vending machine.

"Are you sure you're alright?" Jordy asked, putting his hands on my shoulders, looking into my eyes. His were dark, deep with concerned.

He suddenly seemed very tall, or I was feeling very small. Confused, I looked away, stepped back.

"Wim?" he said, moving with me. "Wim, I know you're scared. I want to help you. I want to make this better, but I don't know how. Tell me! What can I do? I don't know what to do."

Silently, I shook my head.

Nothing, I thought. *You can do nothing.*

He stood there, looking at me, as if trying to read my thoughts, and then he pulled me in to a hug. I stood stiffly for a moment, and then surrendered, folding myself into his arms. He held me tighter, and after a moment began to sway a little, back and forth, like he was rocking me. Pressing my ear against his chest, I listened to the sound of his heart beating, and hugged him tighter still. He buried his face in my hair, his lips brushing my forehead.

I forgot about my BFF Rachel. All I could think of was Jordy's warmth, his heart beating under my ear. I raised my head and looked into his eyes, and everything I had ever felt for him, everything there was, was right there in front of him, and he kissed me, softly, then not so softly, lifting me off the ground, and all my fear, all the horror faded and was forgotten until...

"What are you *doing*?" Rachel's voice was shocked, raw, as the water bottle and her Starbucks cup both hit the floor.

"What are you *doing*?"

We looked at her, her eyes huge, filling with tears. Jordy let go of me so fast I almost fell to the floor.

"Rachel," he began, but she was already going.

"Rachel wait!"

Then Rachel was running, and Jordy was running after her, and I, well, I just stood there watching the best friends I'd ever had disappearing down the wide white corridor of the hospital.

"Looks like we have our man." Det. Hawk appeared, seemingly from out of nowhere, startling me.

"Guess you won't be needing that emergency number any longer," he said, curtly.

His voice sounded angry, or hurt. I didn't know him well enough to tell which. At that point I couldn't really care.

"So you're sure it was Logan?" I asked, distracted, my eyes still following the path of my vanished friends. "Logan murdered Stacy and Luciana?"

In spite of his trying to run me over, I still couldn't accept that Logan shot Stacy, strangled Luciana. Even as I said it, the words just sounded wrong.

Logan?

"Are you absolutely sure?" I asked, again, turning my full attention to him.

"You aren't? He tried to kill you," Hawk shrugged. "Why else would he have done that? Just like I thought, it was all about the money, and in his case drugs. He was carrying, and high, thought if he took you out his problems would be solved."

"That doesn't make sense," I argued, without conviction. After all, he was the detective, and recent events and my own actions would suggest that I was not only grossly lacking in basic skills of observation and extrapolation, but was in fact a complete idiot. "I was going to decline the bequest..."

Hawk looked at me with that same "you're kidding me" look he'd given me when I told him I was attending Harvard.

"You were declining...?" he asked, suddenly concerned. "Seriously? You weren't taking the money? Did anyone know that?"

"I think everyone in the Tau family knew it," I answered, "but I can't be certain. Dr. Tau was having the papers drawn up..."

Hawk was quiet, his face dark. Then he gripped my arm and leaned in.

"Keep my number close, and *be careful*," he whispered, cryptically, urgently. "I've got to get back to it."

Not being sure what "it" might be, I nodded. He left. Feeling confused, conflicted, ashamed, and a bunch of other inadequately defined but definitively negative and self-defeating emotions, I wandered back down the silent corridor to the Neuro ICU, to Logan's room. Dr. Tau was nowhere to be seen. Logan was alone.

Pulling the solitary chrome and white vinyl chair as near to the bed as the cramped space would allow, I gently brushed a black stalk of hair back from his pale, battered forehead. The ventilator hummed and clicked as his thin chest rose and fell. It looked like he'd done it, murdered Stacy I mean. Detective Hawk was certain, and he should know. Logan had certainly tried to run me down, almost killing Chess in the process, but now it seemed would never reap the benefits of his heinous acts. This thought did not in any way provide a sense of relief or justice. There was something wrong about the whole situation, but I couldn't put my finger on it.

At the age of 23, I had serious questions regarding the tenets of organized religion, but my doubts of man had never translated into doubts about God. I might not understand the nature of God, probably never will, but have no doubt whatsoever that God exists. So I prayed for help. I needed it.

When I looked up again, Dr. Daniel Martindale was standing at the door. Though normally only one visitor at a time is allowed in the ICU, Daniel was wearing his white lab coat and would most likely be mistaken for one of Logan's physicians, and so I motioned him in.

"So Logan did it," he blurted, his voice sounding more relieved than sad. "I'm so very glad!"

Shocked by this statement, I simply stared. He was shaking and his face was as white as his lab coat, so I stood and let him have the single chair crowded between the wall and the vent tubing. He didn't argue, but sat heavily, clasping his hands in his lap.

"I'm so glad!" he repeated.

Somehow I managed to squeeze myself awkwardly, protectively between the bed and the chair though it was a tight fit. I couldn't tell much about Dr. Martindale's state of mind, but his behavior was concerning and I wasn't sure I trusted him any nearer to Logan than he already was.

"What do you mean?" I asked, keeping my voice calm, neutral.

He stared at his hands, clasping and unclasping them.

"I was so afraid," he murmured, "because I was sure it was her. Or I thought it might be her... Oh, I don't know."

He was struggling, but I didn't know how to help him, and so I softly repeated, "What do you mean?"

He sighed and drew a deep breath.

"Sierra! I thought... it was her. I thought she did it, killed Stacy and... and Lu. I thought Sierra did it."

The ventilator clicked, and oxygen, invisible but tangible, rattled through blue plastic. Logan inhaled slowly, exhaled. Daniel continued.

"You see when I met Sierra, I thought, I believed she was the most wonderful woman in the world. She was gorgeous, charming, intelligent, fascinating, and I was crazy about her... loved her... thought I loved her... but after we were together..." He hesitated, not sure how much he could or was willing to share about his personal life. I said nothing, waited.

"She's not anything like she seems! The way she thinks is... she's horrible," he gasped suddenly, in a rush. "After a few short months of marriage, I didn't even want to sleep with her, be in the same room with her, her mind is so very vile, it doesn't matter about her looks..."

He was rambling. I tried to rein him in.

"You thought Sierra killed Stacy?" I asked, quietly. "And Luciana?"

He covered his face with his hands and nodded.

"I can't believe I thought that... of my own wife," he breathed. "I'm so glad it was Logan. So very glad! Otherwise, the kids..." His voice trailed off.

I stood in silence, staring at the top of his dark head, but not seeing it. Without thinking, I placed my hand on Logan's thin arm and squeezed. That's when, in my heart, I knew Logan didn't do it. The problem was, I had no proof.

Chapter 28

Dr. Martindale left soon afterward and I took his place in the chair. Propping Stacy's boot heels on the metal frame beneath Logan's bed, I watched him breathe, his eyes taped shut, perhaps sleeping, dreaming without care, the rhythmic sound of machinery soothing me, tempting me to sleep also. I'd been awake for 30 hours straight, a stressful, exhausting, mind-numbing 30 hours. Too much had happened and I was running on fumes, past the shakiness, and approaching what may have been enlightenment. The lights in the room seemed painfully bright, and I had the odd sensation that my thought processes were accentuated to an extraordinary level of clarity.

I realized I needed to search Sierra's room, preferably before she was released from the hospital. She'd been admitted to 23-hour observation and so had several hours to go, but that did not mean the hospital staff would not discharge her early if she was stable and they needed the bed. In the absence of any incriminating evidence, I'd be forced to move to plan B. I didn't much like the thought of plan B.

Rising stiffly, I walked from the room with one parting glance for Logan, then pulled out my iPhone and made the call. She answered on the second ring.

"Mom?" I said, though I knew her voice instantly.

"Hi, Honey," she answered, a bit hesitantly. She knew my voice, too. "I expected a call from you yesterday."

"Mom, can you come to Texas?"

One heart beat, then two.

"Of course," she said. "I can be on the road in an

hour, hour and a half max. Is everything okay?"

My eyes burned, but no tears came.

"No," I answered her honestly, "but everything will be by the time you get here."

"Then I'm on my way."

"Thanks. See you soon."

No questions. No discussion. I hung up the phone.

I knew the killer, and so I knew where the danger would lie. My friends and family could no longer be caught unawares in the crossfire. It was 1pm. I had about eight hours to do what had to be done, hopefully without getting myself killed in the process. When it was all over, I wanted to see my Mom. Straightening my shoulders, I stalked from the building.

Chapter 29

I took a cab back to The Oaks and arrived at the Taus' to be accosted immediately upon my entrance into the house by Dr. Tau. He was waiting for me in his office, appeared as though nothing had happened, as if his only surviving son weren't in the ICU with possible brain damage incurred in an attempted vehicular homicide after allegedly committing the brutal murders of two women, one of whom was his sister. I guess I shouldn't have been surprised, but somehow I still was.

"Wim," he called, eagerly, waving to me with his big hands. "Wim, I must speak with you."

"Of course, Dr. Tau," I agreed, "but can't we talk later? Is Sierra home yet?"

He frowned. "I don't believe she is, but we really must discuss this. It's important."

Reluctantly, I complied, moving across the entry hall and taking a seat in the offered chair. Dr. Tau picked up a thin stack of papers and tapped the ends against his deck, making the edges meticulously even. Then he stapled them together, picked up another stack and did the same. He handed me a copy and I held it in my lap.

"As you know," he began, formally, "I asked my attorney to prepare a document the signing of which will indicate your intent to decline the bequest of monies contained in Stacy's Will."

I nodded.

"After a great deal of deliberation," he continued, "I have decided that you should have this."

He indicated the document, and so I began to read. There were 26 pages, but I didn't get past page 2.

"You're kidding?"

"No." He shook his head. "I am not... kidding."

"But why?"

"Because Stacy... would want... would have wanted..."

My impulse was to argue, but when I looked up at the old surgeon, I was struck dumb. His voice hadn't given him away. His manner was as it had always been, but his eyes, the look in his eyes as he looked back at me, as if he was beyond despair, as if he'd been struck a death blow...

"I'm sorry, Dr. Tau. I really am so sorry," I said, to the man who had started out with everything and now had nothing left. "You know how I feel?"

It was his turn to nod.

"But you still expect me to accept this?"

"Yes," he said, almost meekly, all of his arrogance gone, "I've confidence that you will do the right thing, whatever that may be, according to your own lights, and that I may find a small source of pride in the knowledge that I contributed to some worthy cause, in one way or another. I would consider it a great favor if you would do that, for Stacy, for me."

"Okay then. I can make no promises of doing "the right thing", but I will promise to try not to disappoint you." The time to resist had passed; arguing was pointless.

"That is all I ask."

Dr. Tau motioned to someone outside his door. The young man in the business suit looked like a junior associate from a law firm, and I knew Mrs. Nelson fairly well by then. Both must have been waiting in the wings for their cue. Dr. Tau and I signed and initialed and they witnessed. Then the junior associate notarized, and we were all dismissed. Dr. Tau shuffled a few papers. I looked back at the golden monkeys on the chandelier above his head.

A half-million dollars... What am I going to do with a half-million dollars?

~ * ~

First I went to Stacy's room, left the papers on her dresser, and grabbed a selection of the clothing I'd borrowed from Sierra but not yet worn from the closet. Hurrying down the hall, I knocked lightly, and then tried the door to Sierra's room. It was locked. Fortunately interior door locks are extremely easy to pick. My Dad had schooled me in the art of picking interior door locks when a three-year-old Cal had accidentally locked herself into the laundry room and then couldn't understand how to unlock her way out. He'd used a toothpick. I used the end of one of the metal coat-hangers.

After closing the door behind me and placing the clothing on the bed, I began a systematic search for evidence starting with the drawers of the dresser, careful to leave nothing disturbed. I'd finished with the wardrobe and nightstands, finding nothing of interest, and was approaching her closet when the door swung open and Sierra walked into the room.

Chapter 30

"What are you doing here?" she asked, a bit uncertainly. Her lip was swollen, grapefruit-sized, and her eyes were beginning to look like a raccoon's.

"Oh," I said, forcing a smile. "I didn't know how long you'd be in the hospital. I was just returning some of your clothes. I won't need them any longer. I'll be going home soon."

I pointed toward the garments lying on the bed.

She looked around, slowly, didn't seem entirely convinced, and then tried a smile of her own, winced in pain. As she turned back to me, she lost her balance and reached for the edge of the dresser to steady herself. I suspected she was medicated, and moved to her side.

"Sierra, let me help you," I said, taking her arm and leading her to a chair by the window, "I know we've had our differences, but now that everyone knows Logan committed the murders, now that he's been caught, I hope we can go back to being friends."

Of course we'd never been friends, but I was trying to get out of her room as fast as I could, before she had time to wonder how I'd gotten in despite the locked door or ask questions. She frowned, considering, but then nodded her head.

"Of course, Wim." She attempted another smile, failed again. Her words were slightly slurred. "Of course. You were just upset about Stacy. I was upset about Stacy. Of course we're friends, but I think I'll lie down... just for a minute... feeling a bit... tired... Will you help me to the bed?"

I did as she asked. She lay down and I pulled the white coverlet over her, and then turning I quickly let myself out the door and into the hall, closing the door behind me.

One last place to search, I thought, but I dreaded going and was not at all optimistic about finding anything useful there.

Chapter 31

From the Spindletop Oil Field Gladys City Boomtown Website: Lucas spudded in a well on October 27, 1900, on McFaddin-Wiess and Kyle land that adjoined the Gladys City Company lands. A new heavier and more efficient rotary type bit was used. From October to January 1901, Lucas and the Hamills struggled to overcome the difficult oil sands, which had stymied previous drilling efforts. On January 10 mud began bubbling from the hole. The startled roughnecks fled as six tons of four-inch drilling pipe came shooting up out of the ground. After several minutes of quiet, mud, then gas, then oil spurted out. The Lucas geyser, found at a depth of 1,139 feet, blew a stream of oil over 100 feet high until it was capped nine days later and flowed an estimated 100,000 barrels a day. Lucas and the Hamills finally controlled the geyser on January 19, when a huge pool of oil surrounded it, and throngs of oilmen, speculators, and onlookers had transformed the city of Beaumont. A new age was born. The world had never seen such a gusher before.

The crime scene had been processed and the tape taken down, but to my knowledge Dr. Tao hadn't hired anyone to clean up the garage apartment in the few but endlessly eventful days since Stacy's death. When I went to his office and asked for the key, he rummaged through his desk drawer, pulled out a silver key ring, and then handed it to me without a word. His eyes still had that hollow, lifeless look; it broke my heart to see him that way.

With a feeling of overwhelming dread, I unlocked the door and climbed the stairs; my legs felt like lead and my pace slowed as I approached the landing on the second floor. The smell... I could smell the blood... Stacy's blood... Stacy bleeding...

Forcing myself to look away from the dark, red stains on the rug and hardwood floor, I began working my way around the living room, picking up knick-knacks, touching odds-and-ends, moving things around, knowing that the room had been processed by professional crime scene investigators, knowing the odds of my finding anything of evidentiary value were essentially zero, knowing all that but still compelled to search for something... proof...

Sierra had killed Stacy. I was sure. Logan had said Stacy died because she could not stop talking. Sierra didn't need money, and so must have killed Stacy to shut her up, but shut her up about what? Was Mrs. Tau murdered? Was Sierra involved in her mother's death? If so, why was Sierra so eager to have her mother's body exhumed? Or, was it something to do with Marty? Did Stacy know something about Marty's death? But, he'd died so long ago, and everyone knew it was an accident. Why kill Stacy now? It didn't make sense.

Fortunately for me, I was not left to wonder for long. The person with all the answers had followed me, back to the scene of the crime.

~ * ~

She did make an attempt to hide her approach. I never heard her quietly closing the carriage house's front door behind her, and creeping up the stairs, not until one step near the top creaked ever so slightly as she gained the second floor landing. Still, I was expecting her, and so turned to face her. She had no shotgun this time.

"How did you know?" There was no denial, only curiosity. "How did you figure out it was me and not Logan?"

Sierra casually crossed to the bar, pulled out a stool

and sat, and then reached over and touched the back of the stool next to hers; an invitation. I hesitated, and then moved to sit beside her. If she wanted to talk, we'd talk.

"I didn't know at first," I admitted. "In fact I didn't even suspect it was you until, well, today."

"Honestly?" She seemed surprised, but then extraordinarily pleased. "You didn't suspect me until today?"

I shook my head. "No."

She frowned.

"I guess I should have left well enough alone, then," she said slowly, considering, "but I was afraid you wouldn't stop, or that you already knew, or that Chess might have seen something or remembered something, you know, incriminating... but you didn't... he didn't... All that trouble, for nothing..."

She was quiet for a moment.

"Why did you kill Stacy, Sierra?" I asked. I reached to touch her arm, but pulled my hand back, and shifted awkwardly on my stool. She was a murderer after all. "I still don't understand why. It wasn't for money."

She looked at me with her raccoon eyes, violet icicles glittering in pools of red and black. "Of course not. Don't be ridiculous."

"Did you kill your mother? Did Stacy see...?"

"Please! Now that's just stupid!" she interrupted, impatiently, "Why should I kill Momma? Momma had a stroke. That's all."

I waited.

"It was a long time ago..."

"It wasn't my fault..."

"It was really Daddy's fault, and Marty's..." She stated firmly, and she believed it.

"You see, Daddy never had time for anyone, *except* for *Marty*," Sierra sighed. "Everything was about Marty, and how great he was, and how smart he was, and how special he was. He was nothing but a selfish brat!"

Her open hand came down hard on the bar as her

face reddened with anger. "But I fixed that, fixed him, that day while he was showing off his riding."

"What did you do?" I interjected; pretty sure I knew the answer, though not the specifics.

"It was a very clever plan," she smiled, enjoying the spotlight, boasting to her captive audience, me. "Actually it was brilliant. I'd worked it all out before hand."

"Momma had been talking about the picnic at the stables for weeks. In the morning, we had badminton and archery. After lunch I suggested the game of Hide-and-Seek and volunteered to be "It". That way all the other kids would be hiding, and no one would be looking for me. I made sure I left my bow and arrow set by the paddock fence and grabbed it and crept out into the grass alongside the arena, and when Marty came to the In and Out..." She paused for effect. "I jumped up and shot Prince Tango!"

"You shot Prince Tango? No!" I feigned shock, but felt none. "But how did no one see the arrow in the horse after he fell?"

Sierra smirked; rolling her eyes as she shook her head indulgently.

"Wim... It's not like it was a crossbow or anything. It was a play set. The arrows weren't even pointed, and my aim wasn't that good. The arrow bounced off the saddle girth, but scared Prince Tango enough that he shied and missed the jump."

She seemed very proud of herself, and willing to share, and so I pushed a bit further.

"And no one knew? No one suspected?" But I knew the answer to that question, too.

Sierra frowned.

"That's the rub," she admitted, reluctantly. "Stacy saw me do it."

"How could anyone have planned for that? She was hanging out of the hay loft, not hiding as she ought to have been," she explained, obviously blaming Stacy for this hitch in her otherwise "clever plan". "I made my shot, saw Prince Tango shy, stumble and fall. Marty cried out, tried to roll away but couldn't get out from under the horse. I looked back to watch everyone's reaction and saw Stacy, staring straight at me."

"But you were a child. When you shot Prince Tango, you didn't anticipate the consequences of your actions. You didn't mean to kill Marty, just to shake him up a bit, maybe embarrass him. Why didn't you just explain what happened? And why kill Stacy now?"

Lots of questions, but Sierra loved the sound of her own voice. She sighed, an exaggerated sigh.

"After Marty fell, while everyone was running around and confused, I tried to catch Stacy in the tack room, to talk to her, to convince her not to tell, but that darn Margaret Sheffield, always interfering, dragged us both out and shuffled us off to the house."

"I wasn't able to get Stacy alone until the day of the wake. By then I'd decided I couldn't trust her, even if she did promise not to say anything. Stacy wasn't any good at keeping secrets. I decided I would have to drown her... in the pool... It was a good plan, too, but drowning took longer than I thought it would. I told her I was baptizing her, so when she died like Marty, she'd be born again, like they said in church. I don't know that I believe all that, but I was pretty convincing and Stacy let me dunk her. Funny," she said, her forehead crinkled as she considered, "Stacy was so smart about some things, but she was really dumb about others."

Good thing I don't have a shotgun or a thin wire, I thought, but held my tongue.

"Anyway," she said, returning to her narrative, "she didn't struggle much, and no one noticed. There were so many people milling about, crying and consoling one another, and as usual no one was watching us kids at all. When she started sinking, I let go, climbed out of the water and went back into the house to dry off. Unfortunately Page's daddy saw Stacy and pulled her out too soon. After that, I think my Momma knew it was me, or suspected I had something to do with Stacy's accident and Marty's death."

"What makes you say that? Did she accuse you?" I asked, mildly, as though we were discussing the weather.

"Not in so many words, but she kept Stacy away from me, never left me alone with her. Momma protected me, too, though. When Stacy made up her invisible friend, when she started talking to Paygo, I knew she missed Marty and was trying to replace him. I convinced her that her imaginary friend was Marty, but born again, in a new form like the Bible says. Momma and even Logan played along. Daddy was the only one in the family who wasn't in on the game, but Momma had kept secrets from Daddy before so I wasn't worried about her telling him."

"So Logan knew... that you killed Marty and tried to kill Stacy?" I was skeptical, in the extreme.

"I don't think he did," she admitted, "though sometimes I wished I could tell him. It's not as though we talked about it one way or the other. He probably didn't know, doesn't know even now. He was so much younger. He was just in on the game of Paygo, pretending we could see him, too, pretending Paygo was real."

"Paygo was a good cover. He kept Stacy calm and quiet. Maybe I felt a little bad about Marty, and so I helped give Paygo a full life. Took him places. He even went off to school with me. We had great adventures, or so I told Stacy." She laughed.

"But why kill Stacy now? After all these years? She never told anyone about Marty."

The lines of Sierra's face tightened, and her eyes blazed.

"After Momma died, she was going to tell!" she snapped. "She started saying things. Paygo came back, and she was talking about the bees!"

Over my head...

"Bees?" I said the word with incredulity, not feigned

at this point. "What have *bees* to do with anything?"

"The bees in the barn," Sierra panted, exasperated, "the bees in the barn! Those wood drilling bees, carpenter bees. I don't know what kind they are! I don't care about bees! But I knew, when Stacy brought Paygo home, when she started talking about death and accidents not being accidents, and then hinting about bees, I knew! I knew she was just torturing me, taunting me, trying to make me suffer, before she told!"

"Stacy wasn't like that. You know she didn't think that way, and even if she did, you need not have killed her," I said. "What you did to Marty, and even to Stacy as a child, isn't the same as what you've done now, the cold-blooded murder of your sister and after that Luciana. Even if Stacy had told, you could have explained, that you didn't mean to kill Marty, that you were a child and weren't thinking, that it was all a tragic mistake and accident."

"But it wasn't a mistake or an accident," she said, looking at me with clear, cold violet eyes. "I meant for Marty to die, and I was happy when he did. I wanted him gone, out of my life forever. I could never have convinced anyone that I didn't mean to kill him. I'm not that good of an actress."

Couldn't argue with her there... I sighed.

"And so the idea for the firing range? Not your dad or Chess?"

Sierra tapped her right temple with her index finger.

"Can you say "misdirection"? Can you even spell "misdirection"?

"And Logan, trying to run me down?" I asked, feeling we were reaching the end of our conversation; that everything was coming together. "That's why you were in your Mercedes and not his BMW wasn't it, so that you could reach across and drive using cruise control on the steering wheel. His was a stick."

Sierra laughed. "Congrats Chica, at least you got that one right on your own."

"Poor Logan. He made it too easy. All I had to do was tank him up, dope him up, and prop him in the driver's seat." She laughed again, apparently amused by the memory. "I hoped to kill all three of you, but may still get another chance at Logan *if* he survives and ever regains consciousness. I heard one of the doctors say he may be a veggie... I'll probably not get Chess any time soon... not with Page sitting watch..."

"Sierra," I interrupted, using my hopeful, reasonable voice, though not feeling much of either, "why don't you turn yourself in? Can't you see, if you keep going this way, you're going to be caught. You may never see your children again."

She looked at me and the laughter was gone. I could almost see the wheels turning as she considered her options, calculated the odds. Apparently the odds were not to her liking. She stood up and pulled the Glock from her purse.

"I'll tell them I saw you, going into the carriage house; that I confronted you, and you confessed to killing Stacy. I'll say I brought a gun so that I could force you to turn yourself in to the police, but that you refused and attacked me. We struggled and the gun went off."

Her voice was deadly calm and her hand was steady, but her eyes reflected desperation, even fear. I wanted her to be as calm as her voice.

"Can't you see how *stupid* that sounds?" I spoke crudely, trying to make her angry, as I rose from my seat and backed up a step. Sierra would behave in a much more controlled manner if her blood was running cold instead of hot. "Sierra, no one will believe you. Det. Hawk is not an idiot. You've left a trail of bodies in your wake a mile wide!"

She glared at me, and her eyes turned frostier still. It was working.

"You think you're so smart, so much better than the rest of us, cause you go to *Harvard*. If Det. Hawk was any kind of detective at all he would have suspected you from the first. You were on the spot. You had motive because of the money and Stacy's Will. You should have been the prime suspect!" she shouted. "He obviously is an idiot!"

My heart was hammering so loudly in my ears that I could hardly hear her voice, understand the words coming from her mouth, as I took another careful step backward, and then another. Trying to think... keep her talking... keep her distracted...

"And all that agreeing to sign the money away, that was just for show! You knew Daddy would insist on you taking at least some of the money, *like he did*!"

"How did you know that's the way your Dad instructed his attorney? I didn't know it! Listening at keyholes again, Sierra?" I put as much contempt as I could muster into my own voice, making it sound ugly, trying to keep her focused on arguing with me while carefully working my way around the room toward the door. She saw what I was doing though, and racked the slide with one hand.

"Don't you want to struggle for the gun?" she asked nastily. She waved the gun at me, taunting me, and then relaxed her arm, letting the weapon hang loosely at her side.

"I'll even pretend I don't see you coming." She glanced away from me, slyly looking over her shoulder, giving me a chance to...

Fight or flight... Could I take her? Luciana, her head almost cut from her body... flight, my only option...

"Sierra," I said, taking another cautious step away from her, "it's not going to work..."

That's when she raised the gun, and shot me.

Chapter 32

It happened so fast, I don't know if she meant to hit me in the arm, or if I was turning or raising my hands as I backed away, or if she'd not taken time to aim, or if she'd used a shotgun on Stacy because she simply wasn't any more accurate with a handgun than she'd been with bow and arrow. In any case, the first round tore through the flesh of my deltoid muscle right above its insertion point on the humerus, fortunately sparing the bone, though the precise anatomical location of the hit was the last thing on my mind at the time. I felt the shock, but no pain, as the force of the impact drove me against the bar. I staggered, regained my footing and crawfished toward the door.

"Sierra, wait. Sierra, wait." I was stammering, tripping over my own feet, silently praying.

Oh, God... oh, God...

It was then, from behind me, that I heard the unmistakable sound of a pump action shotgun being racked, a much more authoritative sound than that of the Glock. Sierra froze. Glancing quickly over my shoulder, I saw the last person I expected to see holding the gun. Margaret Sheffield, pink foam curlers pinned carefully in place, looking frail and tiny in a pink dressing gown with navy collar and fluffy pink slippers, was hold a 12-guage Browning with both barrels pointed at Sierra's heart. There was nothing frail about the Browning.

"Aunt Mags," Sierra cried, "I'm so glad you've come. Wim killed Stacy and convinced Logan to strangle Luciana and run down Chess to cover it up. I'm trying to take her in to the police. Help me!" she pleaded.

"I didn't ..." I began, starting to feel a bit woozy,

pressing my hand tightly against my arm to staunch the flow of blood.

Mrs. Sheffield tilted her head, didn't even spare a glance at me, and the gun never wavered.

"Sierra, darling," she said, in her slow, syrupy voice, "I saw the lights in the carriage house from my study window, and decided I'd best pop over to see what it was all about. You do know I can always tell when you're lying, don't you? It's because you're speaking, if you know what I mean. I don't claim to have any idea as to why you would kill your own sister, but you obviously did, and that poor nanny person, too. I don't know how you manipulated that sad boy into running Chess down, but I'm certain you did that as well. You are the puppet master here."

The panic returned to Sierra's eyes, and the Glock shook as she was torn between aiming at me or at her aunt. I could see the wheels turning. She was trying to come up with a story, any story, and that's when the Browning went off in a concussion of sound.

Margaret Sheffield later claimed the gun was too heavy and that she was about to drop it and in trying to maintain her hold on it she accidentally pulled the trigger. The story would have seemed much more plausible if she hadn't managed to fire both barrels. Sierra took two in the chest.

Chapter 33

We left her on the floor, lying less than two feet from the spot where her sister had died. The tiny Mrs. Sheffield helped me slowly down the stairs and out into the ruined front lawn where the Mercedes sat, still buried in the side of the garage. Lights framing the front door of the main house flashed on, blinding us as we both trudged onward, seeking a safe and comfortable place to stop and sit. Mrs. Nelson reached us first, with Dr. Tau, seemingly dazed and voiceless for once, following close behind her. With assistance, I made my way across the yard and sat heavily on the front steps and Margaret Sheffield dropped down beside me. We'd not long to wait.

The EMT guys, by now entirely familiar with the address and route, pulled up before Det. Hawk this time; Mrs. Nelson dialed 911 before I'd time to think to call him.

By the time Hawk arrived, I was sitting in the back of the bus, my arm bandaged and feeling quite a bit better due in large part to the effects of liberally dispensed morphine.

"What the *Hell* were you thinking?" His voice reached me before he'd even climbed from his car. He repeated his question as he strode angrily toward me. "*What were you thinking?*"

I looked at him, his pit bull face tight with frustration and fear, felt inordinately happy to see him, and smiled broadly. Impulsively, I reach out my hand.

"I'm so glad you've come." My mouth moved awkwardly and the words seemed difficult to pronounce clearly. I tried again. "I'm glad you're here..." I grinned, sheepishly. "Don't be mad... at me..."

He stared at me, trying to maintain his glare, his righteous indignation, but lost his composure and laughed, out loud. The first hug Hawk had given me was the coldest, most professional hug I'd ever received. The second was one of the warmest and least professional, allowing for the fact that we were both sitting in the back of an ambulance. He even kissed me, yes, *wow*, in front of the EMTs, Dr. Tau, Mrs. Nelson, Margaret Sheffield, in front of the world. That's when my Mom and Jordy showed up.

~ * ~

It was almost time to go home to Atlanta. Rachel had left the night before, taken Jordy's car, refused to answer his calls or texts, and so he was riding back with my Mom and me. Dr. Tau was in his office and I stopped on my way out the door.

"Dr. Tau," I said, pondering the golden monkeys on the chandelier above his head for the last time, "are you going to be alright?"

He looked up, seemed surprised at the question, then stood up and came around his desk.

"Why of course," he rumbled, with a hint of his boisterous voice. "What makes you ask?"

"Well, after everything that's happened... "

He shook his head.

"Don't you worry about me. I'll be just fine. The hospital called and Chess and Logan are both awake. I never really cared much for Sierra. She'll have to manage her own legal affairs. So all in all things turned out as well as could be expected."

Wow! No response for that...

"But you do care for Logan," I asked hesitantly, hoping against hope that he did, "even though he's maybe not... well... technically..."

"You're asking if Logan is mine?" Dr. Tau seemed mildly amused. "A brown-eyed boy in a blue-eyed family? Of course he's "mine". I never thought of him as anything else."

"But you knew you weren't..."

"His bioDad as they say? Of course, not that it's your business." He smiled. "The things I put that woman through. You think I would begrudge her one small indiscretion? You think I would be so petty as to blame a child for his parentage?"

I looked at him as his face changed.

"Now the man..." His mouth hardened into a thin line. "That was different. I could and did blame him."

I shivered thinking suddenly of Prince Tango.

"Logan will really need your support." I said kindly, shaking off the image of Dr. Tau shooting a horse. "He's going to need lots of help to recover... from all this..."

Dr. Tau cocked his head.

"I've always supported Logan, no matter what he's done. He knows he can count on me. He'll go to the best rehab facility available."

"I mean emotional support." I tried to explain to a man without normal feeling.

"I don't see what else I can do."

And he didn't. But I could do more, and I would.

Chapter 34

Outside, the sun was rising on a beautiful azure-skied Texas morning.

"I'll be back in just a few minutes," I said, stepping off the front porch and heading for the path to the Sheffields'. I wanted to say goodbye to her. She wasn't under arrest, yet, and she had saved my life.

"Wim?" Jordy called after me, but I didn't look back, just shook my head. I needed to go alone.

I left him standing on the porch with my Mom, Dr. Tau, Mrs. Nelson, and Detective Hawk.

Awkward. But I'd deal with all that later.

I walked down the path and let myself through the fence, turned left, entered through the front gate. She answered the door on the first knock.

"Come in," said Margaret Sheffield, sounding just a bit formal. "I'm glad you've stopped by."

She invited me in, and I followed her to the sofa. She offered tea, which I declined.

"I suppose you heard that my son-in-law has improved? He may be out of the ICU later today. Obviously not as bad as it looked... and he's pretty tough." She added the complement grudgingly.

I nodded. "I'm so glad and grateful," I said.

"So you're going home today." She made it a statement, not a question. The *finally* seemed implied.

"Yes," I replied, "but I wanted to thank you, again..."

"No need, no need," she interrupted, waving my words away.

"How is the arm?" She asked, reaching toward but not touching the wide white bandage.

"It's fine, thanks," I answered, rotating my shoulder

slightly to be sure I still could.

We sat silently for a moment, and then she sighed.

"I feel most sorry for that poor, dear boy," she began. "It must have been worse for him than even for Stacy. Stacy may have witnessed murder, but at least she could hide in her own little world. That poor boy must have felt it all, all the tension and distrust, the fear and uncertainty, without ever knowing the reason for it, just sensing the evil... I always knew she was evil, of course, just didn't realize how very evil she was... I'll have to do something for the boy, maybe visit him more... in the hospital... and in rehab... I guess he'll go back there again."

She was wandering, and though I could easily follow her train of thought without the use of proper names, I still had a question.

"So you feel sorry for Logan?" I questioned. "But isn't he... wasn't he... he's not Dr. Tau's biological son. You've always known that, right?"

"Of course," she answered, with a shrug. "Eleanor told me herself. I've always known."

"But your husband... you weren't jealous?" I fumbled, searching for a tactful way to bring up infidelity.

"What on earth do you mean?" She seemed surprised, and looked at me, momentarily confused, but then her brow cleared and she smiled.

Rising from the couch, she walked over to the mantel and selected the picture of a happy couple sitting in a beat up ragtop. She brought it to me and placed it in my hands.

"It's funny. Everyone thought that, at the time you know," Mrs. Sheffield said, shaking her head, "but Eleanor would never have had an affair with *my* husband... and he, Alex, would never have cheated on me."

Wrong again? I was getting used to it.

"But you can't deny the resemblance," I argued, gazing at the face that looked so like Logan's.

"Logan looks just like his grandfather, *on his moth-*

er's side," she stated emphatically. "I thought my father and my grandfather handsome. They were tall, black-eyed, dark-haired, and good men. So I married a man who looked very like the other men in my family. There's nothing wrong with that."

"Well, no," I conceded. *I thought my father handsome, and my uncle Bill could have starred in TV movies, so yeah, I could see it.*

"If you *must* know," she continued, sounding more and more like the indomitable, sometimes condescending Margaret Sheffield of old, "Logan is a half-brother to Chess. Marshall suspected, of course, or maybe he always knew, too, and insisted on having paternity testing performed as soon as the baby was born. Chet Anderson was the father. Eleanor was always attracted to that kind of man, rich, powerful, ruthless, self-centered. I never could understand why she placed so little value on herself."

I was shocked, but not in the way I had expected.

"It's funny, you know," she said, and her voice and face suddenly softened as she gently took the picture from my hand, "that everyone felt sorry for me, that they all thought I was the unfortunate one, the one that "married down", because we were, well, not well off, not like Eleanor, but my Alex," she touched the man's face with her fingertips, carefully outlining his jaw, "My Alex was worth so much more than the combined financial wealth of all the Marshall Taus and Chet Andersons of this world. I would not have traded anything for the life I had with him."

The End